The Wrath of Dionysus

The
Wrath
of Dionysus

A NOVEL

BY Evdokia Nagrodskaia

TRANSLATED AND EDITED BY

Louise McReynolds

INDIANA UNIVERSITY PRESS
BLOOMINGTON & INDIANAPOLIS

The paper used in this publication meets the minimum requirements of
American National Standard for Information Sciences—Permanence of
Paper for Printed Library Materials, ANSI Z39.48–1984.

Manufactured in the United States of America

Library of Congress Cataloging-in-Publication-Data

Nagrodskaîa, E.
[Gnev Dionisa. English]
The wrath of Dionysus : a novel / by Evdokia Nagrodskaia ;
translated and edited by Louise McReynolds.
p.   cm.
ISBN 0–253–33304–0 (cloth : alk. paper). —
ISBN 0–253–21132–8 (pbk. : alk. paper)
I.   McReynolds, Louise, date.   II. Title.
PG3467.N22G513   1997
891.73'3—dc21   97–445

1   2   3   4   5   02   01   00   99   98   97

ACKNOWLEDGMENTS

This project began over lunch with Beth Holmgren in a vegetarian restaurant in Urbana, Illinois. Since it was one of the few times in my life when I ate my vegetables, I had the sense to pay attention to her ideas about the book and I came to share her enthusiasm for Nagrodskaia. Beth also made useful suggestions that helped me to introduce Nagrodskaia to readers. Margaret Dalton's meticulous crosschecking of the translation uncovered errors and modern malapropisms, and the final draft benefited considerably from her judicious eye. Ann Hibner Koblitz and Carol Stimson also read earlier drafts and improved this work with advice about word choice and the narrator's voice. My friends who double as colleagues have helped by encouraging my efforts to make available in English more broadly based materials from turn-of-the-century Russian culture: Daniel Kaiser, Joan Neuberger, Daniel Orlovsky, Donald Raleigh, and Richard Stites. At Indiana University Press, Janet Rabinowitch and Melanie Richter-Bernburg applied the finishing touches with a style worthy of the novel's artist-heroine. I remain happily indebted to Les McBee for his appreciation of cross-cultural experiences.

Several foundations funded my research, and I am grateful to

Acknowledgments

the International Research and Exchanges Board, the Fulbright-Hays Committee, and the University of Hawaii's Office of Research Administration. Pat Polansky, as always, helped me with necessary library materials not readily available in Honolulu. My gratitude for this support is heightened by the present-day assaults on support for funding research in education.

I dedicate this work to the memory of James Baldwin, 1924–87, who would have had much to talk about with Evdokia Appolonovna had their paths chanced to cross in Parisian exile.

INTRODUCTION

When *The Wrath of Dionysus* first hit Russian book stores in 1910, neither critics nor ordinary readers recognized the author's name. The modest print run of 1,000 copies, priced at a ruble and a half apiece, made it simply one of dozens of other so-called "boulevard" novels targeted at Russia's expanding audience for topical, quasi-sensational fare. By the time the book appeared in its tenth edition in 1916, however, the price had almost doubled, the print run tripled, and it had been translated into French, Italian, German, and Latvian.[1] The name Evdokia Apollonovna Nagrodskaia (1866–1930) had become one of the most notorious in Russia's literary world. Not only were her subsequent novels and short stories selling well, she was also adapting their plotlines for the revolutionary new form of popular culture, moving pictures.

Nagrodskaia's star, however, shot very quickly across the Russian cultural horizon. In 1917 she moved with her husband to Paris. Never active in émigré politics, she wrote her last work, *The River of Times,* in exile. An historical trilogy drawn from her experiences in Masonic circles, this saga differed too much from her previous works to generate much attention. More important,

Evdokia Apollonovna Nagrodskaia, circa 1910

it appeared in a different cultural context from the one in which she had been received so enthusiastically.

Nagrodskaia left behind in Russia an important body of work, produced in less than a decade, that was disproportionately influential for such a short career. Her first novel and best-seller, *The Wrath of Dionysus,* stirred up a great brouhaha with a theme that would identify her for readers: confusion about sexual identity. Although today's reader might find the language dated in places, the bigger issues that Nagrodskaia addresses, from mothers having to divide emotions between children and avocation, to the nature of gender identity, and even to the place of the artist in society, remain as fresh today at the end of the twentieth century as they were in Russia when the century first turned.

Sex sells, then as now. What separated Nagrodskaia's novel from the others dispensing various doses of titillation and romance was the psychological complexity of her characters. The novel's title refers to a painting undertaken by the heroine, Tania Kuznetsova. Both the act of painting and the subject matter of the picture presented numerous symbols familiar to the contemporary Russian reader. As a painter, Tania is the consummate cultural figure in a society that privileged artists and other members of the intellectual elite, the intelligentsia. Glorified to the point of a kind of secular sainthood, Russian intellectuals were perceived to be utterly selfless in their devotion to the common good, which they expressed through either art itself or critiques of it. Tania's preoccupation with finishing her masterpiece was thus understood in political terms, as if she were involved in a social reform movement. Her stature also permitted her to live outside normal moral conventions: a widow, she was the common-law wife of another intellectual and mistress to a third man.

Despite a rather thin plot, the story is a rich blend of cultural politics and explorations of sexual identity. The novel begins with Tania traveling south, anxious about meeting the family of the man with whom she has been living in unwed bliss, Ilya. On the train she finds herself uncontrollably and erotically drawn to Edgar Stark, a businessman who is the opposite of Ilya in every way. They separate before the sexual attraction between them explodes, but she finds herself obsessed with Stark. When they run into each other again, she is ultimately powerless against her desires. Without Ilya's knowledge of their affair, she goes to Rome to finish her painting, using Stark as the model for Dionysus, the Roman god of sensualism.

Tania's attraction to Stark and her need to express herself through her painting are part of the same psychological problem, which becomes clear to her when, after completing the painting, she tires of Stark because their relationship was purely physical. She longs to return to Ilya and the life of intellectual contemplation and mutual respect, but she discovers that she is pregnant with Stark's child. Although initially she surrenders the boy to Stark so that she can remain with Ilya, the emotion of mother love further complicates her life. Tania finally accepts a deceitful ménage à trois as the only possible balance for all the people involved, but she is disgusted with herself for having to live this lie. As a Russian intellectual, truth has been her highest goal.

Therefore, Tania's compromise must be understood as it was by her contemporary readers, as a meaningful sacrifice.

Readers of *The Wrath of Dionysus* would already be conversant with the outline of the dilemma posed in the novel, the need to use artistic expression to work through social and personal problems. In this case, by memorializing the Roman god of eroticism and hedonism—the antithesis of the Russian intellectual—the artist-heroine is challenging the moral superiority of the latter. Painfully aware that only a compromise can smooth over the problems she has caused to those whom she loves, and that such concessions come at the cost of her principles, the heroine ultimately chooses to pay the exorbitant price by compromising her standards. In so doing, she raises doubts about how far the intelligentsia's ideals can be applied to real life.

Nagrodskaia's *deus ex machina* for escaping this ethical dilemma is to supply her heroine with a motivation as tangible as it is emotional: a child.[2] Did Nagrodskaia kneel before the dictatorship of domesticity, or did she acquiesce in a reality that readers could understand? How much did maternity temper her message of individual choice? In her work, Nagrodskaia continually delineated the struggle between the ideal and the actual. Tania's sexual behavior might have made her a new woman, but her sense of personal obligation situated her squarely within the context of the nineteenth-century intelligentsia. Two minor characters in the book, Ilya's sister Katia and a Russian émigré artist in Rome, anchored the novel in the intelligentsia tradition with their various criticisms of Tania. Through their presence, Nagrodskaia maintains a necessary element of ambivalence about all of her characters' decisions. This device provides almost as much tension in the novel as the sexual situations.

The Russian reading public circa 1910 was itself as different from the previous generation as was Nagrodskaia, which explains the swift ascent of her popularity. In 1905, the Russian empire had been engulfed in a political revolt against the tsarist government. In the 1890s, the government's policy of rapid industrialization had accelerated the transformation of the agrarian-based social estates of peasantry and nobility into a more pluralistic citizenry that included professionals, factory workers, and a growing number of females in the work force. Frustrated by their lack of opportunity to participate in political decisions, Russians of all backgrounds had lashed out against the autocracy and received minimal concessions. But these Russians had different needs from their predecessors, because they had to learn to negotiate according to changing social rules in the new urban environment. Geographical, social, and occupational mobility were challenging nineteenth-century conventions that had established social and gender hierarchies. Although the absence of readership surveys and the paucity of fan letters has made it impossible to reconfigure the new audience precisely, it is reasonable to assume that readers wanted help in adjusting to the evolving consumer-oriented urbanism and that many had opened themselves up to psychological strategies for dealing with change. The 1905 revolution had sharpened the question of the place of the individual in an industrial society.

Nagrodskaia is representative of the writers who were responding to the needs of this emergent reading public. Writers and readers alike were beginning to value literature as much for its potential to liberate the individual as for its social mission. The intelligentsia contemptuously assigned this group of writers to one of the new urban spaces, the boulevard, which evoked an image of commercial shops and middle-class women with unrefined, middlebrow tastes and pretensions to haute couture. Laura Engelstein has characterized boulevard literature as "a counterfeit of the real thing for those who had neither the material nor intellectual resources to obtain and appreciate the original."[3] But this begs the question that its critics themselves refused to pose: by what other means could those who lacked the appropriate intellectual tools gain access to the culture dominated by the Russian intelligentsia, who were intent upon maintaining a monopoly over those tools?[4] Nagrodskaia repackaged the intelligentsia's message to give contemporary Russian society a unique "means of thinking about itself."[5] Although *The Wrath of Dionysus* was hardly blind to larger cultural questions, it told a deeply personal story of choice and responsibility.

It was not the breathy passages of sexual passion that made this novel the talk of the boulevard. The extremes of sexual tension explored in this novel are not the physical activities of Tania and her lovers but those activities that determine the sexual identities of the various characters. From the outset, Tania is described in masculine terms, and Stark's overwhelmingly female characteristics serve as a complement to what comes across as her male alter ego. The character in the novel who picks up on this gender-bending is Tania's homosexual colleague in Rome, who confesses that he is in love with Stark. Although all of the coupling described in the book is heterosexual, this is essentially a homosexual novel: Tania lives more than one lie.

In addition to confronting its readers with questions of gender, *The Wrath of Dionysus* engaged them in the urgent philosophical debates of the era. The title itself invoked the specter of Friedrich Nietzsche, whose ideas about the internalized human struggle between Apollonian rationalism and Dionysian passion had so engrossed the intelligentsia.[6] Their fascination with Nietzsche quickly filtered down through other literary channels, and the philosopher was sufficiently familiar on the boulevard that the vaudeville houses staged a farce about contemporary philosophy entitled "Thus Spake Zarathustra" in 1905.[7] Other perceptive reviewers connected Nagrodskaia to Austrian sexual theorist Otto Weininger, whose *Sex and Character*, published in Russian in 1909, had proposed a formula for calculating sexual identity based on the notion that all people have characteristics of both sexes and that a key issue of modern life is trying to keep them in balance.[8] Without mentioning his name, Nagrodskaia also discussed Sigmund Freud's ideas of the unconscious, the primal urges of the id, and dream therapy.

Russia's less sophisticated readers were interested in the ideas of Nietzsche, Weininger, and Freud not simply to imitate the intelligentsia but because they faced many of the same problems. These philosophers addressed the problem of momentous change and offered explanations to a confused public. The new groups forming in postrevolutionary society had reason to feel abandoned by an intelligentsia that derided their choice of literature and offered no satisfactory substitute to meet their particular needs. To whom else could they turn but Nagrodskaia and her peers? Here, where readers had confidence in them, boulevard novelists could contribute to the reconstruction of society: they could assist their readers in locating themselves psychologically in the changing city streets.[9] Moreover, authors from the boulevard could help their readers reach higher levels of sophistication, a necessary step in creating a society capable of handling the psychological stress as well as the technology of modernization. It was this combined ability to reflect and to help reshape social reality that gave the boulevard its power.

In addition to Nagrodskaia, many others from this generation used unorthodox sexual scenarios to address the intensifying question of the role of the individual. The revolution had produced a significantly more lenient censorship statute; before that, the kinds of sexual debates in which these writers trafficked had been limited to medical journals. Mikhail Kuzmin's sensational novel *Wings*, published in 1907, described a young man sprouting psychological wings that carried him beyond traditional morality to find happiness in the arms of other men. Kuzmin was Nagrodskaia's close friend and intimately involved with the more famous Symbolist poet Viacheslav Ivanov. Another fictionalization of the love that dared not speak its name also appeared that year, Lidia Zinoveva-Annibal's tragedy of lesbianism, *Thirty-three Abominations*. Mikhail Artsybashev's drama of depravity and implied incest, *Sanin,* was another entry in the catalogue for the lurid literary year of 1907. *Sanin* precipitated more debates than the others because it was read by a much wider audience— probably because his characters were hetero- rather than homosexual.

Nagrodskaia's main characters appeared more inverted than perverted, according to contemporary norms, but homosexual motifs were never far below the surface. Her foray into homosexuality, however, differed in several fundamental ways from Kuzmin's and Zinoveva-Annibal's. First, only one of the characters in *Wrath of Dionysus* acted upon his same-sex longings; and although the author portrayed him sympathetically, this character loathed himself for his sexual orientation and proved unable to sprout liberating wings. Nagrodskaia made the issue titillating but less threatening to readers by framing her story around the search for a sexual persona that would permit a paradoxically natural unnatural coupling of a man and a woman: since both the male and the female had repressed their true same-sex natures, they could satisfy each other.

Her second novel, however, *The Bronze Door* (1911), drew the censors' ire with its multiplicity of sexual deviations from the norm. It featured a homosexual artist pitted against his sister in rivalry for another man's affection. The door in the title drew directly on Freud; in his childhood dreams, the artist turned into a woman when he went behind the mysterious bronze door. Shortly after publication the censors confiscated all copies, and the enraged Nagrodskaia was rumored to have wreaked havoc in the responsible censor's office.[10] Two years later she brought out a second, more temperate version, retitled *At the Bronze Door.* The extremely masculine heroine of a later novel, *Evil Spirits* (1915), suggested lesbianism. This novel also showed signs of Nagrodskaia's interest in the occult, which had parallels in the current interest in the unconscious. Infatuation with the supernatural made evident popular anxieties about the rational, technological world created by industrialization; Nagrodskaia was one of several boulevard authors who tapped into the growing interest in the occult.

None of her later works could match the popularity of *The Wrath of Dionysus,* but the corpus of Nagrodskaia's work provides a useful cultural barometer that measures changing tastes and interests in late imperial Russia, from the more candid interest in sex to the absorption with mysticism and the notions of personal choice that came with the evolution of consumerism. Her novel *The White Colonnade* (1914) used the idea of a recurring symbol to inspire the characters to take control of their lives. The heroine, Kitty, caught only a glimpse of a white colonnade when she was returning from her uncle's funeral. Shining through the rain on the distant porch, with a staircase beckoning her upward, the colonnade came to serve as the symbol of her consciousness of a better life. It would appear to her in times of stress, inspiring her, for example, to free herself from her egocentric aristocratic fiancé. A host of minor characters also came to the realization that they must take action to ameliorate their situations, and those who saw Kitty's colonnade were able to make changes for the better in their lives. A familiar subtheme returned with the actress-mistress of Kitty's fiancé, when she debated that lesbianism might offer an alternative to her current self-destructive sexuality. One of the other characters described how the colonnade worked for him: "There is a moment in a person's life when he can sense, can see clearly, that there's something better out there than the circumstances that surround him."[11]

Nagrodskaia also published several collections of short stories, which offered her a flexible literary forum from which to expand her larger social and intellectual concerns. For example, the title character in "Ania" prostitutes herself to a businessman in order to protect the reputation of her father, who has counterfeited stocks for money to indulge his mistress, a Spanish dancer in a tawdry nightclub. Gradually, Ania becomes aware that she enjoys greater satisfaction from her relationship with this man than she does from her ungrateful father, and she continues the liaison of her own volition. By permitting Ania to make the choice and select the lover over the family, Nagrodskaia created a new twist to the concept of happy ending. The heroine of "The Boy from the Circus" also takes an atypical turn when she decides to opt for a lover she has created in her imagination instead of settling down in a conventional relationship with one of the imperfect men in her adult life. As a child she had met a boy who worked in a circus, and in her memory he remained her ideal, her dream lover. She decides she would rather fantasize about him than experience the disappointments of the real thing. "The Living Shadow," set during the First World War, tells about a problematic love between a soldier and his nurse. The title refers to the memory of the woman who had refused the wounded man's love; he kept her metaphorical shadow between himself and the woman who cared for him in reality. "He," on the other hand, is purely a tale of occult time and space travel, with little about the inner psyche or modern sexual psychology. The title character acquires human qualities when he rescues from an insane asylum a girl who has been considered mad for her fantastic interactions with him. Nagrodskaia made an uncharacteristic descent into the lower depths in "The Nightmare," a story that evokes the works of Maxim Gorky and Alexander Kuprin. This gritty description of sexual depravity in the slums differs distinctively from her usual modernist confusion about sexual identity.

Defying categorization on the basis of either her politics or her gender, Nagrodskaia is best understood as a writer preoccupied with questions of personal identity. Yet contemporary critics rarely addressed her works from this angle. *The Wrath of Dionysus* caused such a furor that they could not afford to ignore this bit of boulevard fare. The attention it garnered and the intensity of the ensuing debates were truly remarkable for a first novel by a completely unknown writer.[12] Most, not surprisingly, had something to say about the homosexual subplot. One critic, who found the book pleasant but hardly as significant as the hoopla warranted, regretted that this extraneous story line made the book popular for the wrong reasons.[13] Another, although he complimented Nagrodskaia's ability to create interesting characters, also cautioned about the dangers of "extremist" feminism.[14] Whether they reproached her for "tendentiousness" or "dilettantism," however, reviewers recognized that she raised the "burning questions of the day."[15] Kuzmin criticized his friend for "some cheap aesthetics," but praised her tact and courage for "taking on dangerous contemporary issues."[16]

The more radical the journalist, the more polemical the critique. Prominent literary analyst Vl. Kranikhfel'd, of the Marxist-oriented *Sovremennyi mir* (Contemporary world), turned out to be the most puritan of her reviewers, arguing that by inserting the homosexual theme, "the author had poured coal tar into a barrel of honey."[17] No one was more mean-spirited than "Nebukva" (I. M. Vasilenskii) at the quasi-radical *Zhurnal-zhurnalov* (Journal of journals), who, in an analysis of *Evil Spirits,* which he compared to *Wrath of Dionysus,* smirked that "having learned nothing, she has forgotten nothing."[18] In contrast, Bolshevik commentator Alexandra Kollontai, whose own personality was split between the feminism of her gender and the socialism of her politics, was Nagrodskaia's most perceptive critic. The only one who caught on to the centrality of individualism as Nagrodskaia's literary leitmotif, Kollontai deplored this in her heroines because it kept them from establishing solidarity with working women. She also recognized aspects that male critics did not, namely, that Nagrodskaia's female characters functioned as agents of their own destinies and were not simply there to supply a reaction to male actions.[19]

Even those critics who treated Nagrodskaia relatively favorably still clung to gender-based presuppositions. Her books always invited comparison to others on the basis of the author's sex rather than the subject matter. Russian females had entered commercial literature somewhat later than their Western counterparts, and in Russia as elsewhere their immediate popularity sparked considerable suspicion about the potential threat of a feminized culture.[20] Lady novelists tended to write "pornography" in the opinion of most critics, who were primarily male and uncomfortable in general with the post-1905 literary candor about sex. They seemed to become especially sensitive when women discussed it. A key sign that critics did not listen carefully to what Nagrodskaia was actually saying can be gleaned from their consistent linking of her name to that of Anastasia Verbitskaia, the most celebrated of the turn-of-the-century female authors.[21] Both wrote about women, to quote their contemporary W. T. Stead, "from the standpoint of Woman."[22] This sufficed for most reviewers to consider them twin sisters. As writers, Nagrodskaia and Verbitskaia had little in common other than gender, a propensity for exclamation points, and the fact that actress Olga Preobrazhenskaia had left the prestige of the Moscow Arts Theater to star in the silver-screen versions of both of their best-sellers, first in Verbitskaia's *Keys to Happiness* in 1913 and then in *Wrath of Dionysus* two years later.

The fact that their female characters took pleasure in conjugal relations set the two women writers apart from their male contemporaries, a fairly conservative group. Superficial similarities, however, dissolve under systematic analysis. Verbitskaia consciously pushed a moderate socialist agenda, creating many politically activist characters. Nagrodskaia, in contrast, distanced herself from party politics and focused instead on the search for the self, a pursuit that was anathema to socialism. The two writers' philosophical differences shine forth in a comparison of their most famous heroines, Nagrodskaia's Tania Kuznetsova, and Verbitskaia's Mania Eltsova, the dancer-heroine of her five-volume sensation, *The Keys to Happiness* (1908–1913). Both heroines are committed above all else to their art, and both have children out of wedlock; but whereas Tania elects to compromise her principles, Mania commits suicide at her young daughter's bedside because she cannot reconcile herself to her human frailties, the most destructive of which is sexual lust. This divergence on the literary use of sex is significant because of its relationship to the two writers' larger agendas. Verbitskaia proclaimed sex to be a fundamental right for women; Nagrodskaia was more circumspect, concentrating instead on the ambivalences of sexual freedom and fulfillment. The two represented the growing complexity of the "woman question," not a unified female aesthetic.

Although Verbitskaia appeared to upstage Nagrodskaia in the nascent movie industry—the film version of *The Keys to Happiness* was Russia's first blockbuster—Nagrodskaia had the greater impact in the long run. In fact, Nagrodskaia's name appears more frequently in histories of the cinema than in those of literature, linked appropriately (if also unflatteringly) with those of Count Amori (Ilya Rapgof) and Anna Mar, two of the most prolific figures in the new genre.[23] Among her own works, she adapted *Wrath of Dionysus*, *White Colonnade*, and "Ania" for the silver screen. In addition, she wrote at least one original screenplay, "The Sorceress." The protagonist in this story is surprisingly insensitive for a Nagrodskaia heroine. When her car breaks down outside a villa, a seductress appears as if by magic to three men in the process of conducting a seance. Tempting all three, a young man, his father, and his prospective father-in-law, the bewitching title character callously destroys their fellowship by arousing jealousy among them.[24]

Nagrodskaia's particular literary style, with its emphasis on psychological introspection, was exceptionally appropriate to the early Russian cinema.[25] Russia's first directors contributed to the development of cinema as a new art form by concentrating more on character psychology than on plot and action. It would be useful to know how (or whether) the directors handled the homosexual undertones of her work, but unfortunately no copies of her films have survived.[26] The film version of *The White Colonnade* was considered sufficiently important to be included in the Russian Golden Series, an array of films produced by the Thiemann and Reinhardt Studio that was intended to be both artistically respectable and commercially successful. The studio had made a fortune from its lavish production of *Keys to Happiness* and sought to repeat its success with comparable film versions of other well-known books. Nagrodskaia's story posed a technical challenge because it depended upon the special effects of the recurring colonnade to convey a mood, not just on the trick photography common to the first silent movies that fascinated credulous viewers.[27] Given the natural affinity between her style and the early cinema, it is regrettable that Nagrodskaia never became involved with the French film industry, as did several other Russian émigrés prominent in motion pictures.

Nagrodskaia deserves to reclaim her pride of place in Russian cultural history because, as an exemplar of genuinely popular literature, *The Wrath of Dionysus* reflects quotidian life in ways that elitist literature does not. It provides insights into the interests and concerns of average Russians not found in the familiar classics of the Silver Age, as the cultural avant-garde movement at the turn of the century was called. Yet *Wrath of Dionysus* offers much more than glimpses into middlebrow tastes. The Nagrodskaia Phenomenon cannot simply be viewed as the vulgar boulevard having its say, and her fiction deserves to be read in its own right because of the way she engaged readers to address the glaring contradictions that beset a society in the throes of modernization: individuals were empowered by increased mobility, but also atomized by impersonal employment structures; consumerism made plain both the possibilities and limitations inherent in choice; the rationalism demanded by public life could not always contain the impulses that prevailed in private.

Cultural significance aside, why should *The Wrath of Dionysus* endure? The canon of Silver Age classics has already been compiled, and it features works by such avant-garde writers as Andrei Belyi and Fedor Sologub, and on the second tier, by such uncompromising realists as Gorky, Kuprin, and Leonid Andreev. *The Wrath of Dionysus* deserves to be placed alongside them, but this requires that a challenge be mounted against the literary critics, especially the Russian intelligentsia, who treated boulevard novelists so negatively.[28] In her study of American nineteenth-century novels, *Sensational Designs,* Jane Tompkins has argued persuasively for the need to reconceptualize literary theory in such a way as to incorporate boulevard novels into the canonical mainstream. Traditional literary theory awards meritorious stature to books on the basis of their ability to withstand the test of time, that is, on their ability to transmit supposedly "universal" values. A text becomes a classic, according to this paradigm, if it does not depend for its significance upon the historical context in which it was written. This criterion, however, rests on the notion that standards remain constant over time and that they remain in force independent of external social and cultural change. Tompkins asserts the opposite, suggesting instead that "a literary classic is a product of all those circumstances of which it had traditionally been supposed to be independent."[29]

Nagrodskaia's characters grappled with the timeless universal of sex but within a distinctively modern context. The manner in which she addressed physical, emotional, and psychological attributes still sounds remarkably contemporary.[30] Returning to Freud, Nagrodskaia gave a number of her characters extraordinary fetishes, especially those pertaining to physical, but detached, beauty—from the symbolic white colonnade to the ephemeral boy from the circus. She fetishized yearning itself, tapping into another fashionable German sensibility—*Sehnsucht,* or longing for its own sake, the desire to desire.

Her straying from the beaten sexual track took Nagrodskaia to a distinctive, albeit sparse, reading public. Khranikhfel'd's comment about the superfluous homosexual theme suggests that he understood neither the book nor the author's intention. Michel Foucault has argued that homosexuality was "invented" in the late nineteenth century; certainly those with same-sex orientations used changes in the legal and cultural structures to generate a "reverse discourse" in which fiction played a central role.[31] "Earnest" (in the parlance of the times) characters in popular novels increased homosexuals' visibility and, however limited, their ability to extend a "challenge to the very power structure that had produced and marginalized (them)."[32] Nagrodskaia helped this select constituency define itself. Her work merits notice on this alone, but it also contains much for larger audiences.

If we consider this novel as an instrument of cultural transformation within the specific context of late imperial Russia, *The Wrath of Dionysus* occupies a unique position in the dominant intellectual tradition. Themes of personal choice recur frequently in Nagrodskaia's works, as they did in the expanding commercial marketplace, and she problematized choice in a way that ran contrary to the prevailing intellectual norms because she showed its potential to liberate as well as to disappoint. Intellectuals who ridiculed lady novelists did so in self-defense: in an atmosphere that was both highly misogynist and threatened by undereducated barbarians at the literary gates, they had to withdraw to the high ground to protect what turf remained. The artist Tania threatened them because, although she refused to commercialize her art, she was nonetheless willing to compromise her moral standards.

In essence, Nagrodskaia was updating much of the intelligentsia's message, but in doing so she necessarily had to change parts of it. Many boulevard novelists may well have been less talented imitators of the great Russian novelists, but the fact that even in the marketplace they patterned themselves according to models that privileged artistic over commercial success suggests the lasting effects of nineteenth-century political culture. Verbitskaia, who left memoirs as well as a substantial body of work, projected a very strong conviction of the writer's social obligation.[33] Nagrodskaia's choice of themes indicates that she held the same principles. She brought to average Russians the principal issues addressed by the avant-garde: the social function of art, the individual in conflict with the collective, and new opportunities for constructing a sexual identity. She contributed not only to a genre that heightened sexual melodrama but also to a style that showed the direct influence of literary modernism with its mix of stream-of-consciousness, interior monologues, direct speech, and symbolism. Her upbringing had taught her that this was what writers were supposed to do.

Nagrodskaia had come by her dual concerns, sexual liberation and the Russian intelligentsia, naturally. She grew up in one of St. Petersburg's most prominent intellectual circles. Her mother's peculiar relationships, however, complicate the task of reconstructing Nagrodskaia's childhood. Avdotia Iakovlevna Panaeva, the daughter of a professional acting couple at the renowned Alexandrovskii Theater, was married for years to I. I. Panaev. The couple worked together with N. A. Nekrasov, a commanding figure among the intelligentsia, on the staff of *Sovremennik* (Contemporary), one of the most influential journals of the revolutionary 1860s. Despite her marriage, Panaeva was widely known to be Nekrasov's common-law wife, and her husband himself wrote feminist tracts. Theirs was an arranged marriage of convenience, not uncommon among intellectuals of that era because women found themselves legally subordinated to fathers and then to husbands: the "arranged" husbands, who had essentially married their wives to liberate them, granted them considerable personal freedom. Evdokia Apollonovna was born in 1866, when her mother was already forty-six. She was the child of Panaeva's second husband, A. F. Golovachev, another secondary talent at *Sovremennik*. Golovachev died when his daughter was eleven years old, and Nekrasov soon followed him to the grave.

Because of the company she kept, Nagrodskaia's mother remains to this day significantly more familiar in Russian literature than her daughter, despite Nagrodskaia's greater immediate impact on her times. Panaeva wrote primarily about women's issues, and for years after Nekrasov's death she continued to hold mini-court in a salon of nihilist intellectuals, passionately at odds with the obscurantist autocracy. Her most famous novel, *A Woman's Lot,* appeared in 1862 but never approached the prominence of the other contemporary novels that identified her generation, I. S. Turgenev's *Fathers and Sons* and N. G. Chernyshevskii's *What Is to Be Done?* Panaeva died in 1893, almost twenty years before her daughter entered the literary world. The mother established the atmosphere in which the daughter developed her values and ideas, but the women did not discuss their relationship in print.

Perhaps, unlike her mother, Nagrodskaia preferred, early in her adult life, the cult of domesticity to that of Dionysus. Although Nagrodskaia's marriages were apparently more orthodox than her mother's, nothing more than a surname is known of her first husband, Tangiev. They had two children, at least one of whom, a daughter, remained in Russia after the revolution and wrote children's stories. Nagrodskaia also had a granddaughter, Elena Alexandrovna Tangieva-Birzniek, who achieved significant national fame as a ballerina in both Riga and Leningrad; the family relationship is not registered in Soviet sources. Already a mature woman when she married Nagrodskii, an engineer in the Ministry of Transportation, Evdokia Apollonovna had no children with him.[34] Like her mother, she maintained a salon, but the daughter's was rumored to be a gathering place of St. Petersburg's sexually experimental society rather than of political radicals. Nagrodskaia was also popular for her seances, which were famous for their moving furniture.[35]

The Wrath of Dionysus brings much of fin-de-siècle literature and politics into focus, and it highlights the middlebrow view of the intense conflicts still unresolved in 1917. Historically, Russian culture had been perceived as a unique space open to the public, which had been denied formal political institutions under the tsars. The intelligentsia established their influence by trying to maintain the democratic integrity of that culture, in defiance of the autocracy. But as education increased the size of the public capable of accessing this culture, competition developed over definition of the agenda and control of the assets. In other words, Russian culture has historically provided the locus for political struggle, and as in any political contest, the issues changed according to the times. Nagrodskaia continued this tradition, but she also challenged aspects of its message by producing fiction and movies that brought ideas about modernity to an increasingly cosmopolitan audience. Like both her mother and her cultural rival, Verbitskaia, she believed that literature served a politicized function, yet her themes differed in significant ways from theirs. The heroine of *Wrath of Dionysus* fought at least one of Nagrodskaia's battles, how to reconcile art—understood to have an intrinsic social value—with selfish pleasures. Another issue played out in Nagrodskaia's characters' actions was the relationship of the individual to the collective. This had proven especially volatile, because one of the central tenets of nineteenth-century political culture had been an idealized notion of abnegation of the self in favor of the social whole. Commercialism hovered above everything with its threat to subvert the moral integrity of a civil society committed to the common good.

Trapped by their own agenda, Nagrodskaia's critics failed to recognize the true significance of her novel. The main weakness of *Wrath of Dionysus* was not, as they argued, that it sold well to an unsophisticated audience, or that the characters were too superficial, or that its homosexual theme was an intentionally sensational commercial ploy, or even Nagrodskaia's tendentiousness. Rather, it was a shortcoming common to all the classics of the Silver Age: the author could point to the problems but not mediate the solutions. Once Nagrodskaia moved to Paris, an emigrant from the cultural sphere in which the questions she raised had profound meaning for readers, her work could not hope to carry the same weight. Her native St. Petersburg no longer existed; the modern individual about whom she wrote became suffocated by the collective in Leningrad.

Translating any text poses numerous problems because languages do not simply provide an assortment of interchangeable words. The translator often finds him/herself caught between competing objectives: remaining true to the text while appealing to readers of a different time and cultural space. I have sought to maintain the precarious balance between the two, changing Nagrodskaia's punctuation, vocabulary, and verb tenses in some places to make her prose flow more smoothly in English. In the process, I have tried not to sacrifice her inflections. For example, she wrote most of the novel in the first person and in the present tense. The present tense works more efficiently in Russian, where it can cover a multitude of English verbal forms. I preferred to use the past tense much more often to improve readability.

On the matter of voice, Nagrodskaia's use of the first person is crucial for two reasons. First, the main character's interior monologues provide the necessary psychological insights to explain her actions. Second, this literary strategy moves the author away from traditional realism and into the developing language of modernism. Tania Kuznetsova, the artist heroine, speaks both to herself and to the implied reader. In order to distinguish between her voices, I have put those passages addressed to herself in italics and kept the present tense; this is my doing, not Nagrodskaia's.

I have taken liberties in several areas in an effort to make this book more enjoyable to contemporary readers. Nagrodskaia punctuated an extraordinary number of sentences with exclamation points, a detail of style that annoyed critics and, given present-day expectations, tends to trivialize her work by rendering it excessively melodramatic at face value. Therefore, I have used them as economically as possible. Punctuation might be one way in which female writers attempted to create their own aesthetic, so readers in search of this must be referred to the original text.[36] Nagrodskaia often repeated the same words; I have varied her sometimes monotonous use of vocabulary with synonyms. In addition, I dropped a number of sentences and short passages for purposes of brevity. I left out nothing that contributed meaningfully to either plot or character development.

In transliterating Russian words, especially names, I have eschewed the formal Library of Congress system, again in search of improved readability in English. For example, I have dropped soft signs and redundant vowels, and I have used an "x" rather than "ks." Opting for common English usage has not changed any aspect of authorial intent.

NOTES

1. Print runs and prices are taken from *Knizhnaia letopis'*, the tsarist government's week-by-week listing of all books published in the empire. The book was originally published in St. Petersburg by N. Ia. Stoikovaia; by the fourth edition, the publishing house Obshchestvennia pol'za was printing and distributing it.

2. Verbitskaia's Mania Eltsova also gives birth in *Keys to Happiness,* but the presence of a child helps to inspire rather than to prevent her suicide because Mania never wants her daughter to have to compromise her principles for worldly desires.

3. Laura Engelstein, *The Keys to Happiness: Sex and the Search for Modernity in Fin-de-Siècle Russia* (Ithaca: Cornell University Press, 1992), 359.

4. Pierre Bourdieu, for example, has argued that the relationship between art and the appreciation of it generates a distinct form of cultural capital, which can be exercised with the same power as economic capital in maintaining political structures. His ideas apply particularly well to the Russian intelligentsia. See Pierre Bourdieu, "Outline of a Theory of Art Perception," *International Social Science Journal* 2, no. 4 (1968): 589–612.

5. Jane Tompkins, *Sensational Designs: The Cultural Work of American Fiction, 1790–1860* (New York: Oxford University Press, 1985), 200.

6. Bernice Glatzer Rosenthal, ed., *Nietzsche in Russia* (Princeton: Princeton University Press, 1986), supplies a broad survey of the German philosopher's influence in fin-de-siècle Russia.

7. "Tak govoril Zaratustra," trans. S. F. Saburov (St. Petersburg: S. F. Sokolova, 1905). Saburov was one of the most active writers and impresarios in late imperial vaudeville.

8. See E. Koltonovskaia's review in *Rech'*, no. 335 and Likhenval'd's in *Utro Rossii*, no. 358.

9. Ayn Rand's work is comparable to Nagrodskaia's on this point. Although savaged by the intellectual elite, Rand raised philosophical questions important to the middlebrow readers who devoured her books. See Claudia Roth Pierpont, "Twilight of the Goddess," *New Yorker* (July 24, 1995): 70–81.

10. S. Savitskii, introduction to *Gnev Dionisa* (St. Petersburg: Severo-Zapad, 1994), 5.

11. Evdokia Apollonovna Nagrodskaia, *Belaia kolonnada* (Petrograd: M. M. Semenov, 1914), 48.

12. S. Dorotin, "Gospozha Nagrodskaia i ee roman," *Vestnik literatury,* no. 11 (1911): 273–75.

13. S. Dorotin, "Roman, o kotorom govoriat," *Vestnik literatury,* no. 10 (1910): 271–73.

14. B. G., "Gnev Dionisa," *Istoricheskii vestnik* 125, no. 9 (1911): 1160–62.

15. See, for example, two reviews in the liberal Kadet newspaper *Rech'*: Sergei Auslander's on July 26, 1910, no. 202, and E. Kolontovskaia's, on December 6, 1910, no. 335. Auslander was Kuzmin's nephew and Nagrodskaia's close personal friend.

16. M. Kuzmin, "Zametki o russkoi belletristike," *Apollon,* no. 9 (1910): 34.

17. Vl. Kranikhfel'd, "Gnev Dionisa," *Sovremennyi mir,* no. 11 (1910): 103–104.

18. Ne-bukva, "Zlie dukhi," *Zhurnal-zhurnalov,* no. 10 (1915): 3–4.

19. Al. Kollontai, "Novaia zhenshchina," *Sovremennyi mir,* no. 9 (1913): 1151–85.

20. In England in the 1870s and 1880s, 40 percent of the authors were women; the comparative figure for the United States approached 75 percent (ibid., 77). On the smaller number of female writers in Russia in the nineteenth century, see Mary Zirin, "Women's Prose Fiction in the Age of Realism," in Diana Green and Toby Clyman, eds., *Women Writers in Russian Literature* (Westport, CT: Greenwood Press, 1994), 77–94.

21. The only reviewer I found who actually discussed this juxtaposition argued that lumping them together was "unfair" to Nagrodskaia, who was the more "interesting" and "significant" of the two (Iu. Likhenval'd, "Literaturnyi subbotnik," *Utro Rossii,* December 24, 1916, no. 358).

22. Quoted in Elaine Showalter, *Sexual Anarchy: Gender and Culture at the Fin de Siècle* (New York: Viking, 1990), 27.

23. N. M. Zorkaia, *Na rubezhe stoletiii. U istokov massovogo iskusstva v Rossii 1900–1910 godov* (Moscow: Nauka, 1976), 159, 231; and S. S. Ginzburg, *Kinematografiia dorev. Rossii* (Moscow: Iskusstvo, 1963), 214, 230.

24. The "libretto," or synopsis, for "Ved'ma" was published by A. P. Panteleeva in Petrograd in 1916.

25. A stage version of *Wrath of Dionysus* was produced in 1913. The authors drew heavily on the long speeches in the novel, but they excluded those passages pertaining to homosexuality and did not attempt to adapt the heroine's interior monologues. Despite repeating so much of the novel verbatim, the play differs significantly from the book. E. Gern and A. Smirnova, "Gnev Dionisa. Intsenirovka romana Nagrodskoi" (St. Petersburg: Severnaia teatral'naia biblioteka, 1913).

26. Vito Russo, *The Celluloid Closet: Homosexuality in the Movies* (New York: Harper and Row, 1987).

27. At least one reviewer found the recurrent image unconvincing, although the sets and some of the acting received good notices. See *Proektor,* no. 5 (1915): 7–8.

28. Tompkins, *Sensational Designs,* especially the introduction.

29. Ibid., 3–4.

30. Engelstein, *Keys to Happiness,* especially chapter 10.

31. Quoted in Showalter, *Sexual Anarchy,* 14–15.

32. Quoted from Jonathan Dollimore, ibid., 15.

33. A. A. Verbitskaia, *Moemu chitateliu: Avtobiograficheskie ocherki s dvumia portretami* 2nd ed. (Moscow: I. N. Kushnerev, 1911; 1st ed. 1908).

34. Biographical material about Nagrodskaia has been taken from several sources. Her obituary in the Parisian émigré newspaper *Vozrozhdenie,* May 21, 1930, no. 1814, provided a few details. Her

publisher and close friend M. I. Semenov wrote a four-page biography that was placed in her minuscule collection of papers in the Russian State Archives for Literature and Art, f. 1118, op. 1, d. 3.

35. Savitskii, introduction to *Gnev Dionisa*, 8.

36. Elaine Showalter, *A Literature of Their Own: British Women Novelists from Bronte to Lessing* (Princeton: Princeton University Press, 1977), 258, discusses Dorothy Richardson's quasi-modernist work, which is mindful of Nagrodskaia's structuring and suggests the possibility of a female aesthetic from this era.

The Wrath of Dionysus

The day was sunny and bright, but my mood was foul. I was infuriated that I, who had never been sick a day in my life, suddenly, today, had to travel to the Caucasus to take the cure.* I can't stand the Caucasus. There's fever everywhere—and wherever there's no fever, there's no greenery or water either. Mother Nature! In order to enjoy a beautiful view, you have to put up with considerable misery and discomfort. This isn't Switzerland; there I can have it all—wild mountains, ragged cliffs, smiling valleys, lakes, and rivers. But here you travel along miles of monotonous terrain, and then more miles in a miserable, uncomfortable saddle, wondering the whole time why you haven't been robbed or murdered. And under foot, poisonous spiders, scorpions. . . .

Nothing could have made me go, if it hadn't been for that damned pneumonia! The doctor insisted that I go to the south.

---

*Many health spas, especially mineral baths, were located in the Caucasus. Fashionable in high society from late in the eighteenth century, the spas were also frequented by a more middle-class element a century later.

There's also a south in Europe, where it's cheaper and more comfortable, much cheaper, but seeing that I'd be there alone. . . .

So, I'm going to *this* south to meet the family of my "future husband." Ilya and I have been living together as soulmates for five years. We haven't been able to get married because his first wife, from whom he separated eight years ago, before he met me, never gave him a divorce. Now she wants to marry again, so they'll divorce this autumn and I will become his legal wife. This obliges me to meet his relatives: a mother, two sisters, and a younger brother. It means I have to get along with them, become one of them, and please them all. Of course I'm not doing this for myself. I couldn't care less. I'm doing it for Ilya, because he loves them so much. How he suffered these five years because he couldn't bring us together; and now I'm going to see them as his fiancée! I'll be one of the family. "They'll take good care of you"—those were his words.

I'll try, I'll try. I can be attractive to people when I want to be, and I very much want to be for Ilya's sake. He adores them, and they in turn idolize him. If only I like them, it will be considerably easier for me to capture the "enemy fortress," and I understand all too well that it is indeed an enemy stronghold. At first they ignored my existence but then, because of Ilya's letters and his trips to them last year, formal greetings and best wishes began to appear in their letters.

I'm not afraid of the sisters, but the mother! She knows all about our relationship. I'm a widow and an artist. That means I'm Bohemian. There was a period of three years between the death of my husband and my acquaintance with Ilya, and any mother could fill that time with horrors. Mothers are jealous. These are all minuses, minuses. She loves Ilya as though he were still a child and takes great pride in his stature as a rising star among scientists. Didn't she fantasize about going to Petersburg, fussing over him, basking in his limelight? And I took this away from her.

When he got married the first time, fourteen years ago, he was still a student and she wasn't so anxious. His wife was the daughter of close friends, an eighteen-year-old student with a dowry. . . . But what came of this? Separation after two years.

Luckily, there were no children or Ilya would not have tolerated the situation until now.

But me? "Tania, my darling, you're not well?" Ilya asked, hovering over me. I see his handsome face, his compassionate gray eyes, his curly blonde beard—I laugh and answer, "No, Sigurd." I've called him Sigurd since one of his female admirers—and among the students he has many—persuaded me that Ilya looks like the hero of a Scandinavian saga.

Many people admire his appearance. His tall, athletic figure always stands out in a crowd. Oh, it was easy to fall in love with him, with such a smart, talented, strong man. I love him so much that it seems I've never loved anyone in my life as I do him; but why don't I have that physical passion to which so many women confess?

"You don't understand it, you're so righteous and unemotional," one of my friends told me.

I don't know how "righteous" I am. Really, when the conversation turns to sexual perversions, degeneracies, I'm never shocked and don't even feel particularly disgusted . . . as long as these deviations don't include children. I can't even imagine stiff enough punishment for the abuse of children, but it's none of my business how two adults enjoy themselves in private. Personally, I don't need such enjoyment and I don't like talking about such things. I won't eat spoiled game hens, but I won't judge the person who savors them; I won't even be surprised by it. I myself eat overripe bananas. I eat them with pleasure, even when they upset my stomach, and don't consider this sinful.

"What are you thinking about, Tania?" Ilya asked.

"I'm sorry to have to leave you," I answered, suddenly aware of how depressed I was to part with him. I threw my arms around him, almost bursting into tears. He stroked my hand, joked, but I could tell that he was upset.

"I hope you'll be comfortable. The conductor said that there's only one other passenger in this car, and at night he'll move to the sleeper. You'll be alone," said Ilya.

I glanced at the luggage rack. It held the exact same suitcase as mine—brown leather, and an elegant toilet case. A gray topcoat and a camera with a strap lay on the seat.

"Ilya!" I cried in despair, "I left my camera in my suitcase!"

"It's because you have a completely masculine dislike of hand luggage," he laughed.

The second whistle. My heart tightened.

"Good-bye, Iliusha. Write." I hugged him, tears welling in my eyes.

"My darling, for God's sake take care of yourself. Send me a telegram from Moscow; and if you're tired, spend the night there."

The third whistle blew. I leaned out the window, nodding my head. Ilya walked along the platform.

"From Moscow, Rostov, Novorossiisk—telegrams. Postcards every day. Please take care of yourself, Taniusha."

He tarried a little, the platform faded from view, but I remained at the window. A feeling of dread gripped me, tighter and tighter. My temples pounded—that would be too much, to have an attack of neuralgia. I turned and sat down. In the door stood the owner of the luggage in the opposite rack. He tipped his hat, and I nodded my head, conscious that he was a foreigner.

When I first board a train I feel disoriented and don't even want to try to make myself more comfortable. I looked out the window at the outskirts of St. Petersburg flashing past me, the factory smokestacks, the fences, the station house, and I felt irritable. Every aggravation wears on my nerves and makes me nasty; indeed, the only two emotions that bring me to tears are irritation and tenderness, strange as that may seem. If my bad mood continues up to my arrival, I can kiss my strategic plans good-bye. Not even close relatives can tolerate my foul temper. At those moments my face distorts into a repugnant mask, and even Ilya has said to me, "Taniusha, how unattractive you are!"—and yet he thinks I'm almost beautiful.

Right now my whole physiognomy must look awful; it's a good thing no one can see it. Oh, my neighbor. I glanced over at him. He was settled into the corner, reading a book with a yellow cover. I have good eyesight—it was Baudelaire. Having nothing else to do, I began to examine my co-traveler. Yes, without question a foreigner. His style of dress, his haircut—not Russian. Simple but elegant. His face was irregular but very handsome. An attractive forehead with prominent eyebrows, thick and velvety, slightly grown together, a straight, blunt, almost snub nose, a soft mouth, with the lower lip almost shorter than the upper, and a wide, jutting chin. And such marvelous eyelashes! His eyes were lowered, but more than likely nice. Too bad I didn't have my camera—I could have snapped a picture right then. That face would come in handy for a painting.

How old could he be? That smoothly shaven face could be deceiving, but he is probably no younger than thirty. He had dimples in childhood. Slight wrinkles around his eyes . . . thirty, maybe younger, but someone who has already lived a great deal. He has such a thicket of hair, combed smoothly and parted in the middle, with one lock curling on his forehead. Dark hair, with a reddish hue and terribly shiny—undoubtedly pomade. I was imagining how much dust it would attract in the course of the journey.

He shifted his position, crossing his legs. His body was very slender, elegant—so youthful, and not tall. He would not even come up to my Sigurd's shoulder. No, he's just a bit taller than I am. What can his nationality be? I would guess a southern Frenchman or northern Spaniard.

The train stopped. My companion looked out the window and then at me. "Pardon, madame!" he said, quickly changing his position.*

"Please make yourself at ease," I said in French. "If you stand on ceremony, I won't feel comfortable." Oh, those eyes, I thought to myself. Dark, deep, big.

"I see," I continued, laughing, "that you want to lie down. Stretch out, smoke if you want to. We won't even notice each other."

He thanked me and smiled. What pretty teeth, a trifle large. When he smiled, his cheeks dimpled lightly. Oh—smile some more, it makes you look so handsome! But rather than smile, he picked up his Baudelaire and immersed himself in it more deeply.

---

*Stark had crossed his legs, a gesture that would have been impolite in mixed company.

I began looking out the window again, contemplating my mission. Ilya hadn't said anything, but I knew how much he wanted them to like me. My notion of this family from Ilya's stories and their letters to him is fuzzy. The mother was widowed just as Ilya was graduating from the university. There had been eight or nine in the family, but the middle children had died, leaving the two oldest, Ilya and Katia, and the two youngest. The mother had no means of support beyond a meager pension and a house with a garden in (the town of) S.[*] In order to raise the younger children, she and Katia had opened a preparatory boarding school for girls. The older sister, who was already twenty-eight, had devoted herself completely to this school. Ilya had described the younger girl, eighteen, as a sweet, fun-loving girl-child. The brother, who had just finished the gymnasium,[**] was a year younger—but he didn't enter into my equation. What could I do to make them like me? What would move them? My artistic talent perhaps? My temples throbbed. My artistry would mean nothing. I'm sure they like only pretentious subjects: a dying mother and a self-important noblewoman, offering charity from her carriage to a beggar and her yellow-green children. In such instances children are always painted in Veronese green, ocher, and zinc white. They won't grasp the significance of execution, the elegance of the coloring. I presume both mother and daughter speak in phrases from the moderately liberal "thick" journals about pedagogy, labor—and all so didactically! No! I've already begun to hate them.

I won't go there. I'll stop in Moscow and turn back. My side hurts. My temples are throbbing. It would be better if I went to Rome. Although I would evaporate in the heat, I was advised to go south, and at least in Rome I have my cool, charming studio. I was planning to go there anyway in the autumn to complete the painting I began last year. I could go there now, be in the south, finish the piece, and then this fall I wouldn't have to be separated from Iliusha.

[*] It is typical of Russian writers to denote cities and towns by a single letter rather than the full name.

[**] A secondary school that prepares students to attend a university.

"Are your sisters pretty?" I'd asked him once, because it was difficult to judge from old worn-out photographs.

"You know," he answered, "I love them so much that to me they're prettier than anyone, except you," he corrected himself. "That sounds like they're freaks, but I love all things pretty and elegant."

I live an ordinary life, except for my art. There's nothing mundane in that—everything's brilliant, every day's a holiday. My art will help me when I get there. I'll paint sketches of the sea, of trees in blossom. And "they" will look at the canvas and ask, "Why are you always painting landscapes and flowers?" Then I'll paint a prisoner being beaten in a country jail, a study of three sheepskins and a pair of felt boots. Indeed, they have. . . . Oh! I'm being malicious again. Why am I so unfair? Maybe "they" are smart, kind, good. . . . How my temples throb. . . . I must not think . . . it hurts, it hurts. . . .

"Madame souffre?"

I flinched. My co-traveler had put aside Baudelaire and was looking at me. Good Lord, what beautiful eyes he has. There's a sort of childlike wonder in those eyes. He looked at me the way intelligent children often look at their elders when they don't understand something.

"Neuralgia," I said between clenched teeth. Suddenly I was seized by a nervous trembling. Oh, these nerves. It's tolerable if it's the nerves, but what if this is a relapse into the fever? Another long illness? No. It would be better to die. I lay down, turned to the wall, nasty convulsions shivering through my body.

Why did I leave Ilya? I'll go back at once. I don't care if this is stupid childishness, I truly am sick. I ache all over, my side, my head, and this trembling. My thoughts were spinning. I sat up and grabbed my head. I was still wearing my hat; I'd forgotten to take it off, and the hatpins had secured it to my hair.

"Allow me to help you." I felt a hand in a soft leather glove on mine. He unpinned my hat and put it in the rack. I started shivering more violently. I wanted to scream, to burst into tears. This weakness, this separation from Ilya, the unpleasant thought of trying to make friends with those people. . . . I was at the point of bursting into tears. And what about this fellow? If he weren't here, if I were alone I'd be able to pull myself together. His presence at this moment was agonizing. The aroma of his cologne mingled with that of a good cigar suddenly went to my head. I was just about to do something to offend him when he began to speak.

"You're very ill. Is there anything I can do to help?"

I collected my strength, trying to get a grip on myself, curled up into a ball, my teeth chattering.

"Do you need a drink of water? Let me ring for the porter."

"Yes, yes." I could barely get the words out, curling up even tighter, feeling as though everything was collapsing in on me. I was struggling with myself, trying to keep from having an attack of nerves. I could handle it. I raised my head. The porter stood before me with a glass of water, which I drank greedily.

"Disgusting! It's warm and stale," I cried. Suddenly, looking at the speechless porter, the situation seemed very comical.

"Oh for heaven's sake, forgive me," I said, turning to my companion, "I've disturbed you."

"Oh, it's nothing," he smiled. "You seem to have poisoned this lady with your water. Do you have any seltzer? No? Bring some at the next station, please."

He spoke very correct Russian, with only a trace of an accent. This made him incredibly appealing.

"How well you speak Russian," I remarked.

"Oh, my father is English, but my mother is Russian."

"Really. I took you for a Frenchman, even a Parisian."

"My parents always lived in France, and I grew up in Paris. Are you feeling better?"

"Completely fine," I laughed. "Except that now I'm embarrassed that I bothered you. I've just recovered from a bad case of pneumonia, and my nerves are playing tricks on me."

I stopped and began to get irritated again. Why was I rambling on? Was it so important to strike up a friendship with the first person I met?

"Should I close the window?" he asked solicitously.

"Oh, no thank you. It's hot."

"Well, at least take my seat." He jumped up, "It's not drafty there. You'll be more comfortable."

I thanked him and we changed places. I pulled out a newspaper. I'd brought a good book, but I'd left it in the suitcase in the rack, and I didn't want to get it down. My traveling companion no doubt would get up to help, but my nerves were still jumpy, and his every movement would irritate me. Sit still, I thought to myself, and hide behind the paper.

He didn't return to his Baudelaire but pulled a cigarette case out of his pocket and stood up, heading for the door.

"Please, smoke in here," I said hurriedly. "You won't bother me. The window is open, and I myself even smoke from time to time."

He hesitated.

"Give me a cigarette," I said, "and I'll light up, too."

"After pneumonia!" he cried.

I found his surprise extremely amusing.

"Oh, please," I affected baby talk, reaching for one.

"But it's bad for you."

"'You only live twice'—do you know that saying?"

"Yes, but there's also another Russian proverb: 'God looks after those who look after themselves'"; he laughed, offering me the case.

When he smiled, his eyes crinkled slightly. There was something wonderfully attractive about his face, more than just his good looks, I thought to myself, looking into his eyes. Suddenly his long eyelashes lowered quickly beneath my gaze. He lit my cigarette and again we settled into ourselves, he with his book and me with my newspaper.

After the spasms I had become terribly warm. My face burned and my head began to swim. At last we pulled into the station. Feeling better, I looked out the window. A group of people waited on the platform: a heavyset policeman, his feet planted apart, standing self-importantly, and at his side two characters in long fur coats groveling about him. The ruddy-faced policeman, with brushlike mustaches, was clearly an important person. The man on his right was thin, haggard, spiteful, fawning all over him with an obsequious smirk. On his left, the other one looked affable, sweating in his diligence, shuffling his feet in place as, ever the menial, he tried to stand still.

What a picture! They're even too stereotypically typical, and good heavens, I don't have my camera with me!

"May I use your Kodak?" I turned to my neighbor in such excitement that he dropped his book. I looked at him imploringly.

"Of course. But unfortunately I've finished this roll of film. I'll put in another."

"No, no. We'll be too late."

I grabbed my notebook and a pencil and feverishly began to sketch the group. I couldn't think about anything, I could only hurry. The second whistle! Give me just one more minute. The third whistle. . . . The train started to pull away—but I was in ecstasy. The cop and his two sidekicks had been eradicated, kidnapped—they were mine! How sweet my success!

"Oh, madame, you are a true artist." I heard a voice and saw my companion's face leaning over my pad. I saw his profile . . . and suddenly went crazy, tormented by the desire to kiss that smoothly shaven cheek. I flinched, apprehensive of these feelings.

"You're an artist?" he asked, still looking at the drawing.

"It's my métier, monsieur," I said, laughing, quickly pulling back, leaving him holding the notebook. He asked to look at it. I nodded. He began leafing through it attentively, and I got down my suitcase and began searching for the bromide. It's disgusting medicine—it gives me pimples—but my damned nerves didn't give me any choice.

"Is this your husband? He accompanied you to the station," asked my co-traveler, holding up a drawing I had made at one of Ilya's lectures about some hieroglyphics from the Yucatán. While he was giving his talk, I was not listening, just sketching his dear, sweet face.

"Yes, it's my husband."

"What a handsome man."

That irritated me. "A handsome man"—is that all?

"Yes," I said. "He's not only handsome but also very intelligent, and that counts for more in a man."

"Yes, of course," he answered, trying to suppress a smile.

I looked closely at his face and thought, if I could draw his face, I would highlight the contrast in his features. That chin—energy and strong will. The mouth, delicate, feminine, revealing the weakness, the softness of his character. Put this together and add those eyes—naive and sad—and you will become a believer in physiognomy!

"You have a remarkable talent. You're a lucky woman, madame," he said to me, bowing as he returned the notebook.

"You're very kind. I don't know how talented I am, but it's true that I'm a lucky woman."

He bowed his head politely.

"I salute a happy person! It's such a rarity."

I became irritated again. Everything I said seemed so terribly foolish. I tossed the notebook down on the seat and picked up the newspaper. I tried to concentrate on what I was reading. I kept shifting around in my seat. It was hot and stuffy. Thoughts kept buzzing around in my head. I had been too weak to travel. I shouldn't have listened to my doctor and left Petersburg, shouldn't have listened to my heart and gone south to visit Iliusha's family. But I won't think about that. As soon as I arrive I'll get right to work on a portrait of Ilya's family. That will make him very happy. I'll also do a watercolor of the cop for him—he loves that comical genre. "Taniusha, you have a quality rare in women—humor," Ilya often tells me. He finds it amusing that I have so many masculine characteristics.

I developed these traits from living independently, from my profession. I love beauty, but not as most women do. For example, when I see factory machinery running smoothly, it takes my breath away; and when I read about some new scientific discovery or technical invention, I am moved to tears. I find great poetry in mathematics. My lack of concern with trifles sometimes leads to a certain disorder, but at the same time, I love beautiful clothes, precious stones, flowers . . . no, I don't appreciate flowers as other women do. I can't grow them, but only use them to decorate a room or myself so that I can appreciate them. I love beautiful women very much, even more than I do flowers. How many stunning women we have here, more than anyplace else; but I so rarely see handsome men—this is patently obvious at crowded functions. But what a multitude of charming female faces one sees at our Petersburg balls! Some, you simply want to kiss. I often want to kiss a beautiful woman's face, but never a man's. . . . Today? I raised my eyes to look at my companion. He was reading earnestly. Very quietly, I picked up my pad, and hiding behind my newspaper, briskly, stealthily sketched the face bent over the book.

The train began to slow down. We approached the station. I quickly shut my notebook. My traveling companion also arose.

⋯⇒◯⇐⋯

I sat in the buffet and ate some borsch. That had been the problem: hunger had upset my nerves. I hadn't had breakfast this morning, I'd been so worried about leaving Ilya. Suddenly, my mood picked up. I looked around me at the bustling crowd, searching their faces for the pretty and the prototypical, enjoying the light from the setting sun as it reflected on the glasses stacked on the buffet table. How lovely the rays falling on the woman in the violet blouse sitting by the window!

"You shouldn't be so careless," someone said, and a hand in a soft gray glove was holding my purse. What was happening? Could I have dropped it getting out of the train car? I keep my passport and money in my bodice, but my billfold, ticket, and baggage check were in my purse.

"What a scatterbrain!" I cried, frozen in shock, spoon in one hand and crust of bread in the other. I laughed and thanked my co-traveler. He ordered something from the approaching waiter and then asked if he could join me. We chatted happily and easily. He laughed at the goings-on of absent-minded ladies, at my appetite, and he assured me that he did not have to worry about my health, although I had frightened him today. He took off his gloves and I looked at his hands. He had rather large hands, not "aristocratic," as they say; but his fingers were long and his nails manicured. On the little finger of his left hand he wore a large gold ring with a fine ruby.

Who was he exactly? Also an artist, a musician or an itiner-

12

ant "distinguished foreigner"? As if he were reading my mind, he jokingly said that it was high time he introduced himself and handed me his card, apologizing that he had only business cards with him.

Edgar Karlovich Stark
Representative, Ogier and Co., Lumber Sales
Paris, Dijon, Marseilles

I had to laugh—I'd taken him for a musician or a distinguished foreigner. I didn't understand it myself, but suddenly I became very gay, babbling incessantly, even making eyes at an army officer, who was twirling his mustache and gazing at me with bedroom eyes.

The whistle. We hurried to the train, now both of us babbling without pause. It was a strange conversation, as if we had to speak very quickly, had to find out each other's opinions on every subject imaginable, to tell each other events from our childhoods and our travels, moving from music to politics, from literature to the theater. We argued and made up. Then night fell; this was during the white nights, when the sun never sets completely. I talked to him about the beauty of this time of year, and he told me about his first impression of these nights, in a forest in Norway, and our conversation became even more bizarre: lines from poems, scraps of phrases, passages from favorite authors . . . yet familiar poetry sounded brand new from his lips.

I was surprised at how well he knew Russian literature and how much he loved it. He told me about his Russian literature teacher, a sickly political emigrant, who had influenced him greatly. A talented, good man, but quite short-tempered: one minute he'd be throwing a book at him and calling him an idiot, the next he'd be kissing and praising him. He told me how this teacher slowly wasted away, dying in his arms.

Suddenly, I became heart-sick, the white night, the sad story. . . . I remembered how Ilya remained at my bedside throughout my illness. I desperately wanted to be with Ilya. I sat silently, looking out at the white night, at Venus shining brightly in the rose-colored ribbon of sunset.

"Next stop!"

I flinched, and then laughed at my fright. The conductor was announcing to my companion that his place in the sleeping car was ready, so he gathered his things.

"Now you'll sleep better, only be sure to fasten the door tightly," he said after the conductor left. "Still, I'd advise you to go to the women's car."

"Oh, I'm not a coward," I answered. I wanted him to stay, but he was in a hurry to go.

"May I have one more cigarette?" I asked.

He took out his case and stopped abruptly. He screwed his eyes slightly, a smile just touching his wet lips.

"I'm afraid," he offered it, bowing his head slightly. This glance, this eye movement, this smile were all filled with a kind of feminine flirtation—not feminine so much as childlike. Blood began to pound in my head.

"As you wish," I said, using all my strength to sound casual.

"Well, ask as you did before," he answered me very quietly.

I wasn't myself at all. I said coldly, "How did I ask before? I don't remember . . . just give me one, please."

"That's not the same!" he winced, offering me the cigarette case. This grimace, and the movement of his head and shoulders, seemed at once graceful and direct. I took a cigarette.

"Good night."

"Good night." I offered my hand. He bowed and kissed it respectfully.

With that barely discernible touch of my hand, my insides began to smolder. Thank God the door was closed and he had gone. Mechanically, I put my hand to my lips and began to kiss it hungrily. . . . *What am I, sick? or just going crazy? What is this?*

⋆⇒◦⇐⋆

I traveled two more days and nights. I ate, drank, conversed with a very nice lady who was accompanying two young cadets from Moscow to Novorossiisk, and flirted a bit with two engineers coming from Rostov. In the youngest cadet's notebook, I drew wild Indians and Nat Pinkerton. Laughing, chatting, but still just thinking about one thing. What's happening? Has this "Representative from Ogier and Co." hypnotized me?

I didn't see him in Moscow. The train pulled in early in the morning. No, I would never see him again. So why all this?

That night I dreamed I was kissing his smooth cheek, running my fingers through his hair, drinking in those eyes . . . bottomless and black. Truly, awake I've never experienced anything like this with my husband or with my lovers. Before I met Ilya I'd had only two other involvements: reckless and brief. Not even with Ilya, my dear, darling, beloved! They all accused me of frigidity. They didn't say this, but. . . . I don't want to think about this because it's disgusting, nasty, dirty.

But why? Because I love Ilya. I have been and will be his wife. His mother and sisters, chaste girls, are awaiting me. Because I don't know that other man, I cannot and will not love him. Because in Ilya I've found my ideal. Ilya's even more handsome: he is strength and power, compared to that slender, graceful, smooth figure . . . yet "he" must be strong, his shoulders are broad—there, I'm doing it again, because it's beginning to get dark. Morning must hurry; I'm afraid of the night.

I separated from my companion in Novorossiisk and boarded the steamship. Off we sailed. The sea was like glass, so calm— even I felt fine, I, who get seasick on the Fontanka Canal!*

One of the engineers got off at the first stop, but the other continued further. Today I took a closer look at him: a nice ruddy complexion with a small, round beard, curly brown hair, and perceptive gray eyes. He was a witty conversationalist, easy to be with. Sitting on the deck, I painted the three pilgrims who, for

---

*The Fontanka Canal is one of the major waterways that runs through the heart of St. Petersburg.

two rubles, had agreed to pose. However, they'd had to ask a monk on his way to the monastery at Mount Athos whether or not this was a sin. The monk thought about it, approved, then decided that he himself would oversee us. He sat next to them and dozed off, his fat hands lying across his enormous stomach. I painted him, for free.

Sidorenko, the engineer, sat next to me, handing me my paints as I requested them. We had a wonderful time, chatting, laughing.

"Such a pity," he said, "that we met, spent these two days together, and will probably never see each other again."

"Who knows? Fate sometimes brings people together in the most unexpected ways. Where are you going?"

"To S."

I began to chuckle. He looked at me in surprise.

"I'm going to S. too!"

"Not really! That's terrific. You must permit me to call upon you."

"Of course. I'll introduce you to the family I'm going to be staying with, the Tolchins. Perhaps you've heard of them?"

"Yes, yes. And I've heard much good."

"I'll present you to some delightful young ladies, and I hope that you won't be bored for a minute."

"You don't need to introduce me to anyone; I'll be coming to see you. It's true, although we've only met, I feel like you're family."

"Viktor Petrovich! You must have an amazing number of such relatives all over Russia." I shook my head.

He blushed suddenly.

"Of course you have every right to laugh at me, but sometimes, well, you can become closer to someone in two days than to someone else you've known for ten years. I'm a very open person, which some people consider a shortcoming. True?"

"Not I," I answered softly.

"You're a special person."

"No, I'm not so unusual, and I cannot stand it when people charge me with trying to be unconventional." My tone suddenly sharpened.

"My God, Tatiana Alexandrovna,* I said nothing of the sort!" he exclaimed.

"You said you found something exceptional in me," I said, staring ahead at the deepening shadows falling across the white kerchief on the young pilgrim.

"You didn't understand me! I simply said you aren't like other people. . . ."

"Worse?"

"Of course not."

"Best of all?"

"Oh, that's not the point. You're, well. . . ."

"You're tripping over your tongue," I laughed.

"You do that to people," he answered, annoyed, and picked up my sketchbook and began leafing through it.

We sat in silence. The older pilgrims dozed, while the young girl gazed into the distance with large, melancholy eyes. What a sweet face! A thick red braid hung under the white kerchief, a small mouth, half-opened. . . . What was she thinking about? How was she reconciling her sadness with her fascination at everything happening around her? If I were a man, I wouldn't be in love with her; but I would want this girl for my sister or daughter. She was clearly one of those persons with whom it is so easy, so comfortable to live.

"That's a familiar face," Sidorenko exclaimed.

I turned around and saw that he was looking at my drawing of "the one." I shuddered, as if from fright, not daring to speak for fear my voice would tremble.

"Who is this?" Sidorenko asked again, handing me the album.

I glanced at it and responded casually, "Oh, someone I traveled with as far as Moscow. An Englishman, I can't remember his name."

---

*The heroine's full name is Tatiana Alexandrovna Kuznetsova. The polite form of address, such as the one used here by someone she does not know well, would include both her Christian name and patronymic, just as she calls him Viktor Petrovich. Ilya and other intimate friends use diminutives, especially Tania, Tata, Taniushka, Tatochka. Many other characters throughout the novel are also called by their full names by some people and diminutives by others.

"Stark!"

I put such a large blotch on the face of the third pilgrim that if my companion had had any feeling for painting, he would have noticed it. But he didn't and, gathering my composure, I answered, "Stark? Why yes, I think so. How do you know him?"

"I met him here three years ago, in the Caucasus. The director of one of the factories introduced us. Stark was the representative of some big firm that bought various expensive woods and exported them to France. He's bright and an engaging conversationalist. I stayed with him when I went to Paris last year."

"So you're good friends?"

"How can I put it . . . we're acquaintances. We can't really be friends because we differ on so many things."

"What exactly?"

"How can I explain . . . we disagree on almost everything, but mostly about politics and women, or the 'woman question,' whichever you prefer," smiled Sidorenko.

"The 'woman question'? How does that interest you?"

"What can I say. I certainly don't support equal rights for women, but I respect them. Stark is just the opposite. He demands rights for them, yet at the same time he personally regards them as so much trash. In Paris, we partied a lot. We behaved, as they say, 'as cavaliers,' but I was always incensed by his attitude toward women: he would pick them up in passing and then drop them just as quickly. True, these women were for sale, but his opinion about proper ladies was no better.

"Once we were returning home from dinner with a family we know. Enchanted with one wonderfully sweet girl, I asked him if he hadn't noticed how much attention she'd been paying him. He shrugged his shoulders and said, 'I never start affairs with young girls and virtuous ladies. Ça pleure!' Now isn't that a nice expression? These gentlemen only understand cold depravity. They cannot love respectable women."

"But a true gentlemen cannot court a nice girl without serious intentions," I answered nonchalantly.

"Well, yes, but you still can't approach every woman with only a lewd purpose in mind. If it so happens you meet a woman you like, maybe even fall in love with, then you won't be worrying about inconveniences and commitments. To worry about those things would not be true love.

"For example, Stark had an affair with a Spanish dancer because he'd heard that she was unattainable. What he didn't come up with! He brought flowers, sat for hours in her dressing room, gave her jewels, paid her bills. I actually believed that he genuinely cared, that this wasn't a joke. He even fought a duel over her! Finally she yielded, and we had to celebrate this event in a restaurant. The three of us were having a great time when Stark received a business telegram. He read it, turned to me, and said in Russian, 'I have some very important business dealings. I need to spend a few days working intensively on some diplomatic arrangements, and I never let women interfere with business. Take the lovely Mercedes for yourself; it would be a shame to waste my 20,000 francs.'

"At first I couldn't grasp what he was saying. Then he turned to her, kissed her hand very politely, and informed her that to his chagrin he had to return home and get to work on some important matters and therefore he was transferring his rights to her to his companion, that is, to me.

"If you could have seen her face! She jumped up, pointed to the door and screamed 'Get out!' Then she collapsed on the table, sobbing. He shrugged his shoulders, wished us good night and left. You tell me—is it acceptable to insult a woman like that?"

"Of course this was a bit cynical, but if this woman had already been paid for," I answered, angry with myself because I felt weak while Sidorenko was talking. I was imagining his face, his eyes, his lips.

"Tatiana Alexandrovna, that's not the point! That poor woman, in the midst of sobbing, assured me that money had played no role whatsoever. From his behavior she believed he loved her, and she was happy because of this love. In general he is terribly cynical about love and doesn't believe in it. Once he arranged an entertainment that simply grated upon my feelings. I can't even describe it to you."

"Not even to me?" I was surprised.

"No."

"It must have been extremely indecorous," I said, "and I'm dying to know."

"One could say that the facts themselves aren't shocking, but the thought behind them is truly pornographic."

"Oh, tell me. I'm no naive young girl."

"I can't."

"Oh. How stupid," I answered, agitatedly gathering up my paint and brushes. I couldn't paint any more, so I slammed the box shut.

Sidorenko looked at my sketch closely and said, "You are a bona fide artist, Tatiana Alexandrovna."

That's the same thing "he" had told me!

"A lot you know," I blurted out. I could barely contain myself, almost tearing the sketch out of his hands and turning to go away.

"Tatiana Alexandrovna! Why are you so upset?" he asked, following me.

I felt that I had to explain my rudeness and said angrily, "You've infuriated me. What is this, getting a person interested in something and then dropping it. If you can't complete the story, don't begin it in the first place. I'm very curious . . . and I despise it when people converse with me as with a young girl. . . . I appreciate true collegiality. Listen, I won't speak to you again until you've told me the story of Mr. Stark's crime," I added teasingly.

"I just can't. I can't without insulting your feelings."

I wanted to say, what does someone like you know about my emotions? but instead added peevishly, "As you wish. It's your affair," and went into my stateroom.

Once in the room I tore off my smock and buried my face in my pillow. It was torment, I wanted to see him so much. I wanted to kiss his eyes, his lips, the cheek above his neck. I wanted to smell his cologne. Why had I started talking about him? I certainly hadn't heard anything positive. Oh, let him be whatever he wants, a fool, a lecher, a drunk! At this moment all I wanted were his smiles, his kisses! But Ilya?

I jumped up, grasping my head. My temples throbbed. I started to weep from a combination of fury and shame—but then calmed down. What kind of idiocy is this? What am I thinking? This is gibberish, a sickness. Of course I love only Ilya. All this nonsense is not love! If someone told me at this moment that "he" had died, I would rejoice. It is agonizing for me that he exists.

Okay, Tatochka, I told myself, are you fifteen years old and have you fallen madly in love with a handsome stranger? No. At fifteen I only fell for actresses, dancers, and beautiful women. My first man was my husband. I was married at seventeen and a widow by age twenty. I had fallen for his hussar's uniform and his liquid tenor as he serenaded me with gypsy romances. It mattered a great deal to me that all the women who frequented my mother's salon went crazy for his mustache. And he thought he could pay his debts from my dowry!

What an idiotic marriage. Within six months he had returned to his old flame. I was so insulted! That's exactly what I was, "insulted." Then it became a source of entertainment. One of my girlfriends and I found her letters to him in his desk and read them, then baited him with allusions to them. I drew caricatures of the two of them and mailed them to him. He didn't dare ask me directly—he was flustered, confused. And I loved it, I really did. I could be as capricious as I wanted. I could paint for hours, and he couldn't forbid me to enter the academy, and he couldn't force me to spend time with his boring society friends. I lived exactly as I wanted to.

I did, however, have one great sorrow—that my children did not survive. Strange as it may seem, this man didn't leave me any memories. Not long ago I had trouble trying to remember his name. His first name was Alexei, but no matter how I racked my brain, I couldn't come up with his patronymic.

There were two others after him. I can't say why or how I got involved. I certainly didn't love them. One dumped me because he was jealous of the other, and that one I tired of in less than a week. But it seemed that they loved me.

Ilya! That's the one I love, and only him. How close we have become, how well we work together. He's like a brick wall that protects me, my truest, most dependable friend. I couldn't survive losing him. He's not only my husband, but also my friend, brother, and father. Indeed, I have no close relatives. Everything that's good in me I owe to him. All that I live for is my art and him. He loves me, too, as both a friend and a woman. Maybe he's even too passionate. What am I lacking? I. . . . "You're so righteous," he sometimes says to me in the height of passion, "that you seem cold to me." I kiss him and assure him that he's dearer to me than all else. This is true; I never lie to him. Sometimes I want to respond to his sensual embraces with the same. . . . I can't. . . . I don't know how. . . . Am I so pure, I ask myself? And now I know I'm not! How vile! There's the dinner bell—I don't have to think about it any more. Time to make up with my engineer; I was extremely rude. Yet I still want to know . . . surely Sidorenko will tell me now?

"What are you going to do, Tatiana Alexandrovna?" asked Sidorenko, climbing up with me to the deck.

"Haven't you forgotten that I'm not speaking to you?" I turned to him, mustering all my flirtatious skills.

"You still haven't exchanged anger for kindness?"

"And I won't!"

I leaned my elbows on the railing and stared into the sea. The moon had begun to rise, the western sky was crimson, and waves were rising slightly in the sea. They would soon be tossing more heavily. How I love golden moonbeams! Chasing all thoughts from my head and drinking in the beauty of the evening, I hummed softly.

"Tatiana Alexandrovna," said Sidorenko, "isn't it a sin to tease on a night like this?"

"I'm not spe-e-eaking to yo-ou!" I sang.

"And if I cannot tell you the story?"

I said nothing, just continued humming.

"You don't want to understand my problem."

I gestured to him to leave.

"Okay, okay. I'll tell."

"You're such a darling," I said in the voice of an excited

schoolgirl. "But please, give all the details and tell it as you would a literary tale. What kind of story is it?"

"It's not exactly a tale."

"Well, make it one. Come on, Viktor Petrovich."

"Tatiana Alexandrovna," he admonished me, "I had no idea you were such a tease!"

I put my hand on his sleeve and looked into his eyes, "Is it really so dreadful?"

"I don't know. You confuse me so that I no longer know what's good and what's bad. You're a most paradoxical woman!"

"A paradoxical woman! I like that, Viktor Petrovich. I applaud you. Now, down to business. Get on with the story."

"There's no getting away from you, is there? Okay. Do you know a Baron Z., a stockbroker and music patron?"

"I've heard of him. Continue."

"When Stark was in Petersburg they met at a party hosted by someone in high finance. Do you know Baron Z.'s reputation?"

"I've heard something wicked about him but can't remember what."

"He has a questionable moral reputation, although in business he is irreproachable. Well . . . uh . . . I don't quite know how to put this . . . he became passionately smitten with Stark."

"What do you mean?" I asked, astonished.

"There, I knew you wouldn't understand," Sidorenko cried desperately. "How can I explain this?"

"No, don't worry. Now I get it. Continue!"

"Okay. While still in Petersburg I told Stark, 'What makes you go to see this gentleman—what will people think?' He answered, 'I only go to his house for dinner and evening concerts. I never go alone.' 'It's obvious that he's courting you!' Stark laughed. 'That amuses me.'

"Once Stark and I went to Paris, and Baron Z. showed up there. Wherever we went, so did he. This bothered me a great deal, but Stark nearly died laughing. Once, returning from the races, we decided to walk through the Bois de Boulogne and catch the metro at Pont de Neuilly. The weather was marvelous, the woods were crowded, and we hadn't gone halfway before we saw Z., riding in an enormous carriage. 'Wait,' Stark said to me, 'I'm going to put on a show.' Before I could intervene, he had insisted that Z. come with us. Stark was terribly obliging, suggesting we go to the Cascade restaurant for a bottle of wine. Z. was ecstatic. While they were chatting I grew livid with Stark for putting me in a position where I would have be in the company of that man. When they turned toward the restaurant I made up my mind to leave, but Stark whispered to me, 'Careful, Z. will think you're jealous.' Tatiana Alexandrovna, what would you have done in my situation? What could I do? Let that vile creature think such disgusting things about me? At that moment I despised Stark for putting me in such an awkward situation. I could do nothing but go with them. Z. must have remained of this opinion, because I was clearly in agony watching this comedy. Stark was purposely trying to convince Z. that his desires were not in vain; he took on the role of a flirtatious woman. I became more stunned than angry. At one point Stark turned to me and said coquettishly, 'Sidorenko, shut the window. I feel a draft.' And you know what, Tatiana Alexandrovna, I stood up and closed that window. I even hurried to do so. Only later did I come to my senses and spit in disgust. Some time passed. I don't know what they were talking about; Z. was speaking softly to Stark. All of a sudden Stark jumped up, grabbed a glass of wine and threw it in Z.'s face. Then he pulled out one of his business cards and said to me, 'Viktor Petrovich, give the baron one of your cards, too, so that he can send his seconds around, in case he demands satisfaction.' When we left, Stark was in ecstasy. 'Oh, that was fantastic! What's Z. going to do now? He can't refuse the duel because I insulted him in front of witnesses. And now he has to fight with someone he considers his "beloved woman"!'

"'Listen, Stark,' I said, 'I have no idea why you dragged me into this and why you now insist that I act as your second.'

"'Oh, dear Viktor Petrovich, this is so much fun, please humor me.'

"'Drop that tone, Stark, I'm not Z.'

"'I'm sorry. It's hard for me to drop the role-playing.'

"There was no duel. Z. left town without sending his seconds. Stark was quite chagrined."

"I just see it as a boyish prank," I said, and returned to my cabin. What a dreadful night! It didn't help that I was seasick.

I slept late the next morning. I was in a foul temper, not wanting to get up and dressed. I felt completely worn out, my temples pounded. Horrible! After breakfast we will arrive in S. I will have to smile, be pleasant, pretend I care. Am I worthy of the love of these women and the boy? I had soiled myself with my imagination. I didn't like recalling the pictures my mind had painted for me. No, I've got to end this once and for all!

I jumped out of bed and dressed. But my countenance! Dry lips, circles under my eyes. I packed my suitcase and went out on deck. Thanks to Sidorenko my nerves had calmed down considerably.

We approached S. Sidorenko grabbed my suitcase and swung it up onto the deck, saying cheerily, "Does this mean you're inviting me to come see you? Indeed, I'll be there tomorrow!"

"Of course, of course," I said hurriedly, looking closely at the crowd on the dock. Ilya had asked me to send a telegram from Novorossiisk so that someone would meet me. I was trying to guess which ones they were. And I was right. His mother and Katia greeted me very cordially, but with reserve. Zhenia, on the other hand, threw herself around my neck and I adored her immediately. Andrei watched me sullenly. The mother was a slight brunette who looked younger than her years. Katia, also a brunette, was tall and full-figured. She looked the same age as her mother. However, I am not good at telling the age of such women.

Katia had fine facial features and could have appeared beautiful, but she did nothing to enhance her appearance. With the coquetry peculiar to this kind of woman, she had made herself look homely. She combed her hair in such a way as to make her graying temples noticeable. In addition, she wore an ill-fitting corset and fastened her dress clumsily with a leather belt. Her face was austere, with thick eyebrows and a large nose. She wore a haughty expression—not proud, haughty.

The mother's face was softer, plainer, but also showed repressed discontent. More than likely with me.

If only they'd shown me a spark of warmth! I would have responded with all my heart. But now? Now we all tried to be sociable.

Zhenia resembled Ilya, also big and blonde. She was a darling, with a wonderful complexion and beautiful eyes. Glorious in her youth and freshness, she could have been even more lovely if she had had the know-how. Andrei also had brown hair. How I despise youths of his age. They're either rude on principle or as pesky as fox terriers. He was already showing signs of animosity, something he'd gotten from his older sister.

The mother was well-bred and tactful, Zhenia delightfully dear, and I scarcely saw Andrei. All would have gone smoothly had it not been for Katia!

My trunk arrived and Zhenia helped me to unpack. She delighted in my clothes. Katia made a wry face and could not help saying contemptuously, "That lace dress must have cost two months of a professor's salary."

"You're mistaken, Katia," I answered lightly, "this dress cost the head of a charming child and a basket of mushrooms."

"What kind of head and mushrooms?" she scowled.

"I bought it with the money for a painting I sold entitled *The Girl with Mushrooms.*"

She pursed her lips, then added, "How many people that dress could have fed!"

"Really? They could eat lace?" I feigned naiveté.

Zhenia snorted with laughter and Katia flushed. I sensed that I had gone too far and said cheerfully, "You're so stern today, Katia. Here's a new issue of your favorite journal. Read the article by your idol, L."

"Thank you," she said dryly, and taking the journal, she left.

I was sitting in the garden, painting the magnolias. Zhenia, sitting next to me, chattered nonstop about the gymnasium she had finished last year.

"In the fall I'll begin at the Pedagogical Institute. At first mother planned to go with me, but then she changed her mind."

I knew why she had changed her mind—she realized she couldn't live with her son.

"Of course you'll live with us, Zheniusha."

"Oh I'd love to, but Katia thinks it would be better for me to live alone."

I found Katia and asked why she objected to Zhenia living with us that winter.

"Why do you think," answered Katia, "I'm sure it's very noisy at your place."

"At our house?" I was flabbergasted. "It's almost deathly quiet. I'm in my studio as long as there's light, and in the evenings I either sculpt, paint, or read. Do you think Ilya could work there if it were noisy? Occasionally we go to the theater or a concert, but we rarely entertain."

"And if Zhenia grew accustomed to your extravagance?"

"Katia, you don't understand how expensive Petersburg is. Ilya earns approximately three thousand rubles a year, and I about the same. You know how generous Ilya is—he helps out many people. I assure you that we cannot afford to live in the lap of luxury."

"I was judging by your clothes and trinkets," she was getting a little flustered.

How young you are, my dear, I wanted to say, but continued, "It's true, I love beautiful, elegant things. But laborers such as Ilya and I cannot afford many extravagances. Don't forget that I was sick all winter and couldn't work."

She couldn't restrain herself, "Looking at you it's odd to hear those words: laborer, work. . . ."

"Why?" I asked naively.

Her mother looked anxiously at Katia.

"Your work is entertainment, pleasure for you."

"And why are we supposed to hate our work? Do you hate your students, your job?" I was surprised.

She tried to say something but I wouldn't let her. "It's true, my work pays better. There are fewer artists than teachers."

She began to redden.

"You manufacture luxury items. I don't know if that can be considered labor."

"Does that mean you discount the toil of the poor factory girl who sits all day, hunched over a skein of silk, because she's producing a luxury item?" I exclaimed, shocked.

"But that worker receives only a pittance!" remonstrated Katia.

"Again, because there are many workers. You should also take into consideration talent and creativity. The scribe receives kopecks in comparison to the writer."

Katia grew quiet. Her mother watched her uneasily. I returned to my work, but I was upset. Katia was too weak a sparring partner. Was it worth it to aggravate her mother with these exchanges? Wouldn't it be better to keep my mouth shut? This bickering was for old ladies.

What a spectacular night! I was in the garden, where the quiet and perfume were marvelous. The sea was pounding in the distance. I would have gone out to the shore but the gate was locked, and I would have had to wake the entire house if I'd gone looking for the key. How could people sleep through such a night? How could Zhenia be sleeping—at her age I could have stayed out all night long.

"Tatochka, aren't you sleeping?" I heard her voice from the terrace.

"Yes, I'm asleep, sleepwalking in the garden," I answered in a hollow voice.

Zhenia laughed and ran to me, dressed in her robe with a large flannel shawl wrapped around her.

"You're so careless, wearing only that thin dress. You'll catch a fever."

"True. Despite all the natural pleasures of the Caucasus, fever still stands over us as a reminder of death."

"Take part of my shawl," she said, wrapping it around me, and we walked slowly through the garden.

"Tatochka, I absolutely adore you," said Zhenia, bending down to kiss me. I'm not especially short, but she's taller. "Maybe you don't believe me, but I fell in love with you at first sight. No— it was even before that, when Ilya began to write to us about you. I love Ilya so much—more than I do Katia or Andrei."

"Ilya's better than the others," I laughed.

"Oh, yes, he is, and you're exactly the sort of wife I had wished for him."

It was just childish prattle, but it made me so happy and warm that I kissed her in appreciation.

"You're not at all like the other women we know. You're so— well, so bright. Mother and Katia have said you aren't pretty. But to me you're lovelier than anyone else I know. Katia thinks that your clothes and your hair style are too theatrical, but they seem so pretty to me. Among us, Katia is the most demanding. She dismisses everything as 'frivolous': clothes, entertainments . . . isn't that a kind of prejudice?"

"Zheniusha, don't scorn other people's prejudices. It's diffi-cult to stop once you've started. Dress, clothes—these are trifles. But if you begin to reject other things . . . my dear, listen to Katia and your mother, and you'll live peacefully, happily, without troubles." And, I added to myself, without passion.

Now I always take opium at night and sleep like the dead, without dreaming. In other words, I can fight "you." In the daytime, with the strength of my will, and at night, with opium. I'm recovering, getting well!

Sometimes I even feel sorry for Katia. She's completely disconcerted. She's dying to be able to justify to herself her hatred of me. Her integrity makes her suffer because she knows how unfair this is, how she has no legitimate grounds for this hate. Agonizing, she's looking for something that she can sink her teeth into, but no. There's nothing. I've committed no sins in which she could take comfort.

She tried to get me on my political convictions—but ours turned out to be exactly the same. I really wanted to pretend to be a partisan of the extreme left, but I restrained myself so that there would be fewer pretexts for confrontations. Our arguments clearly upset her mother, Maria Vasilevna. Even my help to the needy is more generous, since my income is larger. Only the issue of my dress remains problematic.

Somehow we began talking about N., her favorite writer. Ilya and I had been friends with N. for a long time, and I gave her a book of his stories. He had signed the book with a very friendly inscription, typical of what authors say when giving a copy of their books to an admirer: "To the talented, sensitive, and clever Tatochka, from a friend."

Of course the good-natured Ivan Fedorovich wrote the same thing to a hundred women, but for Katia he was a god and his words, sacred scripture. Her unwarranted aversion to me tormented her conscience even more. When she read the inscription her entire face changed, and I felt so sorry for her that I wanted to shout, "Katia, I wear mascara! Does that make you feel any better?" She didn't understand herself, but I certainly did. Her antipathy was organic. I embodied what she detested most physically, and none of my virtues could counteract this. Even if I had performed an outstanding feat in the name of humanity, she still would not have been able to overcome her loathing for me— which was entirely physical, instinctual. Heart, soul, mind— these mean nothing. How often do we hear someone say, "He's irreproachable in every respect, but somehow I still don't care for him." Or the opposite, "He's a drunk and really something of a scoundrel, but still an amiable fellow." Physical instinct! When the body cries out, there is nothing reason or intellect can do with it. The only thing you can do is to restrain yourself from displaying your emotions, be they sympathy or antipathy.

Katia will neither beat nor poison me—she's "restraining" herself. She might not understand this, but I do very well. Katia—during the day, you should be acting upon your strength of character, at night take opium. Surely then in your dreams you will quarter me or roast me on the spit! Take opium at night!

I've only been here two weeks and am amazed at how well I feel. The neuralgia is gone, and no traces of my illness remain. I work, climb the mountains, eat—I'm eating indecent amounts.

The mother is softening noticeably. If only she were capable of accepting affection, I would give her a great deal because I honestly like her very much. Zhenia never leaves my side, while Katia and Andrei steer clear.

Sidorenko came to visit, and Katia happily perked up, unconsciously hoping to catch me flirting—but that did not work. If I flirted with Sidorenko it was so lightly that neither he nor Katia noticed.

I've been trying to coax an Abkhazian woman I met at the bath house to pose for me. Good Lord, what I wouldn't have given if she had agreed! What a body! Great shape and beauty! She had an ugly face, though, dull with a broad nose. To hell with her—I'll toss her head back and change her face. I've never seen such a back, breasts, legs—a suntanned Venus.

But, she refused to pose, the fool. I begged and pleaded with her, gave her a bracelet, visited her every day, and listened for hours on end about how to make the local dishes.

How I love to paint the female body; and I do it well because it's so beautiful. I've been exhibiting for only three years now, and my nudes have made my reputation. Because I'm a woman, it's easier for me to find models. My female friends pose for me quite often and gladly. Oh, how I would have painted my Abkhazian, all stretched out, body turned slightly to one side, lying beneath the bright sunlight against a dark rock! I can even see the sunbeams on her dark, perfect body, on her shoulders and thighs. She has refused, damn her!

Tomorrow I'll take my camera and snap a few shots of her while she's sunbathing. At least then I can get her body, if not her coloring. The simpleton! I've been walking around all day in a bad mood, telling everyone that I have a headache.

I begged her again, offered her my diamond brooch, but not even that helped. I've already seen the picture in my head. When I'm "pregnant with a painting," as Ilya puts it, I can't think about anything else. As soon as I finish my piece in Rome this fall, *The Wrath of Dionysus,* I'll get to this. I will take a huge canvas, more than eight feet high. . . . The sea . . . the rocks . . . the women . . . a lot of women.

I won't make the mistake most artists who paint female bodies make; they use just one model in various poses. In the foreground I'll have a magnificent redhead, even a little on the heavy side— one of the risqué women of Petersburg. She's posed for me once already. It's as they sing in *Bluebeard:* A Rubens, a famous Rubens!* She'll be lying down, tossing her red mane. I'll put my Abkhazian next to her, that strength, those muscles—a real Diana! And on the other side I'll put one of the students I know, Nadenka Flok, who's light, soft, and supple. Nadenka isn't pretty, so I'll need someone else's face. . . . Oh, the pilgrim from the boat! And the others, dancing, running, swimming, and playing in the water. And in the right foreground I'll put an old woman: naked, withered, repulsive. . . . "And You Will Become Like Me" is what I'll call it. The toothless mouth will smile scornfully, and what mockery will gleam from those evil, red eyes!

Preoccupied with my painting, I paced about, feverishly sketching the sea and the rocks. I thought about asking Zhenia

---

*Tania is referring to a song in Jacques Offenbach's operetta *Bluebeard,* as popular in Russia as in France.

to pose for me, but she won't do. Her breasts are shaped like small protruding cones, she doesn't have a flat stomach, and I love a straight line! Her backside is low, like a horse that has fallen to its hind legs. But her hands, shoulders, and skin are absolutely marvelous. I'll place her in the water, only her head visible, her hair flowing loosely and violet petals falling from a wreath onto her shoulders—it will be captivating! She'll be swimming, smiling.

Sidorenko was singing, accompanied by Zhenia. He has a nice baritone, and he sang with taste and feeling. I loved to hear him. They were singing "Dreams of first love. . . ."

I must draw my pilgrim alone . . . in the meadow . . . a bouquet of wildflowers tumbling out of her hands. She's standing completely still, her eyes raised upward . . . all around is silence . . . open space. . . .

"Dreams of first love. . . ."

My first love was a young woman who lived across from us. She was a lovely brunette, and I couldn't have been more than eight. Sometimes I sat at the window for hours, late at night, listening very quietly so that my nanny wouldn't come in and send me to bed. I looked into the opposite window, where my idol was playing the piano in a brightly lit living room.

Sometimes I'd run into her on the stairs, where my heart would stop and then pound rapidly. Oh, how I daydreamed then! I was a healthy, lively girl, and loved to play noisily, especially with boys. But then I began to hide in corners, sit on the stool in front of my mother's vanity in her boudoir—and fantasize. I dreamed that I became friends with my idol, that we went for walks, painted together, lived at the dacha. . . . I imagined it down to the minutest details—our conversations, adventures, travels. . . .

When her family moved away I became feverish, delirious, and spent a week in bed. Then, of course, I forgot all about it. But her face, the face of "my first love," still appears to me; I could paint her from memory. A pretty brunette.

No, it can't be! But it is: a blunt nose, a sharp chin, a mouth . . . dark eyes . . . big. . . .

I'm not myself. I'm trying to sort out all those people to whom I've been attracted. Maybe it's only my imagination, but every face I've especially liked, that attracted me to it, has had one or more features of "that" face. This must mean that there's a specific "type" that I'm attracted to, and when that "type" became personified, I was startled. I must not think about that, I must not, or God help me, it will begin again.

But isn't this a fascinating psychological question! Does Ilya have any of these traits? He must have one. Yes, of course, his forehead: straight, with a prominent brow. Indeed that sort of brow has always appealed to me, and I always kiss him on his forehead. Oh, "that" face I wanted to kiss all over, everywhere. . . .

I jumped up, crying "Zhenia, Zhenia!" My voice must have sounded strange, because Zhenia and Sidorenko came running in, a bit frightened. I got hold of myself and said with a nervous laugh, "Over there, on the railing, a scorpion!"

Viktor Petrovich grabbed a stick and Zhenia the fire tongs.

I was embarrassed by my foolishness and said calmly, "Let's forget it. It's cooling down, so let's go for a bike ride."

I had taught Zhenia how to ride a bicycle. She took to it quickly, as she had earlier learned to ride horses and to sail. Katia declined. It seemed that she enjoyed the sport but simply couldn't stand the fact that it had been my idea.

We leaned our bikes against a tall hazelnut tree and sat down to rest. The road was in terrible condition, even worse on the incline. We were hot and tired and didn't even want to talk. The evening was serene: no wind, and the sea reflected the rosy sunset. Zhenia gazed meditatively into the distance, fanning her face with her kerchief. I put my head in her lap. Sidorenko lay propped up on one elbow, chewing a blade of grass.

I couldn't stop thinking about the bizarre coincidence of my attractions, and to try to chase these thoughts away, I sat up and said petulantly to Sidorenko, "What a boring conversationalist you are today, Viktor Petrovich. Read us some poetry or sing us a romance."

"I can't just like that. Zhenia Lvovna, what's on your mind?"

Zhenia flinched, startled. "Oh, nothing. . . . Why am I being so timid? I'm thinking about 'him'—you know, about 'him in quotation marks,' as Viktor Petrovich calls it."

"Oh," exclaimed Sidorenko, "Zhenia has a 'him'!"

"No, not really, that's not the point," Zhenia answered in such misery that we laughed.

"Okay, Zhenia Lvovna, for three weeks now I've been singing romances, reading poetry, I've saved three kittens from the water, given you a mandolin and 'eyes' from American potatoes, and even ate the toffee you made without making a single face. Do I finally have the right to be placed between your quotation marks?" Sidorenko asked with great feeling.

"Oh, no, Viktor Petrovich," Zhenia answered very earnestly.

"Why not?"

"I love you very much, but I will not fall in love with you," she said, shaking her head.

"Why not?"

"You're not my type."

"You already know your type?" I interjected swiftly.

"Of course!"

"And I'm not your type?" Sidorenko asked with farcical disappointment.

"No, you've got light brown hair, and I like real brunettes. You've got a beard, and I prefer mustaches only—a thick mustache. You're only medium height, and I prefer them very tall. No, I'll just not fall for you."

Sidorenko made a helpless gesture. "Okay, okay. You've described him physically. But what about his soul?"

"If he's smart and a decent man, that would be very good."

"That means he can be wicked, just so long as he has a mustache. Ah, Zhenia Lvovna, and you consider yourself a serious woman."

Zhenia's face betrayed her exasperation. "Of course I can't

explain all of this very clearly. I haven't thought much about it.
I don't even like novels where all they do is talk about love. But
this is my opinion: in the beginning, you like someone's exterior—you can even be attracted to a homely person, if you see
something good in it. Then you fall in love. And then all the bad
qualities make their appearance. You fall out of love, and that's
painful. But that's how it is. I just can't say it better."

"So true, Zhenia Lvovna," Sidorenko said suddenly, very
quietly. "So true. And if this person is good and smart, then. . . ."

"Then that'll put an end to it," said Zhenia decisively, "and
then—happiness!"

"But if it's suffering instead?"

"I don't know. As far as I'm concerned, love is happiness,
even unrequited love."

We all sat silently, looking at the sea.

"Oh, Zhenia, what a lecture you've given us on love," said
Sidorenko, with a slightly exaggerated jocularity.

The end? No, my dear, innocent girl, you still don't understand that there are two kinds of love, and one of these you can
very well suppress, because it does not give happiness.

⟶⊷⊶⟵

Sidorenko was going to Tiflis by way of Batum. All of us,
except Katia, accompanied him to the felucca. Zhenia could
barely keep from crying, asking him not to forget to bring her
some yellow leather *chuviaki.*˙ In fact, we'd all made so many
requests of him that he had rather a long list. Sidorenko promised
that he would definitely return in two weeks, and he pleaded
with Zhenia not to fall in love with a grocery clerk.

"He'll have mustaches like two fox tails," he assured her, "and
my chances will be ruined."

Sidorenko was jittery, in a nervous good humor. It was time to

---

˙*Chuviaki* might best be characterized as Caucasian leather slippers.

board, but he was moving slowly, repeating his good-byes. He finally had to jump in the felucca as it was leaving, and cried back, "Zhenia Lvovna! The end of it!"

We returned home.

"Tatochka," Zhenia asked me in a strange voice, "what did Viktor Petrovich shout?"

"I don't know, Zheniusha, something about an 'end,'" I answered, almost tripping because Andrei, who was walking behind me, had stepped on my dress in his heavy swamp boots and had ripped it. Maria Vasilevna chastised him, and Zhenia, trying to help me, said angrily, "You could at least apologize instead of gawking!"

Andrei just stood there, staring at me sullenly.

"Apologize to Tatiana Alexandrovna," his mother said sternly.

"I don't consider it necessary," he blurted out.

"Have you lost your mind? Go home!" Maria Vasilevna grew pale.

I was laughing, making jokes, trying to smooth over the incident. But Maria Vasilevna was extremely upset. On the way home, she tried to explain to me that she had neglected her son's upbringing. There was no gymnasium in the town where they lived, so she saw him only on vacations. I tried to soothe her, pointing out that all boys between the ages of fourteen and seventeen were rude. It was simply youthful behavior.

It was boring without Sidorenko—he's such a pleasant person. That evening Zhenia and I wrote him a letter, that is, I wrote and Zhenia added an inordinate number of exclamation points. It turned out to be a long and entertaining letter; we were anxious for him to return.

Andrei is becoming intolerable. I hadn't paid any attention to him before, but now he constantly interrupts my conversations and says nasty things to me. Maria Vasilevna turns alternately white and red. Zhenia gets angry. Katia is suffering; she recognizes that someone else is being unfair to me, and she's both ashamed of him and of herself. She's too equitable for her own good.

⊹⊱⊙⊰⊹

Zhenia was sewing something and I was finishing a sketch. It was hot, and we weren't conversing.

"Tatochka, do you love Ilya very much?"

"Where did that come from? Of course I do," I answered, surprised.

"More than anything else in the world?"

"More than anything else. Why do you ask?"

"I read a story in a back edition of an old magazine, which ended with that question. In America someone even surveyed readers to see which door they thought he picked. Wait, I'll tell it to you. Once upon a time there lived an emperor and his daughter. She fell in love with a commoner—she loved him terribly. When the emperor learned of this he became very angry and wanted to put the man to death. The princess wept, pleaded with her father, and finally he decided to settle the matter thus: in the circus arena he would build two doors. Behind one would be a tiger, fierce and hungry. Behind the other, a woman."

Zhenia laid her sewing down on her knees.

"The woman would be beautiful, in a word, more beautiful than the princess. The man would be brought to the arena, where he would have to choose at random between the doors. . . . If he opened the one with the tiger, death would be instantaneous. If he opened the one that the woman was behind, he would win her, lots of money, and a ship to sail to a far-away land. . . ."

Zhenia put down her sewing and stared off into the distance with those big eyes of hers, so much like Ilya's.

"So, what happened?" I asked.

"Everyone gathered at the circus. A huge crowd. The princess. They led in the condemned man. He had to choose! Oh, I forgot to tell you that the princess knew which door hid which. He begged her with his eyes, 'Help me!'

"She paled, then blushed. She raised her hand several times, dropped it, then suddenly jumped up and pointed to a door."

Zhenia stood up. "What, Tata, do you think was behind that door?"

I said nothing. Zhenia was extraordinarily agitated.

"Why are you so quiet, Tatochka? Answer me."

In her voice I could hear a plea: if you had been the princess and Ilya were standing in the arena?

"The woman, of course!" I said assuredly.

"Really? Oh, how wonderful."

"Child, why are you so pleased?" I was astonished.

"Tatochka, dear, let me tell you about my romance. It's very simple and short, but I had an affair," she laughed.

"Please, tell!"

"Maybe it won't be interesting to you."

"How can this 'page of life' not be interesting?"

"Well, it's only half a page. I was in my last year at school, when I returned home for vacation. I met a law student; his mother keeps a dacha here. A terribly important lady. He and I became very close. We went riding together, boating. I don't know exactly how, but we fell in love. He told me that he loved me and that next year, after he'd finished school, he'd marry me. Then he kissed me. That was the last time I saw him."

"Is that all?"

"With the romance, yes, but the story continues. The next day his mother came—so proud and powerful—she was almost on her knees before me, begging me to reject her son. She said that we were both young, that I would not feel comfortable with his crowd. That he would become ashamed of me, would become unhappy . . . that the family was in debt and that he already had a fiancée, a beautiful girl, wealthy, from high society. She said that if I really loved her son I must refuse him.

"I'm giving you only the most basic details. She was very subdued, elegant, convincing, so that it became clear to me that it would be better for him to marry the other girl. I wrote to him, turning him down. I cried a lot. I kept thinking that I must not have loved him very much or I wouldn't have spurned him.

Other women kill their sweethearts rather than allow them to go with other women."

"No, Zhenia, true love doesn't kill. You honestly loved him. It isn't love that inspires murder, but passion."

"Aren't they the same thing?"

"No! A thousand times no!"

"Explain it to me, Tatochka, I don't understand."

"It's inexplicable, Zhenia."

And if that graceful, smooth body, that passionate and tender mouth, those eyes belonged to me? And "he" stood in the arena? Would I hesitate? Oh no, not for a second. The tiger.

⋆⇥◗ ◖⇤⋆

I was writing to Ilya, feeling good, peaceful, but also a little sad because I missed him. I was telling him all this. The door creaked, so I turned to see who opened it. Andrei stood in the doorway. I looked at him quizzically. He blushed, pulled at his shirt, and said in a quavering voice, "I've been sent to you to beg your pardon. . . . Mama wants me to. . . . I'm doing this for Mama. . . ."

"That's very nice, but I'm not angry with you," I said light-heartedly.

"I don't care whether you're mad or not. I'm asking this only for mother's sake. I don't care about your opinion."

"That's great," I said, and sat down to continue the letter.

He stepped into the room and stared at me with big, malicious eyes. The vein in his forehead throbbed.

"Haven't you said what you came to say? Now get out of here and close the door. I don't want a draft," I said.

"I hate you!" he cried out suddenly, in a strange voice.

"What? Why?" I asked reflexively.

"Because you're an arrogant and pretentious woman. You pretend on purpose not to notice me, and my hatred for you," he stepped toward me; "you treat me as though I'm not even human, a fly or some other insect that isn't even worth your noticing," he screamed hysterically.

40

"Andriusha, Andriusha, dear, please forgive me," I tried to settle him down. "I certainly didn't realize that you were so temperamental."

I put my hands on his shoulders and wanted to kiss him. Suddenly he threw his arms around me and we toppled over on the couch, his hands pressing down on my shoulders. An unpleasant smell of homespun wool mingled with the sour smell of a child poured over me. I pushed him away with all my strength and he fell to the floor. I stood up but was too disgusted to speak.

He jumped up, looked at me, flustered, and threw himself toward the door. I heard him run up the stairs to his room and slam the door.

I drank water in great gulps. "What a rotten, loathsome, snotty kid," I whispered.

Then the abhorrence and uneasiness of the incident passed, and it seemed rather stupid. Still, it was extremely unpleasant. I must tell Maria Vasilevna. It would alarm her, though, and there was nothing she could do. Such hysterical people sometimes take their own lives. . . . Then people would say, "She drove him to it, she destroyed a young life!" And I hadn't even noticed that "young life" before today. It hadn't entered my head. I don't care what people say. If such a hysterical wretch were to shoot himself, it would be no great loss for humanity. But—he is Ilya's brother!

What if he was upstairs hanging himself? I climbed the stairs hurriedly, listened quietly, and pushed the door ajar. Of course, everything was as expected. He was writing at his desk, and on his desk, a revolver! Oh, you bastard!

I entered quickly and called to him. He jumped up and grabbed the gun.

"Go away! Leave now or I'll shoot you, too," he cried in a squeaky voice.

"Please give me your German lexicon," I said evenly.

"What?"

"Your German lexicon. And do you happen to have the books by Malinin and Burenin?"

"No, I have Evtushevskii," he answered, unnerved.

"Well, then give me Evtushevskii. I need it very badly."

Automatically he put down the revolver and went to the bookshelf. I grabbed the gun and stuffed it in my pocket.

At my motion he jumped back toward me.

"Give it back, now!"

"You sit down and we'll talk about it, Andriusha," I said sternly. "You shouldn't behave like such a hysterical girl, such a spineless creature."

"Me, spineless?" he screeched. "Give me the revolver!"

"Of course: cowardly, weak-willed. At every trifle you would want to shoot yourself."

"And you think I could live after what happened?"

"What happened? Nothing significant," I said calmly.

"Was it so trivial?" he said drawing back, his mouth agape.

"Of course. You need a woman, and I'm the only one in the house you're not related to. Just find some other women and you'll see, these feelings will vanish as if by magic."

"But . . . but it's shameful to buy a woman for money."

"It's even worse to throw yourself at the first one you meet."

"My God, can one never do without that abominable act," he fell into his chair and covered his head with his hands.

"Of course you can. Don't dwell on it. If you keep reading books about 'how to retain your virginity'"—I pointed to some brochures on his desk—"then you're not going to be able to think about anything else but that. There's an old Tatar fable about a man who was told not to think about monkeys, and he ended up thinking only about them. It would be better for you to have some sort of physical exercise, gymnastics maybe. All you do is read scientific books and live in a placid environment. You're old enough to get married. You're so smart and sophisticated," I lied shamelessly, "yet you don't seem to appreciate that human life is a very valuable thing. And if your life isn't important to you, then at least expend your energies on something more serious than feminine hysterics."

I stopped talking. He sat at the desk, his nose buried between his hands.

"I'm so ashamed of myself in front of you," he muttered, almost in tears.

"Don't be embarrassed. It would have been much worse if you'd been with an innocent young girl. Andriusha, I think now we will become true friends."

"Yes, yes!" Tears in his yes, he suddenly reached out both hands to me, "Forgive me, I. . . ."

"Never mind—it's now as if nothing ever happened. Let's go to your mother and tell her that now we are friends."

"Yes, let's go. Oh, you're so wonderful. Now I'm going to work harder, and get out more. . . ."

Arm in arm, we walked into the living room. Maria Vasilevna was sitting at the window, lost in thought.

"Mama," I said softly—it was the first time I'd called her that, "Andriusha and I have made up and now we're friends."

"Love me a little, too, for Ilya's sake," I whispered more quietly, embracing her. She trembled, clasped my head and drew it to her breast. She had tears in her eyes. Victory! Complete victory! Andriusha looked at us and suddenly buried his face in his mother's lap and began to sob. He howled like a tiny baby.

"What an appetite you have, Tatochka," said Maria Vasilevna, "at least don't eat the dessert! After the salted fish, there was goose, and after the goose, the fruit dumplings. All that food so late in the evening—what's going to happen to you?"

"It's not my fault that everything's so delicious," I answered plaintively.

I love to eat and admit to this openly. I'm a terrible housekeeper and am also candid about this. I never know where my money disappears, my maid is spoiled and lazy, although always pleasant and polite. But I'm an excellent cook. Ilya has always insisted that it's possible for a person not to recognize my artistic talents, but still remain my friend. But woe to those who doubt my culinary accomplishments—they are enemies for life!

Maria Vasilevna has ordered for tomorrow a menu of foods that I don't particularly like, so then I'll fast a bit.

We heard steps on the terrace. Zhenia jumped up and ran to

the door. Sidorenko stood there, his arms filled with bundles and packages. We greeted him noisily. Zhenia began tugging at him so that he dropped the parcels, mumbling incoherently that he'd seen our light on, and at first had decided that he wouldn't disturb us, but then he couldn't help himself because he wanted to see Maria Vasilevna so badly. It was obvious that he was terribly happy to see us all.

Zhenia tore into the packages, adored the *chuviaki,* chided him about the ribbons, ate the candy, and asked about the opera—all in one breath: "Oh! they're so pretty and comfortable! . . . I told you I needed eight *arshins** . . . did she sing well? She has the voice of a nightingale . . . and wider, much wider . . . this one has liqueur in it . . . and the tenor and baritone sang well? . . . If they get dirty I'll clean them with benzine. . . . Do you want a chocolate toffee?"

I repeated her words to Zhenia. She laughed, and then remembered the sheet music. Sidorenko clutched his head; he'd forgotten it! But Zhenia didn't want to wait till tomorrow to sing, so she sent the cook after the music.

"You must sing, sing now!"

"What kind of a voice do I have after that trip?" said Sidorenko.

But Zhenia was insistent. She opened the piano and lit the candles. Maria Vasilevna went up to bed. I went out on the terrace and sat in the swing. Sidorenko followed me. His liveliness had faded and he looked depressed.

"What's the matter, Viktor Petrovich? You've returned from Tiflis unhappy. Business?"

"No, Tatiana Alexandrovna. Everything went well and I'm very glad to be back. I got so lonesome, and I wanted to see you so badly . . . all of you. It was terrible without all of you. Is your husband coming soon?"

"Ilya Lvovovich?" I corrected him, "yes, in two weeks."

That's one of my pet peeves—for some reason I hate it when

---

*An *arshin* is equal to 28 inches.

mistresses say "my husband." It makes me furious, as though a civil servant had called himself a general. Once I even became ashamed when Ilya introduced me to someone as his "wife." It was at the beginning of our relationship.

"I've got a name and a surname, Ilya. Are you ashamed of me?"

"God forbid, Tania!" he was flustered, "I was only doing it for you. . . ."

"That means you think I'm ashamed that I love you. I find it worse to assume titles that don't belong to me. I don't want to advertise our relationship, but there are people who would disapprove and I don't want to try to deceive them."

"Well, Tania, maybe unsophisticated people. . . ."

"Why do you say that? Maybe they're overly moralistic."

"Pharisees."

"What do you mean? Be fair, Ilya. I consider myself your wife, and I know that I'm more of a wife to you than many others are to their husbands. But that's not my title. Case closed. I don't call myself 'Countess' Kuznetsova."

Sidorenko stared at me intently. What could he want with Ilya?

"Tatiana Alexandrovna," he suddenly broke the silence. "Why am I afraid of you?"

"Me? What a joke!"

"Sometimes I've wanted to ask you certain questions, but I've always been apprehensive. . . ."

"I simply don't recognize you, Viktor Petrovich," I laughed, "you must have gotten seasick on that ship."

Zhenia ran out on the terrace with a packet of sheet music. Her face literally shone with excitement. She loves and appreciates music. She should have been preparing for the conservatory, but Katia had decided that she must attend the Pedagogical Institute. I don't want to argue with Katia, but it's a sin to waste such talent.

"Grieg—that's yours, Tatochka. 'The Lark' by Glinka, my Rakhmaninov? a new one? You must sing this today, Viktor. What's this, Chopin's waltzes?"

"And preludes and ballads. That's my present to you, Zhenia Lvovna."

"How clever you are! I just don't know how to thank you. Now I've put you between quotation marks," cried Zhenia in ecstasy. "What's this? A romance for a mezzo-soprano: 'Love is an Enchanting Dream' by Pavlov."

"Oh, I almost forgot. That's for you, Tatiana Alexandrovna. From Stark."

It was as if I had fallen off a cliff. Did I hear correctly?

"What Stark?"

"Don't you remember? We argued because of him on the boat. Your traveling companion as far as Moscow. You must still have the sketch you made of him."

Chatterbox, stupid chatterbox. Did he tell him about the sketch?

"I don't understand, Viktor Petrovich," I said evenly, delighted that I could keep this tone; "how did he know that you and I were acquainted?"

"We talked about you."

"I don't see how your conversation led to me!"

"Quite simply. I ran into him at the Oriental Hotel, and we had lunch together. They delivered your letter as we were eating. I was so excited! I was reading and laughing at your description of your trip to Olginskoe, and of the fat Caucasian tavern keeper who was chasing after Zhenia Lvovna—did he have a mustache?"

"A beard."

"Thank God. I wanted to shoot myself. Well, Stark wanted to know what I was laughing at, and I gave him your letter. Then. . . ."

"You let him read my letter?"

"Why not?"

"If I'd known that you were going to give my letter to the first person you met, I would never have written you," I said indignantly. "I wrote solely to you."

Viktor Petrovich looked surprised, and then his surprise turned into a happy smile.

"Dear Tatiana Alexandrovna, forgive me. I had no idea that this would upset you. On the boat I'd been unfair to Stark. He's really a nice fellow. I'm ashamed that I gossiped about him. In Tiflis he worked like a dog, walking all day, or riding horseback to Borzhom or some other place . . . we rarely got to spend any time together . . . he's truly a good fellow."

"How quickly you change your mind about people!" I said, surprised by the sudden elated tone in his voice.

"True, there's something very kind about him . . . you're attracted to him maybe even against your will. It's a pity that you never noticed his smile—he's amazingly handsome when he smiles."

The familiar tremor seized me, and irritated with myself, I said angrily, "You're talking nonsense. What else?"

"Yes, yes. He read your letter and said, 'A witty woman wrote this, and if she's not bad looking, then I understand your. . . .'" Sidorenko stopped, blushed, and continued. "Then I remembered about your encounter on the train—he remembered you immediately, asked a lot about you, and then we went together to buy the music. He wanted to know if you could sing, what kind of voice you have, and he bought this song and asked me to give it to you."

"Quite a singer you found," I said spitefully, "and what sort of a voice do I have? And this, what's his name, Stark, is he in Tiflis?"

"Yes. But in a couple of days he's going either to India or to Brazil."

"So, what are you going to sing?" I asked after a few minutes of silence. I had noticed that Zhenia had been looking back and forth at us, very quietly and soberly.

"What shall I sing?" Sidorenko asked jovially. "What do you want to hear, Zhenia Lvovna?"

"I don't care," Zhenia answered in a strange voice.

"Sing this," I handed him the first romance I found.

They went back inside. My temples were pounding. I clutched the sheet music. "The usual romantic words," I whispered and suddenly noticed a small mark by the last verse:

I love you, and I do not await an answer,
I love you, and do not await a kiss,
Indeed, there is only one pleasure,
The dream, the dear, sweet dream.

I sat motionless for a few minutes. Was this mark unintentional? No, it was too sharp and clear. How to explain it? "The dream, the dear, sweet dream." Did that mean he had noticed the state I was in? What shame! But how could he have been aware?

He knew, he must have, I whispered to myself, as if delirious. That's why he lowered his eyes. . . . Was it just a stupid flirt, or was he trying to make fun of me? Or did someone else mark the song?

The singing had stopped; they would be coming out here soon. I ran through the garden, used the servants' entrance to get to my room, and threw myself on the bed. Had I really not disentangled myself from this insanity?

A knock sounded at the door.

"Who's there?"

"It's I, Tata. Why did you leave? Are you sick?"

"I feel a bit feverish, so I left without saying good night because I didn't want to upset your party."

She stood at the door, as if mulling something over. I said nothing.

"Tata, may I come in for a minute? I want to ask you about something," I heard her voice through the door.

"Zheniusha, dear, I don't feel well. Tomorrow."

I heard several steps move away, but then she turned back and said, "Please, for heaven's sake, I can't sleep and I'll be upset all night long. I simply must talk to you."

Her voice sounded so desperate that I jumped up and opened the door.

"What happened?"

She wore only her nightgown and slippers. I jumped back in bed and wrapped myself up in the blanket. Zhenia stood silently in the middle of the room for a few minutes and then sat down on a corner of the bed.

"What's the matter with you, Zhenia?" I was a bit alarmed.

"I came. . . ." she began, then stopped and looked at me intently, then threw herself around my neck.

"I want the truth. . . . I'm afraid . . . ," she whispered, tears streaming down her face.

"Zhenia, what are you afraid of? Tell me, child."

"No, it would be too horrible . . . it's only my imagination . . . you're too good. You love Ilya . . . and not someone else."

I grew cold. Could she, Zhenia, this child have guessed my predicament?

"Zhenia, tell me what you mean. You're scaring me."

"It seemed to me . . . that you loved him."

"Who?" My heart fell.

"Viktor Petrovich of course."

I stared at Zhenia in disbelief and then burst out laughing. Me in love with Sidorenko! I wanted to say something, but looking at Zhenia's baffled expression, I started laughing again. Her face began to brighten.

"This means it isn't true," she cried, "it isn't true! Now I see!" She clapped her hands and began jumping around the room, then threw herself on me again. We laughed and kissed each other.

"Now tell me, Zhenia, where did you ever get such an idea?" I asked, wiping my eyes.

"Oh, a long time ago. Remember when he was leaving, and he cried out 'that's the end of it'? I guessed right then that he was in love with you, Tatochka."

"With me? I thought he was in love with you, Zhenia!"

"No, I figured it all out. Yes, of course, I'm sorry for him, but he shouldn't fall for other men's wives. I was watching, though, when he returned. Everything was fine, but then I got scared. . . ."

"Of what?"

"I don't know myself. When we were going through the sheet music on the balcony, you had such a strange look on your face."

"Can you describe it?"

"I don't know. I can't really say. You became so angry when you learned he had given your letter to someone else to read. And your voice when you said, 'I wrote it solely for you.' At that moment he became so happy, his face shone, and he even began to praise the other guy. It put him in a great mood."

"You don't mean that, Zhenia."

"Yes, yes," she bounded, "I notice such things immediately."

"Even that I love Sidorenko?"

"Tatochka, dear, forgive me. But you had the expression of a woman in love."

"What are the signs?"

"Oh, I don't know, something about the eyes."

"Yes, my fever had just begun."

"I understand now, but I was terribly jealous then."

"You wanted Sidorenko?"

"For Iliusha's sake. I was prepared to tear Viktor Petrovich's head off last night." She began to kiss me again. "But please, Tatochka, don't flirt with him," she implored.

"When did I flirt with him?"

"No, no. You didn't know then that he isn't indifferent to you. That, by the way, is something I'm also guilty of. When friends tell me that someone 'is not indifferent' to me that I hadn't noticed before, I start imagining things, drawing them out of proportion, fantasizing."

⊷══◦═⊷

Today the entire house is in an uproar. Sidorenko suggested a picnic, and a few of the Tolchins' closest friends agreed, plus a whole group of young people turned it into something of an all-night excursion. We spent the day baking pies and making sandwiches.

How lovely it was! A campfire on the beach. Moonlight on the water. The picnic was a stunning success. Everyone was happy. The young people were dancing to an orchestra comprised of three mandolins and two guitars. The men began jumping through the fire, trying to show off their skill and daring.

Maria Vasilevna, a fat and jolly colonel's wife, a young, very pleasant doctor's wife and I sat on a grassy knoll, our backs to the

50

woods. The doctor's wife's young son buried himself in my lap and was sleeping soundly, as babies do when they've been playing hard all day and then simply fall asleep where they drop.

Sidorenko was always trying to be beside me, but Zhenia had made a pact with her friend Lipochka—they wouldn't leave him alone for a minute. But the two of them had become so involved playing catch that they had momentarily forgotten him, and he sat on the grass at my feet. He was very somber and sat silently.

"You're a rare success story. Your rich uncles keep dying, you keep rising unexpectedly in your profession, you organize a picnic, and the weather couldn't be better if you'd ordered it."

"But loneliness?" he asked.

"What loneliness? Everyone loves you—look at all your friends."

"And what if this means nothing to me? What if I want a woman's caresses, a family. Don't judge from a distance, Tatiana Alexandrovna."

"What's preventing you from having a family? Look at that bouquet of charming girls. Why don't you even try? Maybe I'm partial to you. You're such a good man, Viktor Petrovich, that I would advise all these girls to fall for you."

I spoke the last sentence with a touch of sadness and a little sigh. Sidorenko grasped my hand and kissed it passionately.

"Maria Vasilevna," I said, "order Viktor Petrovich to be in a better mood!"

"Oh, I'm happy, I'm deliriously happy!" he jumped up. "Maria Vasilevna, if you would like, I, in my position as a State Assessor, will roll down this hill."

It was like a signal. All the others ran to the knoll squealing and crying out. The men flew down, one after the other. The women applauded and made wreaths for the winner of this new competition.

Sidorenko, his cap pushed to the back of his head, clambered back to us, and we welcomed him with applause. Suddenly he stopped, his eyes looking behind me, and exclaimed, "Where'd you come from, Stark?"

I drew my shoulders up around my head as though I were expecting a blow from behind. I probably lost consciousness for several seconds, and when I recovered my senses, Sidorenko was introducing him to Maria Vasilevna and the doctor's wife. Stark was telling them about some sort of profusion of nuts on the ground; his horse had become lame, which had forced him to walk. Coming into the woods, he'd spotted our campfire.

Composure—no, not composure: inside I flamed and shook at the initial sound of his voice, but then found an inner strength. I took myself firmly in hand and began chatting about trivialities, about what a small world it is. And again those bottomless eyes were staring straight into me, as if testing me.

Ah, I thought to myself, you want to know what kind of effect your prank with the sheet music had on me. You'll never find out. I didn't notice a thing. Your mockery went for nothing.

Sidorenko certainly doesn't understand people! He portrayed Stark as some sort of fatalistic hero in a novel, a Don Juan, and I believed him. Stark is very amusing, very well bred and clever, but he's a "simple" man. That's obvious at first glance. The young people and the doctor's wife's children flocked to him. Even Katia spoke to him very sweetly; she used the same tone that she does for her young students. Is it possible that she cares for that elusive childlike flirtatiousness, which occasionally brightens his slightly melancholic air?

And when it's serious, it's a sad face. What elegance in all his movements! He was apologizing for his outfit, but he's simply dressed as a tourist and those high leather leggings look marvelous on his slight, slender body. I was watching him stretch out at Katia's feet. His face, how it smiled about something they were discussing! I was overwhelmed by a passionate tenderness. At that moment I wanted to put him on my lap, like a small child. . . .

Shouldn't I run away? Now? Is there a boat today? No. Give this night to revel in the bliss of seeing him. I've never experienced anything like this. It seemed to me that until this moment

I had lived only in my art. Tomorrow I can get a grip on myself and leave, if necessary . . . but now I want to live and to love.

"Life is wonderful! What a fabulous night!" said Sidorenko.

"Oh, yes, yes, life is good," I exclaimed loudly.

He took my hand and kissed it several times, saying, "What a lovely, happy face you have at this moment."

And "those" eyes looked sharply in our direction, and just as quickly lowered. Did he think that we were in love? He must have a poor opinion of me, since I'm sure that Sidorenko related to him my complete biography. And what would it matter if I were such a woman? A woman who doesn't think about duty and honor, but lives by her instincts.

And how I envy you, women unhampered by responsibility and conscience! I applaud you as lucky women, as a coward applauds heroines!

What is he, a sorcerer? He's cast a spell over all of us: Maria Vasilevna, Zhenia, the servant, and even Katia, dour, sullen Katia! Oh, Katia, you have forgiven him his debonair attire, the flower in his buttonhole, his gloves, even his cologne. You would never have tolerated these airs in another man. As soon as he'd departed, after his visit, and the doctor commented on the part in his hair, you declared immediately, "There's nothing artificially stylish about it! When he leaned forward, his hair fell across his eyes, so he shook his head and it fell back into place. Completely naturally. It's you, doctor, who have feathers sprouting out of your head."

"Why Katia, you're in love with Stark!" exclaimed Zhenia.

"No, I'm not in love, it's you who may fall for him."

"I could never go for him. If I hugged him, I'd squash him," Zhenia proclaimed decisively, "a man like that."

"And what a pair you'd make: an elegant gentleman with a sledgehammer like you," laughed Katia good-naturedly.

"Yes, a real man has to be athletic, so that when you cuddle up to him you just sort of disappear into him. You've got to be smaller . . . ," the doctor's wife added romantically.

"Exactly," Zhenia concurred.

Funny. I'm smaller than Zhenia, and more feminine than she. But I never want to disappear into a man's embraces and feel myself so petite. . . . Oh no! I want to grasp my beloved in my arms myself, and even make him suffer!

It was a holiday. The quay was crowded, but we had found a table on the rotunda. Zhenia ordered three servings of ice cream—one for me, and two for herself. I saw Stark and Sidorenko in the distance. Zhenia jumped up to call them over, but I stopped her.

"Why not, Tata? They were probably at our house and Mama sent them over."

"Let's sit together alone for a while. Today I'm not in the mood for a lot of noisy conversation."

Something must have sounded odd in my voice, because Zhenia acquiesced sweetly, "All right, Tatochka."

We sat quietly for a few minutes, listening to the military band playing a duet from *Faust*.

"Tatochka," said Zhenia, "are you lonesome for Iliusha? You must miss him terribly."

"Oh, how I want to see him!" I almost burst into tears.

Darling, how wonderful it would be if you were here! All the sorcery would vanish, like smoke.

Zhenia tenderly stroked my hand as it lay on the table.

"Oh, my angel . . . allow me to have a cup of coffee with you."

It was Sidorenko, beaming because he'd found us. Stark was with him. We exchanged greetings and they sat at our table.

Sidorenko had been extraordinarily happy these last two days, after the picnic, making farcical declarations of love to Zhenia. I looked at him, thinking, he's nice looking, intelligent, a nice man—but women don't care for him. I wasn't thinking about myself. None of Zhenia's girlfriends, except one, notice him at all. And the one who does thinks it's time she got married and that he is an excellent match. But another girl tells her, "He isn't very interesting."

How he can jabber away with Zhenia about idiocies! I was surprised that the women weren't after him, as he can converse with them for hours. Not long ago he had a Georgian woman laughing and entertained for an entire dinner, although she didn't speak a word of Russian. I'm amazed at his talent. And what's stranger still, they all suspect each other of being in love with him. Such are his manners and looks. He's like the "juvenile" in a melodrama.

"Did you like the romance that I drew up the nerve to send you?" asked Stark, his head bowed solicitously.

Oh no, it's begun! I thought to myself, and answered in the most polite tone, "Oh, yes. Thank you very much. The music is lovely."

Why did I mention the music? It was as if I were avoiding the words.

"Yes, and I also liked the words very much, they are very pretty." I looked at his profile, his eyelashes lowered. He was putting a spoon on the table.

That means he was indeed the one who marked the refrain; I thought, just hold on.

"The words?" I said, slowly, as if trying to remember. "Oh, yes, they went very well with the music."

He looked up sharply and then lowered his eyes again.

"I hope that you will give me the pleasure of hearing you sing."

"I don't sing at all—that's just Viktor Petrovich's gossip," I laughed, and joined in Zhenia's conversation.

Zhenia wanted to lead us home via a shortcut through the outlying vegetable gardens. Of course the "shortcut" turned out to be twice as long. The path was narrow. Sidorenko led the way, singing a march, followed by Zhenia, who was pretending to beat a drum. They were cutting up something terrible. I walked behind Zhenia, and Stark brought up the rear.

My dress got caught in a blackberry bush—Stark untangled it. I could feel his presence behind my back, and the former madness gripped me tighter and tighter. I wanted to see his face; he had stepped back a little. I turned my head and saw his lips, going mad with the desire to kiss them at that instant, and then turned away and continued on.

A moment . . . something clasped my arm above the elbow, and a quiet voice broke the silence: "I love you. Oh, how I love you."

With superhuman self-control I wrenched my arm away and ran—I almost knocked Zhenia down as I seized Sidorenko's arm. But the two of them were cavorting about so that they interpreted this as a joke. Sidorenko took my arm, beginning the dance steps as he hummed a polonaise. Zhenia almost died laughing.

"We've lost Stark," she said, coming out onto the road, "and I wanted to invite him to tea with us."

"He didn't even say good-bye?" Sidorenko was surprised.

"He said good-bye to me and then turned back," I answered calmly.

"What a pity. Well, tomorrow drag him along when you come over. I want to play the piano with him," said Zhenia, parting with Sidorenko.

He's come over today. They're all sitting out on the terrace, and I'm going to join them. If I could control myself yesterday, I have nothing to fear today. What happened yesterday? mockery? a test? a sudden burst of passion?

They were calling me. I walked serenely out onto the terrace. Stark got up from the railing, where he was sitting. I greeted him, extending my hand as though nothing had happened. His every touch was torture, but I controlled myself.

Katia had already left, and Sidorenko and Zhenia were heading off to the living room, to the piano. I wanted to follow them.

"Will you forgive me if I ask you to do me a kindness, and

listen to my explanation of my behavior yesterday?" Stark said quietly.

I heard such music in his voice, but I answered dryly, "Would it make any difference?"

"Yes. I beg you to hear me out. I don't want you to think me impertinent." He stood before me, his eyes lowered, biting his lips gingerly.

"Isn't it better to consider the incident settled? You've apologized. . . ."

"No! I'm not apologizing!" he said with proud determination. "I'm innocent, and I'm asking you to hear me out."

I wanted to cry out—I can't, I don't want to listen! But despite myself, I pronounced the word "speak."

Languorously, I leaned back against a column and tossed my head back so that it was partially concealed behind a grapevine. He couldn't see my face. The leaves hid me, so he couldn't detect my consternation.

Reclining against the railing, he held a cyprus branch. The moon bathed him in light.

"I'm blameless," he began softly. "When I saw you then, in the train car, I suddenly lost my head. At first I didn't even attribute it to your presence. But then I inadvertently touched your hand . . . and I was instantaneously gripped by desire, by reckless, blind passion. If you had not been a proper lady, I would have propositioned you on the spot."

I made a move to leave.

"Oh, don't go. Let me explain. I know that my words might seem callous to you, but I'm not at all cynical. Yes, I've known many women. I used to change women almost every day. All of them, even the most devoted, those I cared most about, nevertheless seemed weak and lachrymose, or petty and capricious. But in you I sensed something strong and powerful. I can't explain it, even though I've often reflected on it," he said in exasperation, breaking the branch.

"My desire for you grew stronger every minute. I've known women a thousand times more beautiful than you! But something in your movements, in your eyes . . . in your narrow hips and full breasts, the curve of your back, the nape of your neck. I don't understand it myself, but I lost my mind! You turned out to be so clever and educated, but it wouldn't have mattered to me if you had been ignorant and common. I wanted you, your lips. . . ."

I began to sway.

"Forgive me," he implored. "I intended to say something else to you. You can't imagine how much will power it took for me not to grab you in my arms when we parted then. I hurried to leave you, when I wanted so desperately to remain with you; but I was afraid of what I might do.

"What a horrible night that was! Several times I got up, wanting to go to you, to plead with you, or to break down the door of your compartment. Then my agents met me in Moscow, and in the light of day I laughed at myself. But at night! I cursed myself for not asking your name. Indeed, I knew nothing about you—who you were, where you were going.

"Little by little those feelings began to fade. But sometimes, at night, a single remembrance of one of your movements or words, and it would begin all over again. At those moments I would take a woman, thinking that might help. Don't be angry! I would close my eyes so that I could pretend it was you . . . but those poor creatures would destroy the illusion with every word or action. And then suddenly I met Sidorenko. Like a lovesick schoolboy I sent you that sheet music. I don't know why I did it. You didn't understand, and how could you? I had important business to attend to, but I sent someone else in my place. And here I am.

"I know that you belong to someone else, and that you love him. I have no expectations of you; I'm not as naive as poor Sidorenko. I had decided not to say anything to you, but yesterday, when I was walking behind you and you turned around. . . . I don't know. Something in your eyes. . . . I went crazy, and had to tell you that I love you."

He fell silent and looked out into the garden.

And I? While he was speaking, I was experiencing things I'd never felt in a man's arms. It was like being in a blistering whirlwind. When he stopped, I came to my senses. My legs were shaking, but my voice, curiously toneless, was calm when I said, "Please leave here."

"I can't."

There was such imploring in those words, a childlike plea, and those bottomless eyes looked at me with such sweet sorrow. Oh, no, don't let him leave. I wanted to cherish him a little longer, to be with him. I said softly, "All right, stay. But I hope that there will be no more conversations like this one. I'm counting on your discretion."

I'm so happy, deliriously happy. I can't think about anything, do anything. It's as though there's nothing but insanity all around. I am not alone with him even for a minute. We're always with a large group, but I see his eyes. It's as if I'm drawing my composure from his passion. All day long I'm cool and controlled. But alone at night it's another matter. No one sees, no one knows. Those around me don't notice a thing, not even my naive, "experienced" Zhenia.

Stark is playing on the swings with Zhenia while I am drawing his portrait. I have a whole album of such sketches, which I hide from everyone. In three weeks I'll return to Petersburg, and everything will be over, but now I'll let things remain as they are. We only live once! And who is hurt by my love? No one knows anything about it.

He's been gone for three days. Sidorenko said he went somewhere in the forest. Then Andrei turned up yesterday and informed us that Stark had been out at the sawmill with him for the past three days, and that they had returned together. Oh, and even Andrei is under his spell! All he can talk about is Stark. He recounted word-for-word every conversation with him and his opinions about various subjects and people. It's odd that the youth Andrei understands Stark better than the adult Sidorenko.

I was lying in the hammock, while Andrei sat next to me on the stool, gesticulating and speaking animatedly: "We talked about everything—we sat up almost all night talking about everything, especially about you!"

"About me?"

"Yes, Edgar Karlovich speaks about you with such admiration. He asked me about you, and I told him about the time you persuaded me to change my mind."

"Really? In three days you became such close friends?" I asked.

"Just imagine, I have a lot of friends at school, but I would never tell any of them. You might call it friendship, but I tell you I love him like a brother. How do you think that happened?"

"I don't know, Andriusha."

"I myself don't understand. And I feel such tenderness toward him. He's strong enough to tie a poker into a knot, yet when we got to the ford in the river, I almost suggested carrying him across it in my arms! It's true, isn't it, that he's very handsome?"

"Come, come!" I teased Andrei, trying to get him to talk more about Stark. It was so wonderful for me to hear about him.

"Oh, you women, all you want are athletes! But he was stronger than all of us, except the young Chalava, even though he looks like a woman," Andrei retorted, irritated, and then continued, "you should see him chopping logs! Your beau is no match for him."

"What beau?"

"Sidorenko, of course. You aren't going to try to tell me that Sidorenko is better looking than Stark."

"Of course he's better looking."

Andrei spat in exasperation.

We were coming back from one of the gardens situated on the outskirts of town. There were a number of us; Stark, Andrei, and I were bringing up the rear. I was carrying a large sheaf of roses that Sidorenko had cut for me.

After the discussion with Zhenia, I had asked her to do what she could to keep him away from me. Why expose myself to declarations of love, and feel uncomfortable thereafter? He had taken my arm as we left the garden. Zhenia, walking with Lipochka, quickly remembered her charge and grabbed him, dragging him ahead with her. He could only look helplessly back at our party.

Stark offered me his arm, but I refused. I couldn't have stood that. I've managed excellent self-control, but I could not retain calm if he were holding my arm.

Andrei was walking between us.

"Oh, Andrei, I left my walking stick back on the bench where we were sitting. Would it be too much trouble for you to get it?" asked Stark.

Andrei headed back. I wanted to call to him, but I didn't want Stark to suspect my weakness.

"I left for three days, tried not to think about you, but nothing helped," he said, not looking at me.

I quickened my step, saying nothing.

"You ordered me to be quiet, but I can't. Give me at least your hand—it's such a trivial thing, a crumb from the banquet of the rich man whom you love. He's so happy, so wealthy. How I envy him!"

I was almost running.

"Understand, my dear, what a kindness you would be doing, one clasp of the hand, one glance. Darling, I love you, I love you!"*

Running, I reached the rest of the group.

"Tata, you have a fever again," said Maria Vasilevna; "take my shawl. All your stylishness! It's evening, and you're parading around in décolleté."

I wrapped myself in the shawl, shivering.

Bless you, Caucasian fever! Beneath your guise I can tremble,

---

*At this point, Stark has stopped using the formal "vy" (you) with Tania, switching to the casual "ty" as a sign of their intimacy.

*my cheeks can burn, and I don't even have to answer questions!
As soon as I get home I can go into my room, bury my face in
my pillow, and listen to the passionate whispers reverberating in
my ears.*

Hooray for the Caucasian fever!

⟿⟾

The heat was unbearably oppressive. The air was dry. On the
horizon, over the ocean, dark clouds were building up. We were
going to have a thunderstorm. The same as a cat, I can feel a
storm approaching. In such weather it's taxing to walk across
the yard, but the indefatigable Zhenia had dragged me into the
hills to "pay a call" on Sidorenko. She was so sweet in her frisky
mood that I couldn't refuse her, so I dragged myself up the hill
after her, to the little white house where Sidorenko lived.

"Tsk, tsk, Tata, we're going to catch them undressed, and
really startle them," Zhenia whispered to me. I started to turn
back.

In the shade, Stark had spread himself out in a wicker chair,
beneath the spreading branches of a tree. He had hung his white
suit jacket from one of the branches and had taken off his vest,
opening the collar of his light blue shirt. Sidorenko, in a dark,
unbelted peasant blouse, also with his collar open, was mixing
some sort of drink with ice. I saw Stark's soft white neck, which
contrasted so sharply with his sunburned face. It was wrenching
for me; I wanted to run away, but it was too late.

Zhenia flung open the gate and announced, "A detachment
of Cossacks has entered a peaceful Chinese village. You're captured!"

Both men jumped up. Sidorenko wanted to run inside, and
Stark grabbed his jacket.

"Stay where you are!" cried Zhenia, putting her parasol
against her shoulder, like a rifle. "One move, and we'll . . .
disappear!"

"No, no, for heaven's sake, don't go! We're so happy to see
you," said Stark.

"But we can't remain dressed like this in the presence of ladies," mumbled Sidorenko in despair.

"You, Viktor Petrovich, are permitted to put on your belt, but Mr. Stark, you could go to a ball in those white shoes and blue socks. You are permitted to fix your décolleté," Zhenia declared decisively.

"At least let us put on our ties," implored Stark, "we can't be such scarecrows with ladies around!"

"Ladies and gentlemen, look at this man! He's coquettish enough for ten women, even for our Tatochka. He knows very well how charming he is, and how much light blue becomes him. Oh, you," she added, waving her hand.

I was terribly grateful to Zhenia for her chattiness. It gave me time to collect myself.

Sidorenko didn't know where to put us, what to feed us. He ran inside to pester his servant, a sleepy, slow moving Turk. The table was soon set with wine, fruit, and cookies.

Stark cut some flowers for us and quietly, almost imperceptibly, laid several budding tea roses in my lap. He said almost inaudibly, "They are also pale with passion."

It was lovely. Indeed, all his lovemaking was exquisite. Why was I willing to believe immediately that this was true love? Why didn't I think for a moment that he was lying, pretending? I, who am so cynical in these matters, believed completely in this fabulous love. I feared only one thing. In order not to give myself away, I tried not to look at him. He was so handsome today.

Forgive me, my dear Sidorenko, if I flirt so foolishly with you, trying to conceal how my passion is gradually overpowering me.

Zhenia, having eaten of everything that was put on the table, remembered her plan to allure Sidorenko. She attempted to look languorous, but couldn't sustain it; and when she looked over at me we both started laughing.

"I haven't seen you so lighthearted in a long time, Tatiana Alexandrovna," said Sidorenko; "lately you've been so pensive and irritable."

"That's just how it seemed. You weren't looking carefully."

"You think so? You have such an expressive face that one can read it like an open book."

That struck me as so funny that I could barely contain myself. "What did you read in this book?"

"If you want, I can tell you what I'd like to read in this fine, intelligent book. . . ."

Zhenia stuck her head between us. "Are you two telling secrets?"

Her face was so sweet in its naive cunning that I spontaneously kissed her rosy cheek.

You're such an idiot, Viktor Petrovich. Don't you have eyes? There's such a charming creature right here, next to you, and you want to read a book written in a language you could never understand.

⇥⟫⊙⟨⇤

Zhenia didn't deviate from her plan. If Sidorenko tried to get me aside into a private conversation, she would immediately join in. He began to get angry, while she exulted. Stark said very little. He sat leaning on one arm of the chair, his chin propped in his hand, gazing off into the distance. Was he posing? He looked extremely handsome. Why did I believe him? Because it didn't matter to me whether it was the truth or a lie. What difference would it make?

Kinto, Sidorenko's setter, ran in. Zhenia began to play with him, forgetting her host.

"Tatiana Alexandrova, I have to talk to you about something very important to me," Sidorenko said, twisting around the back of his chair.

"Speak."

"Not here. I don't want anyone to disturb us. Let me come to you tomorrow evening."

He was agitated. I knew what he wanted to discuss, and I wanted to say—Don't bother, it's all in vain—but that would have resulted in a long, drawn-out conversation. Tomorrow's fine.

Now I just want to look at those eyes, partially covered by thick eyelashes, those sad, sad eyes. And those velvety, scowling brows. At that supple physique sitting in the other corner of the porch.

I had said "okay" simply because I wanted Sidorenko to leave me alone, but he wanted to continue talking. Zhenia, remembering her duty, pulled him off into another room to look at a Caucasian violin. I also got up, but Stark, not changing his pose, said, "Don't go. I won't say anything to you. I won't even look at you. Would it be too difficult for you to do me one kindness, to let me be near you for a few minutes? I'm leaving tomorrow."

My heart stopped. Look, look, I thought to myself. Look for the last time. It's so lovely, so bright, and you can't endure it. You regret, you skinflint, that you aren't willing to pay for this broken life. You're afraid for yourself. You want a rock-solid foundation, so you're setting free the butterfly with the beautiful wings. For the last time . . . you're looking at yourself! you're not looking at me, because if you really were, you'd see how my breast is heaving—how my whole being is straining toward you . . . but I can't, I can't. . . .

He made a movement, as though he wanted to stretch, to throw off a weight. His motion enveloped me in a red fog that covered everything. I jumped up, reached out and cried, "I can't! My dear, I can't any longer!"

Then in a flash—reason returned. Panic. I don't know how I did it, but I ran into the house, fell into Zhenia's arms and, as if in a dream, demanded, "Let's get home as quickly as possible. I'm suffering from sunstroke."

Yesterday the frightened Zhenia brought me home half-dead. Everyone believed my story about sunstroke, even the doctor who wrote me a prescription and warned me against the dangers of drinking white wine in the heat. Sidorenko and Stark dropped by in the evening to find out how I was doing. They were told that I was fine and that I would probably get up tomorrow. I did get up, but I won't leave my room until he's gone.

I sent Ilya a telegram, begging him to come immediately. I told him I was very sick and unable to endure the heat. I went to the telegraph station myself; it was dark, so no one saw me. I felt better—I had buried my fantasy.

I made my way home carefully. Sidorenko was there, waiting for me to come out of my bedroom. I was walking very quietly, hoping to slip into the garden through the back gate. Then I made out a figure against the fence. Stark! I recoiled. My strength had left me. I put out a hand, as though trying to defend myself from a blow, and said hoarsely, "For God's sake, for the sake of all that's holy, don't come near me."

"Darling," he said, "what are you afraid of? I want to show you how much I love you. My desire is strong, but my love stronger still. My love is tender, devoted, true. Leave everything and run away with me. I will live only for your happiness."

"No, no! Can't you understand that I have only passion for you, not love. I love another," I sobbed, "have pity on me, once and for all! You know that you could make me follow you without thinking. Do you want me to be contemptuous of myself for the rest of my life? Do you want to take advantage of my weakness, my sickness at this moment? No, a thousand times no!"

"My precious, you have to understand that this isn't simply attraction, not just desire. I love you, love you . . . of course you don't believe me! How can I prove it to you? I know what I'll do, I'll leave today on the first boat. I don't want to take advantage of what you call your weakness, your sickness. Two months from now I'll be waiting for you in Rome. You told me that you must go there. Will you believe me now, believe in my love? I could be happy at this moment. Darling, I'll wait for you in Rome. You'll come, I'm certain of that. During our separation, you'll realize that you are mine and must be mine. Do you believe me?"

I nodded.

"I'll write to you; you must allow this. Oh, I won't expect answers to my letters, but I must be able to drop you a few words. True, dearest?"

That voice was such sweet music to me.

"Yes," I whispered, as if in a dream, gazing at him.

"Don't look at me like that, Tata," he said, closing his eyes,

"I'm afraid that I'll throw myself at your feet. I can't even kiss your hand, or I would lose my head from the very nearness of you."

He grabbed his head, reeling. I started instinctively toward him.

"Don't come any closer, Tata," he said, straightening himself out; "I want you to believe me, and now I can't be responsible for my actions for a moment longer. Remember, I will wait for you! Go, go!" He nearly shouted as he ran away from me, along the precipice, jumping across the bushes. Rocks flew out from under his steps.

I reached out, whispering, "Come back, come back!"

Passing myself off as ill, I stayed in my room and remembered, remembered. . . .

Why is everyone being so nice to me? Zhenia, Maria Vasilevna. I know that they love me, and I feel terrible about this. The ties that bind me are getting tighter and tighter. How can I leave? It's no longer just Ilya, but also his mother, sisters, and brother.

Ilya finally arrived. I threw myself on him and sobbed. I, how could I betray him, forsake him and his family, who had become like my own! I had gone out of my mind. Of course I would never forget that wonderful illusion, but let it remain a dream. I have a stable life, and a real, solid love, and an obligation. But "it" still smolders within me. "It" will pass. I don't need a single memory.

Time is the best medicine. Time and Ilya. He's so happy seeing me with his mother. He is moved by seeing Zhenia and her attachment to me, although he won't admit it. Katia troubles him, and sometimes he looks at her rather harshly.

"Katiusha," said Ilya, "I don't understand why you treat Tania as an outsider."

"We're such different people," she answered.

"But Zhenia, mother, and Andrei have befriended her."

"Zhenia and Andrei are still children, and mother is simply a very kind person."

"So you think that only children and especially good people can love Tania?" Ilya asked derisively.

"I didn't say that, Iliusha. But I'm not an especially demonstrative person; one could even call me morose. I can't make friends very quickly, and especially not with those who appear to me completely unacceptable."

"In what way do you find her unacceptable?"

"In everything."

"That's not an answer."

"Okay, maybe it's because for her, beauty, pleasure, and enjoyment come first. I look at life more seriously."

"What! I always think of Tania as a woman who lives for art and family, and now it turns out that she only wants to dress up and tell jokes," said Ilya contemptuously. "You want her to walk around in a black dress, with a pious expression, and push her education, knowledge, and talent on everyone."

"I don't recognize you, Ilya," said Katia defiantly. "Are you saying that I'm forcing my education on anyone?"

"I don't recognize you either, Katia," Ilya blazed. "Excuse me, but it seems to me that you're jealous of a smarter, more attractive woman."

"No!" exclaimed Katia. "I'm only jealous of the fact that she has taken you away from us. And don't demand that I love her."

"She's taken me from you? That's a lie. I love all of you as before, and you are very well aware of that. But why am I supposed to deny myself personal happiness? Why can't we all live together, caring about each other?"

"That can never be. I used to dream, Iliusha, about how you and I would live together, and suddenly this woman, alien to me and unsympathetic. . . ."

"Enough, Katia. Sorry, but your words sound bizarre to me, as though you were fantasizing about some sort of material comforts. Let's end this conversation, because I don't see what can be salvaged from it."

He turned and went in the house. Katia, defeated, insulted, sat in silence for a few minutes. Then she put her head against the back of the bench and wept bitterly.

⊷⊜⊶

Relations were so strained between Ilya and Katia that Maria Vasilevna was suffering. It was time for us to go. I said nothing for a couple of days, and then brought it up to Ilya. I pointed out that he wasn't being fair to Katia by calling her mood "an old maid's caprices." I tried to explain to him that just as there can be love that is exclusively carnal, Katia's attitude toward me was the opposite, a kind of "hatred of the flesh." But he said jokingly, "Taniusha, you might understand psychology, but it's Chinese to me."

"Does that mean we're supposed to live solely by instincts?"

"No, and reason."

"And when reason isn't functioning?"

"Then it's time for the madhouse," laughed Ilya.

"Don't joke, Iliusha. Let's talk about this at least once. It seems to me that you're afraid of these questions."

"Yes, Taniusha, I'm an ignoramus on all these finer points. It reminds me of the fakir contemplating his belly button. Don't be angry, child," he grasped my hand.

I wasn't angry. I know he's a simple, commonsensical person. But should that prevent him from trying to understand other people's feelings?

I wanted to leave so badly, but I couldn't ask Ilya because it had been so long since he'd seen his family. He was trying to convince them all to move to Petersburg and live with us. I didn't care. I loved them all, even Katia. Of course, a month ago I wouldn't have wanted this. Then I feared the introduction of any outside element in our life, but now I'm happy. Give me more to worry about, more attachments, more obligations. The more the better!

I ran to the garden to sit among the azalea bushes and read the letter. Why? It brought me nothing but pain and the realization that it could never happen. I see now that I could never part with Ilya, that life without him is unthinkable. One can live without flowers and fireworks, but not without food and warmth.

But my, fireworks and flowers are beautiful!

The second letter has arrived. He's already in Italy. His letters make it all sound so pretty, what with his descriptions and the impressions he's sharing with me. But these are words. Just words. Maybe.

"My dear, write me at least a line on a postcard here in Florence. Just a few words: I'm healthy, I remember . . . and I will know that your hand held the paper. I'm writing you with a pencil on a bench in Giardino Boboli.* In front of me, the city is fading in the sunset. Roses are all around, and you . . . you are always with me.

"You are so deeply a part of my life, my body, my soul, that I can't separate myself from you. I try to look at everything beautiful in nature and art exactly as though you were looking out of my eyes. In museums, I make it a point to stop at those statues and paintings that you mentioned in conversations. I stand there for hours, thinking, let her feast her eyes on it! So I stand some more. Are you content, my dearest darling? Recently in the square I almost said out loud, 'Let's sit with our backs to the tram so that it can't spoil the effects.'

"In the countryside I gather together a whole crowd of ragamuffins and feed them pasta and sweets, telling them that a wonderful signora sent them from Russia.

"At night . . . don't worry, my love. I can only put my head on your knees and dream about your kisses and caresses. I dream in my dreams, dearest.

"In Hungary I was incredibly busy from morning till night, walking around the forests with my interpreter. I negotiated contracts, wrote reports, made sales, but you were there with me, near my heart, hiding in my chest because you didn't want to be involved with the business. You would raise your head only in the woods, where I cut an autumn bouquet for you.

"I've never experienced your kiss, but does it matter? My dream, my beloved dream. . . ."

*These are famous gardens in Florence.

I sent a postcard to Florence: "Good-bye. Forget."

I don't need any more letters. I burned the two with the cyprus branch which, in a burst of sentimentality, I had picked up after he had snapped it. I also wanted to burn the album with my sketches of him but couldn't bring myself to do that, so I wrapped it in paper, tied it with a string, and hid it in the bottom of my trunk. I won't think about it any more—it's over. I severed myself from all that was beautiful and elegant.

Who can say that I don't love Ilya? Now I am his, body and soul. If I profaned my soul, I kept my body pure! I never even kissed the one I love. Men need only that. I must get back to work because I haven't finished all I need to do. My despondency is terrible, suffocating, but it will pass.

I have almost completed the family portrait, and it's turning out nicely. Maria Vasilevna is at the window, sewing. Zhenia and Andrei are toward the back, at the piano. Katia is standing in the doors to the terrace; she looks quite impressive. I flattered her, trying to tease her. Ilya is standing next to his mother, a newspaper in his hands. I painted it in his absence, from memory, but as it turned out his figure didn't need any alterations, just a bit of touching up.

I'm doing a pen-and-ink portrait of Sidorenko, which is almost ready; but lately he has been coming by so seldom that I haven't been able to finish it. . . .

The picture I painted of Zhenia's head, her hair cascading down, peering through a bouquet of azaleas, is terribly charming; but I won't make a gift of it to her. No, this will make a fine decoration for my studio in Petersburg.

Today I am in such a serene and pleasant mood that I gave in to Andrei's and Zhenia's request that I put together an "exhibition" of all the paintings I've done in S. They carried everything out to the gazebo, including canvases that just had a few brush strokes on them. They hung them around the walls, stood them against chairs and even on the benches in front of the gazebo. We were ceremonially invited to the "grand opening."

Goodness, but I had painted a lot in the last two and one-half months! Ilya was surprised and congratulated me. The doctor's wife was touched by the portrait of her mop-headed spouse. "No photograph has ever been able to capture Ignasha's pugnacious expression," she said, "but Tatiana Alexandrovna, as a true artist, captured it immediately."

She was terribly put off, though, by the pictures of naked women. "Really, Tatiana Alexandrovna," she asked naively, "you don't paint men naked?"

"Sometimes, Anna Petrovna. At the academy we were supposed to."

"Completely naked?"

"Completely."

"How can you? I would faint," she exclaimed.

Katia had been quiet, but then she turned to me. "You've immortalized all of us, Tata, even Mikhako and Kintoshka. I'm surprised that you didn't notice what an interesting face Stark had."

"Yes, Tatiana Alexandrovna, you missed something on that score," exclaimed Andrei.

"Somewhere in my album I have a sketch of him," I said disinterestedly.

"If I were an artist I would have painted him," observed Katia.

"If you want, I can give you the sketch, if I find it," I smiled.

"Yes, please look for it and give it to me. I'll have it framed and hang it in my room," Katia answered coolly.

"No, give it to me," cried out Andrei. "Why Katia? He's my friend."

"I'll draw you another one."

"Make mine so that his eyes are plainly visible. He's got eyes like this," Andrei held up two fists.

"He's got an appealing face," Zhenia commented.

"You don't have such an appealing face," declared Andrei.

Zhenia started to say something back to him, but Maria Vasilevna insisted vehemently that they stop arguing.

Today Zhenia found Sidorenko on the embankment and, as I had requested, brought him back so that I could finish his portrait. He seemed put out—can his feelings for me really be serious? If so, it's too bad because I never wanted that.

"Viktor Petrovich," said Zhenia, "did you know that I'm going to Petersburg with Tata and Ilya?"

"So I'd heard, and I don't know what I'll do without you! It'll be so boring. And in Peter you're going to find so many men with mustaches. All my hopes will be dashed. But don't cry. I'll take a leave and come visit you."

"Come in January because Tata's going to be in Rome in October and November."

"I'm not going to Rome this year, but somewhere north. Norway, maybe."

"Winter in Norway?" Ilya was surprised. "You haven't seen snow before? You can see snow around Petersburg. Or maybe the snow in Norway is warm?"

"Maybe you can't see the difference, but I can," I shot back, annoyed.

"In the spring you can have an exhibition with two identical paintings: Norwegian snow and Petersburg snow. Your critics and disciples will begin to argue, and the admirers will discover the finest shades of difference. Only be careful not to mix up the titles."

I flared up and shot Ilya an evil eye, for which I was ashamed a minute later. But Sidorenko suddenly beamed.

Don't misinterpret, dear, I thought to myself. I'm just not a nice person.

We're leaving tomorrow. Last night we were up until 2 A.M. trying to persuade Maria Vasilevna to join us. She gave us the excuse that she didn't want to leave Andrei alone while he was in school, but that wasn't the truth. She knew that Katia wouldn't be going and could stay with him.

Zhenia was alternately crying, kissing her mother, and bounding with joy. How I envy her! She has so many unknown pleasures awaiting her: good music, theaters, even the stores and the streets. Ilya helped me, but it didn't take much to convince the family. After her conversation with her brother Katia had given up, had surrendered—not to me, but to inevitable circumstances. She'll be bored without me. Her life is so miserable that at least her hatred of me gave her a passion of sorts.

"Next year I'll come to live with you when I start at the university," Andrei pressed my hand, following me and sighing. He must have already had his cry in private.

My plans were set: I'd go to Petersburg, get Zhenia settled in our modest household, enroll her in the conservatory, get some of my old friends to keep an eye on her, and then get ready to go abroad. I was thinking about going to Scotland because I know nothing about it.

I simply must go to Rome. My unfinished painting is urgently calling to me. I spend two months there every year. My teacher, the renowned Scarlatti, and my friends write to me, invite me . . . but I don't want to go. I told him to forget me, so will he try for a rendezvous? I doubt it.

But . . . God protects those who protect themselves.

Back on the ship. Yesterday, just before departure. I received a letter from Scarlatti, insisting that I come to Rome. He was celebrating his jubilee and wanted "to see his dear student without fail."

Ilya read the letter and commented, "It's odd that you're not going, Taniusha. You'll hurt the old man."

It might hurt Scarlatti, but it'll hurt me even more. My paint-

ing is almost half finished. What's holding me back is the model for the central character, Dionysus. My friend Verber, though, wrote to me not long ago that he had found a deliveryman who would do. Still, I don't want to go. Why not? Surely "that" is completely over and "he" has no reason to come to Rome.

"I'll see," I said.

"You're just being capricious," said Ilya. "After your illness your nerves have become unglued. You used to talk about your painting all the time. Even when you were sick, you ranted on about it. And now for some reason you just don't care."

"I just don't want to," I retorted stubbornly. "Don't push me; it's as though you're turning me out. If it's necessary to you that I go, I'll go," I added, ready to burst into tears.

"You know that you're speaking rubbish, Tania. You're behaving like an infant."

"Yes," I said maliciously, "that's how you always look at me. As far as you're concerned, I have only whims. You don't care about my soul, my nerves." Tears poured from my eyes as I got up and went into the stateroom.

Sidorenko, who had come to see us off, was standing close by. He had heard our conversation and felt filled with hope. *How wrong you are, "observant" Viktor Petrovich!*

⊶⊜⊜⊶

I was lying down in the stateroom when he came in quietly, thinking I had fallen asleep, to look for something on the table.

"Iliusha," I reached out to him, "forgive me, dearest."

He took my hand and kissed it hard. "I'm not angry, Tania."

"Sit here," I said, making room for him on the settee.

He sat down; I took his hand and, pressing it against my cheek, I said, "Please don't tease me."

"Good heavens, Tania, what's on your mind? It's impossible to contradict you," he laughed. "Everyone pampers you: fate, the critics, friends and admirers—we have become so spoiled that it's gotten out of hand."

"It's true, everyone indulges me except you, Ilya."

"That's a nice thing to say!"

"I love you so much, so much that I'm prepared to sacrifice everything for you—even art," I said, sitting up and nestling up against him.

"I'll never demand any sacrifices of you, Taniusha," he said tenderly.

"At this very moment," I implored him, "I want you to tell me that you love me with all your heart."

"How you love words, Tania! Hasn't my whole life, all of my relations with you, made this plain?" he asked reproachfully. "Do you really still need words? Oh, Taniusha, my silly little girl. Stop teasing, kiss me, and let's go out on deck. You really are my little dreamer, and you are getting carried away."

I know that in the last five years you have always demonstrated your love, but now, at this moment, I need something else. Maybe the words that you can't say to me, despite all your love, Ilya.

⟡

I found a stack of letters waiting for me in Petersburg, among them a long, thin envelope. I recognized the distinctive handwriting immediately. Should I read the letter? Just throw it in the fireplace. But. . . . I opened the envelope.

"You wrote me: forget . . . good-bye. We won't talk about what I think, how I feel. I simply want to remind you of your promise.

"When I left you, mustering superhuman strength to conquer my desires, there, at the walls of your garden, you said you would come to Rome. I'm waiting.

"I left then so that the passion which had seized us both would not throw you into my arms against your will and your judgment. I behaved honorably, didn't I? Now in the course of the last two months you've been able to think it over, get control of yourself, sort out your emotions. I want you to tell me to my face: forget, good-bye. You don't even have to offer me any explanation, which in any case would be unpleasant. Come, and I will be able to tell at first glance.

"Send me a telegram. I'll meet you at the station and will know by your eyes what answer you have brought. I won't speak a word of love. You won't hear any entreaties from me. People will be all around us. I'll accompany you to your hotel, say good-bye, and disappear from your horizon forever. I can even emigrate to America or Australia if you'd prefer; I have my job and my money.

"You see, I'm not threatening you with suicide. Remember, I won't permit myself either a single reproach or a tender word. I even hope to conceal my anguish. But I ask you to come. You must come! I behaved honorably; do the same for me."

I am behaving honorably, dear, and I believe you. I must refuse you, refuse myself, but I'm not afraid. My love for another is as strong as my love for you. In my heart they're identical. I'll come and tell you straight out that a dream must remain a dream.

Everything is falling into place, as though fate is driving me to Rome. I received another letter from Scarlatti and an official invitation to his jubilee. I also received a second very flattering invitation: I have been selected to serve on the jury for an exhibition. A sculptor I know, and with whom I wanted to study modeling, has agreed to postpone his departure a month for me. Even the beautiful Lucia Pesca, a popular nightclub singer, has agreed to pose for one of the bacchantes if I come to Rome before November. I'm going.

The train, huffing, hissing, and bellowing out puffs of suffocating smoke with the nonchalance of Italian trains, pulled into the dirty terminal in Rome. I had traveled the whole route thinking that I was coming to bury my dream. I prepared myself for the funeral, and a thousand times planned how I would act at our meeting. Nevertheless, when I saw his figure on the platform, my heart stopped. Couldn't I hide out on the train, go as far as Naples and return from there? And what about my word?

No. I want to see him once more, for the last time, to look at him, to hear his voice. It will all be over in half an hour and we'll part forever. I jumped onto the platform.

He saw me, rushed toward me, grabbed my hands and began kissing them. Just a little more effort and the funeral will be over. I took a breath and said calmly and deliberately, "How nice of you to meet me. Will you do me one more favor? Here are my tags, please get my luggage."

He let go of my hand immediately. He was probably looking at me, but I was looking for something in my handbag and continued, laughing, "Rome, however, has not greeted me especially cordially—we're having better weather in Petersburg. Of course, I'm bringing you numerous greetings from the family. Zhenia even wanted to send you a jar of blackberry preserves but, forgive me, I was afraid to bring yet another suitcase."

My stupid chatter, my laughter—those were the funeral bells. The porter was the torchbearer, the chugging automobile, the hearse, and the stench of the incense burning on Piazza Termini. What a prosaic funeral I am giving you, my love! There are no tears. I'll cry later, in the hotel room. The sky, the gray sky, is weeping for me.

⋆⇒ ⇐⋆

It was difficult to remain silent. Very politely, I chattered on and on about Zhenia's musical successes, about the latest political news. . . . He occasionally turned his eyes to me and then silently looked back out the window. His face was pale, lips pursed, and he was scowling, but he was so handsome, surprisingly good-looking with that expression of repressed grief. My heart was breaking, my head spinning.

How foolhardy I had been to rely on my own strength! What was I doing? And Ilya, Zhenia . . . the family . . . my duty . . . reason . . . will? Oh, let it all go to the devil! Let it all disintegrate!

I put a quivering hand on his shoulder, leaned toward him and, gazing at his lips with hungry eyes, whispered, "Don't you really want to kiss me?"

A sound came from his chest, not quite a moan, not quite a cry. He grabbed me, and kisses gushed forth all over my face, hands, and dress.

"Oh, how you frightened me, you wicked woman! Dearest darling!"

The automobile stopped to let a tram by. I began laughing nervously and tried to pull away.

"Slow down, they can see us through the window."

I had to persuade him, like a child, to take me to the hotel where they were expecting me.

"Why? Let's go to my place. I've already gotten it ready for you."

"Impossible," I told him, so happy that I could lean against his shoulder, kiss his cheek, his eyes, and revel in his touch. But I had better control of myself than he did.

"You mean that it's not all finished 'there'?" he asked, moving slightly away.

"Dear, that's all for later. Now I have two months," I said, smoothing his hair. How long I had fantasized about doing this.

He looked at me reproachfully.

"Do you know that I came here with every intention of saying 'no'; I was very confident."

"Evil woman!"

"But when I saw your eyes, your eyelashes, this spot between your cheek and your neck. . . . I forgot everything. I love you!"

He was looking at me with inordinately wild eyes. I closed them with my hand, saying, "Now we'll go to the hotel. Get yourself in hand. In an hour I'll be wherever you want."

"Move away from me. . . . I'll be there, on the corner. I'll be waiting exactly an hour from now. Don't torture me. We have so much to talk about, to ask . . . it's funny to think that we know so little about each other. I'll let my servant off and we'll be alone."

"For God's sake, dear! We've arrived."

Oh, what a slowpoke you are, Beatrice. Why is it taking you so long to prepare my bath? Forty minutes have already gone by with all this commotion. Hurry. . . . I won't be dressed in time. I can't make him wait, but at the same time I want to look my best. Am I thinking about something? No, all that's in the distance. I'll worry about it later . . . later I'll suffer remorse, cry, anguish over this, maybe even regret it, but at the moment, hurry! He's waiting for me.

And he was waiting for me. He looked pale. He took my arm and we walked in silence. Suddenly he stopped. "I can't go on. I'll call a cab," he sucked in a breath.

"Stop being a baby," I laughed. We continued in silence. At the gate he took out his key, but his hands were shaking so badly he couldn't get it in the lock. I took it and opened the gate. He led me across a beautiful marble terrace and into a large, austere living room.

"You're at my house, Tata, and yours!" he said. "Take off your cloak and hat and be the mistress of the house. Order me about!"

He opened the door to the bedroom—it was big and light. I saw masses of roses everywhere, in vases, on the spacious bed, on the vanity, and simply scattered about the floor.

I stood in front of a large Venetian mirror, fixing my hair and getting intoxicated from the smell of roses, the warmth of the fire place, and the handsome face behind my shoulder reflected in the mirror. I looked at him, and in the mirror offered my arms and lips. That instant he grabbed me, tore at my dress and whispered, choking, "Forgive me, forgive me. . . . I'm a savage beast, a primitive animal . . . but I can't. . . . I've waited so long!"

It was evening, almost night. I'd sent a messenger to the hotel with a message to send my things to my studio, where Verber was still living, and to say that I would be there day after tomorrow. He demanded for himself tonight and tomorrow.

I agreed to everything, but this conversation sobered me up. I reminded him that we hadn't eaten since two o'clock that afternoon. From the closet he took out a fantastic costume made of silk and lace, and then tied the wide ribbon around my waist himself. "I myself will dress you, Tata, I've dreamed about it so often."

How beautifully he makes love! We had a cold supper in a small dining room with Louis XIII furnishings—it was like a poem. He fluctuated between passionate caresses and child's play. His laughter was infectious, and his kisses made me drunker than champagne. We ate from the same plate and drank from the same glass, in which he mixed rose petals he had strewn on my breasts.

I don't know what had happened to me, but this wasn't love, nor passion—it was insanity.

We were exhausted, could barely move. We just looked at each other with voracious eyes. He was lying on the floor on a white bear rug, reclining against my knees. He looked at me with those bottomless eyes, chattering incoherently about his love. I looked into those eyes, leaned toward him and listened greedily to his voice. I could see his half-naked body, with the soft folds of an Arabian robe draped across one shoulder. . . .

I could feel it. . . . I knew that in one more minute we would go crazy. I feared for my sanity and said, almost delirious, "Quiet, be quiet! Madness is coming toward us! Can't you hear its steps? I'm terrified."

Noon. Slivers of sunlight, like golden thread, shone through the lace curtains and fell through the crack in the heavy silk drapes. It slid along the white back of the low bed, fractured, elongated, and fell across his head. He was sleeping and I was reclining on a pillow, watching him.

His face had a serious, almost sorrowful expression. But he

was so handsome—not classical good looks, but something else. Strange. Stark didn't look very much like Byron, yet at the moment he reminded me of a portrait of the poet.

My gaze took in the entire body lying before me: one hand lay under his cheek, and the other was flung out. I could make out his slender, beautiful legs under the thin blanket. Watching him, I leaned forward to kiss his perfect throat but stopped. The artist in me overpowered the lover. I was already thinking about how to sketch him, how to capture that pose, that face.

Noiselessly, I slid out of bed. I remembered that yesterday, when we had left to eat, he had shown me a cozy little corner by a large Italian window, set off from his study by flowering plants.

"That studio is for Tata if she wants to paint here," he had said. He had wrapped his arm around my waist and I felt his breath on my shoulder; I paid no attention to that corner. But now that I remembered it I ran there.

His sweet thoughtfulness and attention touched me. I had everything there I needed: watercolors, crayons, even a stack of canvases and an easel. I grabbed some colored pencils and quietly returned to the bedroom. Stark opened his eyes quickly and began feeling around for me. He started to jump out of bed. . . .

I have found my Dionysus!

"For God's sake, don't move! Stay as you are!" I cried excitedly.

He made a charming grimace and struck a pose, looking at me slyly; he knows how handsome he is and that I love him.

When I'm in my studio or simply wandering off somewhere, I come to my senses and can think about it: what exactly is it about him that drives me out of my mind? Now I feel very positive that it's his femininity. His movements are very feminine; he flirts gracefully and has a careless, languorous laziness that complements a childlike liveliness and gaiety.

The artist in me delights in his body: at once tender and strong, a slender waist, flawless hands and feet . . . it's also feminine, but that is precisely what I need for my Dionysus.

⋅→═◗ ◖═←⋅

Today I wanted to sit all day and work, but I had just gotten everything laid out when Stark came and dragged me away for a walk and then to his house. I reprimanded myself: I still haven't finished anything, Lucia Pesco is soon going on tour to England, and I'm overpaying the models—but he comes and pouts, "I've been waiting a whole hour for you, Tata."

"Sit here with me for while, darling. I simply have to work."

He sat down, but looking into his eyes and hearing his voice. . . . I tossed aside my brush and said, "Let's go for a walk."

We went outside the city and there, nestling up against each other, we lingered through the blooming autumn flowers, filled with desire and making such pretty speeches to each other that our heads were spinning, our eyes dimming.

⋅→═◗ ◖═←⋅

I had to write home some sort of explanation. I've been here three weeks, but have only dropped a few postcards, saying how incredibly busy I am and that I'll send details later in a letter. It's offensive, appalling of me not to tell Ilya the truth. But I can't, I simply can't. It'll be better, easier for him, if I explain everything to him in person, when I return. But I can't think about that now. Today I managed to get the whole day to myself, persuading Stark not to come by.

"A whole day without you?" he said in his whimsical, child-ish voice, "I won't bother you. I'll just sit still."

"Dearest, when you're there, I can't do anything, can't think of anything else but you. If I were sitting next to you, do you think you could do your calculations?"

"Of course not."

"Then please let me prepare what I must today, and I'll spend all of tomorrow with you."

"Well, okay. I'm beginning to hate your art. I can't do anything—it makes too powerful a rival. Anyway, I've let my business slide and I have letters to write."

"Excellent."

"But tomorrow, Tata, I'll come earlier. All right?" he plucked the pale lilac chrysanthemum from his buttonhole, stuck it in my hair, kissed my cheek and moved toward the door. At the door he stopped and, touching the head of his walking stick against his lips, said reflectively, "However, you won't be drawing tonight."

"No, but I want to go to bed early tonight so that I can get a good night's sleep because I have to get up tomorrow at eight."

"But if we go to bed early, you'll get your rest."

"No, no, please," I said hastily, "leave me alone today."

"Tata, I'm a primitive creature, an animal—I know that. But today, you'll see, I'll be quiet as a mouse. I'll only kiss you here"— he touched my forehead—"you'll see."

I looked at him. What was he doing to me? And Lucia Pesca, and the two models with physiques like Hercules but rather dull-witted countenances, who were now sitting in my kitchen playing cards? And Ferelli, who would be waiting for me tomorrow in his studio at nine o'clock? And the other appointments I had to meet? But he's looking at me! Well, I'll go this evening, but what time will I get up tomorrow morning?

We were walking along the Appian Way on a moonlit night. We'd left our car at a church and were walking arm in arm, snuggling up to each other.

"You know," I said, "that would make a wonderful subject for a painting: this ancient road, bathed in moonlight, and a person in contemporary dress, a pedestrian or on horseback— no, a car. A car with two headlights would be best . . . and all around, lit by the moon, the ghosts of Roman senators, patricians, soldiers. And Metella* herself would be looking down from her tower, struck with wonder."

He said nothing. I could sense that he was disgruntled and pulling away from me.

"Tell me, what's the matter?"

"It's so silly."

"I want to know, tell me!"

"I'm jealous," he said heatedly. "I'm jealous of your damned art. Because of it you continually forget about me. It means more to you than I do, and it's constantly pulling you away from me," he added in his capricious tone.

What do you know! And I thought he was the one pulling me away from my art!

Today I can work all day long! Stark wasn't able to get out of visiting the family of a friend he bumped into yesterday. But even so I could barely convince him to spend the day with them. He made me swear that I would come at ten.

I can draw until dusk, and then turn on the electric lights and finish the bust I'm making of Scarlatti, which my instructor says is coming along very well. It's my present to the Master on his jubilee.

I'm so happy to be working that since early morning I've stopped only to exchange a few words with Verber. He made coffee for me and was making sandwiches when he started to reproach me: "Mama, you've abandoned your work, and even me, sinner that I am. It used to be that a day wouldn't go by without your swearing at me, and now three days have passed and you haven't called me a fool once."

"Dear Vasilii Kazimirovich, I can't worry about you now."

*Nagrodskaia was referring to a well-known landmark, the tomb of Caecilia Metella, a noble Roman matron of the first century B.C.E.

"I know, Mama, I know. I can see what's happening and I'm not getting upset."

"Good—no need to."

"I'm not upset because it won't last long."

I put down the brush, surprised, and looked at him. He stood before me, tall, emaciated, his hands thrust in the pockets of his ragged pants, wearing an unbelievably greasy jacket, his sharp nose high in the air. His whole face, covered in tiny wrinkles and a moist red beard, was laughing happily.

"What makes you think that?"

"I just know that it won't last long. You lost your head over the shape and the coloring. It won't be for long."

"You're an idiot, Vasenka."

"Thank God, you're finally swearing at me and calling me Vasenka. Your 'Vasilii Kazimirovich' depressed me greatly. You'd tossed me aside."

I looked him over carefully and realized that I had indeed neglected this man who was like a son to me: only the jacket and the pants remained from the suit I had bought him last year, and they were in dreadful condition and too small for him. And he was terribly thin. My conscience pricked me.

I'm spending almost all my time now with Stark; but before, when I came to Rome, Vasenka ate most of his meals with me and worked on his paintings in my studio. I even dressed him. He was as attached to me as a dog, and I had maternal feelings for him despite the fact that he was fifteen years older than I.

Yes, I need Vasenka as a mentor. He has such delicate artistic sensibilities, such an understanding of art, and such broad erudition in the various epochs and styles. And how he can develop a subject, arrange the poses, the details. What talent!

Vasenka himself can only paint bad watercolors for stationery stores. Foreigners gladly purchase the paintings, which gives him a meager income. All the paintings depict the same scene: Rome at sunset, an Italian girl in a red skirt leaning against the columns of the Forum, and the Colosseum in the moonlight. He assured me once in despair that he would never be able to paint anything good.

"I can't, Mama. You see, I've studied, I've tried, I know how to draw, I see every mistake . . . but when I try, it still doesn't come out right."

Vasenka is one of the few Russian painters who got stuck permanently in Rome. In his youth, he was in love with a model, and then habit and the lack of discipline to do otherwise kept him here. Once I considered taking him back to Russia, but then I realized that he would starve there. He would never accept financial help. Money insults him, but he'll accept payment in kind: food and clothes. Once when the wind blew his cap into the Tiber he came to me and declared, "Mama, let me do you a favor. You may buy me some kind of covering."

Even then, he'll accept this kind of payment only from someone he loves, and there aren't many of them. He won't accept anything from someone to whom he is indifferent, and he is indifferent to almost everyone. Moreover, he won't take help from anyone he hates, and he hates as strongly as he loves. Sometimes I've sworn at him for his rudeness and badgering of people he meets in my studio. Because of him I lost a female acquaintance with whom I was becoming quite friendly. Another time he said awful things to a general from Petersburg who was visiting me in Rome. I wasn't surprised that Vasenka had picked a fight with the general; the latter was an important man who liked to show off, but the woman was sweet and congenial, not at all pretentious.

"What about her didn't you like, Vasenka?"

"I just didn't like her."

"That's no reason to say spiteful things to a person."

"Well, why did she have bows all over her dress?"

"The bows bothered you?"

"Well, yes. That was enough."

"You buffoon, you've driven away all my friends."

"And that's so bad?"

"For me it's very unpleasant."

"Oh, they just hang out and bother you."

"That's my business. Now I'm asking you sincerely to leave them alone, Vasilii Kazimirovich."

He concentrated on his work, grumbling, "She put bows on everywhere, and then started chatting! Imagine! As if she were a normal person!"

I was torn between laughter and anger.

He started calling me "Mama" three years ago, when I brought him to my place from the hospital after a severe illness. He was so weak that I had to feed him with a spoon, like a baby. His mother was Russian and his father Polish, but he was convinced that his ancestors were Germans, and he was avenging himself on them with his slovenliness—he hated Germans.

"My burghers are turning over in their graves. They're beside themselves, with such an heir. It's too bad I can't drink or I'd have become a drunkard to spite them!"

We had an ugly scene today. As we were returning from a stroll, a young couple was walking toward us. She was a lovely redhead with her hair in a braid, and she was carrying a basket; he was a handsome soldier. They made a splendid pair. Her cheeks glowed as she lightly swung her basket from side to side, listening, laughing, and lowering her eyes at whatever her picturesque cavalier was saying. He twirled his mustaches as he leaned toward her. It made a somewhat clichéd scene, but they were both so full of vitality, joy, and youth, that I feasted my eyes on them and turned to follow them with my gaze. Suddenly Stark grabbed my hand and hissed through his teeth, "You can't stare like that."

I opened my mouth in amazement.

"What's the matter with you?"

"Nothing. It's just that I don't want you looking 'that' way."

"You mean I can't look at a face I like?"

He didn't answer. I wanted to get angry, but I could see such pain on his face that I felt sorry for him.

"You're a strange person. What's the matter? A pretty girl walks by me. . . ."

"You weren't looking at her."

"I was looking at her, and at him."

"No," he said stubbornly.

"What—no?"

"You weren't looking at him like you look at other people."

"This has gone too far!" I erupted, "Think about what you're saying and you'll be ashamed."

He was silent. Obstinately, I turned and headed home.

"Tata, please don't get angry, but this has been bothering me for a long time."

"What?" I was surprised.

"The way you sometimes look at men."

"I?!"

"Tata, do you remember, when we were still in S., and I rushed toward you? We were still on the path, and I told you that I loved you."

"Of course I remember."

"Your glance drove me insane then, and sometimes I see you look at other men with that same glance. It says, 'Come to me. I want you.'"

"You're crazy! I'm leaving."

"No, Tata, don't be mad. You do it unconsciously, but when a man sees that look he'll turn and follow us . . . he'll forget everything, that you aren't alone, that you. . . ."

"Listen, you need a doctor. Did I just glance at that soldier like that?" Unrelenting, I walked through the entrance and began to climb the stairs. Boiling mad, I tore off my hat and jacket and sat down at my easel. A minute later he was on his knees before me. I had no will power left with him. I should have thrown him out, taken offense—but I was stroking his hair.

"You've forgiven me?" he said happily, clasping his arms around me.

"No, I don't forgive you," I answered, smiling. "If you thought about it, you'd see how you slandered me. You think that I'm prepared to throw myself into the arms of the first man I meet on the street, at first sight."

"But you yourself told me that the first time you met me, on the train, you felt passion for me, and that was 'at first sight.' You didn't know me," he said softly, looking me in the eyes.

I said nothing. That wasn't true, I thought bitterly. I had found in him the incarnation of the type most attractive to me, my ideal of beauty. When I tried to explain this to him, he shook his head sadly.

"Yes, Tata, but you're talking about physical desire, and that will pass. I can already sense that your intensity is weakening. But me? I gave you my whole heart, my whole life. Because you, you are not only a woman, but life itself. Tata, I'll go out of my mind if I lose you. I want you to love the person inside me at least a little. Tata, my life, love me, if only just a little. I can't live without that love."

He raised his head. His eyelashes were wet, those long, curly eyelashes. I kissed them—they're so beautiful.

We remained in that position until it grew too dark to work. Vasenka came in, and Stark slowly started to get up from his knees.

"Don't disturb yourself, handsome Dionysus," Vasenka said, shaking Stark's hand; "the weather is miserable. If it's okay with Mama I'll start a fire and make you some punch."

Feeling a little chilly, we gladly accepted his proposition. His face was very jolly and he was rubbing his hands together.

"Why are you so happy, Verber?" Stark asked.

"I had a good time while you were gone."

"What were you up to?"

"I'll tell you while I'm making the punch," he said, stoking the fire.

I made myself comfortable on the ottoman, piling the pillows up around me. Stark was half lying next to me, leaning on my shoulder. Vasenka poured our punch and then sat, glass in hand, on a stool close to the fireplace.

"How nice it is to sit with good friends around a fire. Warm, comfortable, no 'outside forces' intervening . . . to your health, Mama."

"And to yours, son. Were you a good boy in my absence?"

"Depends on your point of view. I told you, I was enjoying myself."

"How?"

"Do you promise not to swear at me?" asked Vasenka, wrapping his arms around his boney knees and contorting his face into fine wrinkles.

"Uh oh, he's made another mess," I said uneasily.

"If you get upset beforehand, I won't say a thing."

"You must tell me, Vasenka. You've done something terrible."

"Nothing of the sort. I clashed with outside forces."

"Are you going to tell me or not?"

"Handsome Dionysus, hold Mama down and make sure she doesn't throw a pillow at me."

I tried to jump up, but Stark, laughing, pinned me down. His laughter always soothes my nerves—it's so happy that it's contagious. I fell laughing, my chest on his knees, and said, "Vasenka, I won't touch you. Just tell me what you've done!"

"Nothing special. I just had a heart-to-heart conversation with a compatriot."

"With what compatriot?"

"I don't know. He was tall, wearing a suit, and had a stu-u-pid expression on his face, and he had a tiepin in the shape of a horseshoe. As soon as I saw that horseshoe, I knew he was a fool."

"You're the fool."

"Oh, Mama, no! If you're going to try to be elegant, at least show some taste. Ask Dionysus over there if he'd wear a horseshoe."

Stark was laughing, but I was getting annoyed.

"And if he did," Vasenka continued coolly, "you'd lose all interest in him."

"I'm telling you, get on with the story."

"When I saw the horseshoe, I squinted and said nothing. He asked me in French, 'Whom have I the honor of meeting?' and I answered him in Italian, 'Don't speak French.' He asked me in French, 'I must see Madame Kuznetsova,' and I answered him in Italian, 'She's gone for a walk.' He said in French, 'I can't understand you,' and I answered, 'And I can't understand you.' It was all very polite, Mama, and I would have politely shown him the door, except that he muttered in Russian, 'fool.' I answered him in Russian, 'I hear a fool!' and set about my business. 'Kind sir,' he said, 'here is my card.' 'A duel!' I said. 'All right, but I still don't have mine yet with the proper ducal insignia.'

"He became embarrassed. 'No,' he said, 'I'm giving you this card for Tatiana Alexandrovna.' 'Then give it to her servant and then go to hell!' I replied.

"Then he started fuming. 'Who are you, kind sir?' And I answered, 'Tatiana Alexandrovna's roommate.' You should have seen his face!"

"Verber, how dare you!"

"Don't get so upset, Dionysus, you've got a dirty mind."

"What?"

"Keep listening. Stunned, he started muttering, 'That's impossible.' 'What's impossible?' I was insulted. 'That I live with Tatiana Alexandrovna? We eat, drink, and work together, and sometimes I spend the night in her kitchen.' 'Oh,' he said, 'I was thinking. . . .' Immediately I began to glare at him. Getting up from my stool, I yelled, 'It seems you interpreted the word roommate in its most perverted sense. How could you think that about Tatiana Alexandrovna? You've insulted her with the most vile suspicions! Go, and get your filthy imagination out of here, kind sir!' He stumbled backward toward the door and left, the mangy coward."

"He must have thought you were a lunatic," Stark laughed, but I was upset. What kind of stupid joke was this?

"Give me his card," I said angrily.

Vasenka picked it up off the table and handed it to me:

Viktor Petrovich

Sidorenko

How inopportune.

⊷═◦═⊶

Sidorenko came again today, but he didn't find me. He left a note asking when I would be home.

"I've got to see him, there's nothing else I can do," I sighed. I was sitting on the bed, eating grapes. Stark was lying next to me on a pillow, holding up a plate of fruit.

"Of course we'll see him," he said.

"I'm surprised that you aren't jealous," I said, feeding him a grape.

He shook his head thoughtfully, holding it between his large, white teeth. Those white teeth, set off by his pink lips, were so pretty that I leaned forward and with my own mouth took out the grape.

"Darling," he whispered, embracing me, "I'm not jealous of him at all. I'm not simply jealous of every man, without differentiation. Sometimes I'm even jealous of myself."

"That doesn't make any sense."

"How can I explain it . . . sometimes I. . . ."

A knock at the door interrupted him. A business telegram. He jumped up from the bed and wrapped my red shawl around himself. He had such a marvelous body that it looked pretty draped around him. He reminded me of someone—who?

He tried to read the telegram by the flicker of the blue lantern which lit the room, but it was too weak. He turned on the wall lamp, read it and, with one hand holding the shawl against his hip, he reached up to turn off the electricity.

"Stop!" I cried, "don't move for a minute. Did you run away from the Academy Museum in Florence a long time ago?"

"I don't understand you."

"Did you live before, in the fifteenth century, and pose for Sandro Botticelli. Do you remember the youth in his painting *Primavera?* Mercury, picking oranges! You're so handsome in that pose—come, kiss me, hurry!"

He turned off the light and said dejectedly, "No, Tata, I don't want you to kiss me just because I remind you of one of Botticelli's models."

"Why are you so capricious today? What's the matter?"

"Listen, my dearest, what if I suddenly became crippled or hunchbacked, if I became outrageously fat or thin? Would you still love me? You wondered why I'm sometimes jealous of my-self. At those moments I'm ready to disfigure myself. I know that you don't love me but my looks. It hurts me, Tata, that because of my body you don't see my soul. That's very, very hard on me."

It's no easier on me; this is already our third scene today.

⋆⇒◎⇐⋆

I was expecting Sidorenko. Vasenka was with me because I didn't want to meet him alone. I was reading letters; Ilya thanked me for the "sweet" and "detailed" letter. True, it had been detailed with an account of my work, descriptions of the models, Scarlatti's jubilee, but I don't know how sweet it was. . . .

The letter had not contained any of the previous loving words or petty niceties. Of course I had begun it with "dear" and ended it with "kisses," but it had none of what I used to fill my letters with. Yet Ilya still found it "sweet"; did this mean that he didn't need the kinds of affectionate phrases I used to write to him?

Does Ilya love me? Can it be that on those occasions when I sober up from my passion and my conscience bothers me, my feelings of guilt are actually unnecessary? Maybe it wouldn't be any great sorrow for him to lose me. Katia and his mother would come to him; with his loving family all around, maybe I'm completely expendable. Why does that thought make me de-pressed instead of happy? It would be a thousand times better. Do I want Ilya to be hurt? No, of course not. It would be better if Ilya didn't love me. Zhenia had added a postscript: "Dearest Tatochka, I sense that something is not right with your work. Or maybe you're so consumed by your painting that you've forgot-ten the rest of the world. But when you have time, please remem-ber your sister Zhenia, who loves you so very much."

My dear child, this is so hard for me. How are you going to bear the grief that I am preparing for your nearest and dearest? Your faith in people will be shattered. I'll take away your happi-ness and joy in living, if not forever, at least for a long time. Oh, how this torments. I wish Stark would come. He's like wine for me: I get drunk and forget all else.

"Why are you so sad—knock it off," said Verber.

"My heart is heavy, dear friend."

"Nonsense. If the letter did this, pay no attention."

"Oh, Vasenka."

"Of course I know what's going on. You've gotten tangled up with Dionysus, and now your conscience is bothering you about 'Trajan's Column.'"*

"Stop this foolishness."

"Nothing foolish about it. What are you going to do? You'll go back and forget all this."

"You really think that I can just go back home?"

"Why not? Will Dionysus bite off your nose? The same person who left can return."

"You're crazy."

"Oh, Mama, don't ruin your life! Dionysus won't keep you satisfied for six months. Then you'll be sorry."

We sat quietly for a few minutes.

"Mama, let me go out for a little while."

"Sit where you are."

"At least let me do something—this is boring. Let me wash your brushes."

We still had an hour to wait for Sidorenko. *Poor Eddy—you aren't the one bothering me now!*

⊷⊜⊝⊶

The doorbell; Sidorenko had arrived.

"Behave yourself," I begged Vasenka.

"You'll see, I'll be refined à la Dionysus."

"For heaven's sake don't be 'à la' anyone!" I exclaimed.

Sidorenko walked in with such rapid steps and such a happy look on his face that I felt ashamed. He kissed my hand several times, chattered on incoherently about all he's been doing in S.,

*Here Nagrodskaia invokes another familiar monument, the column of the emperor Trajan. Verber ironically uses it as a metaphor for the very tall Ilya.

and how bored he was without me and Zhenia. Suddenly he saw Vasenka and stopped. I said hastily, "Please let me introduce you: Vasilii Kazimirovich Verber—my best friend, who is very sorry for his joke. Hoaxes and practical jokes are his passion. Sit down, dear Viktor Petrovich, and tell us why you're in Rome."

I was trying to speak as cordially as possible and was chiding myself for not allowing Vasenka to leave. I could already see the familiar spark of irrational hatred flickering in his eyes.

"I came to Rome," said Sidorenko, "on very important business."

"I hope that your business won't prevent you from visiting me. For example, tomorrow evening I've invited the local Russian colony over, artists—I hope you won't be bored."

He stared intently at me, started to say something, but then looked at Vasenka and decided against it.

"I'm extraordinarily busy, and squandering my energy something awful—as usual. Two portraits and a painting. It's the picture I started last year. I've used three female and four male models, but still haven't found one for the central figure."

"Are these the sunbathers you were telling me about last summer?"

"No, this is my long cherished dream, *The Wrath of Dionysus*." I forgot about all else and began talking about it. "Dionysus is incensed! And everyone around him is drunk on his anger, they've all lost their heads—everything has collapsed into chaos. They're running, jumping, crying, laughing. He has deprived them of all reason! The whole crowd becomes intoxicated immediately! The only ones who have kept their heads in this crowd are the panthers, and they look at the people with such contempt. . . . And above them all, Dionysus, feminine, yet majestic and furious, half rising from his golden settee. . . ."

"Oh, how I envy you, Tatiana Alexandrovna," said Sidorenko, "you can get so caught up in your art that you forget everything else around you!"

"Not always," I sighed.

Sidorenko pricked up his ears, and I quickly changed the subject. "Have you seen our family recently?"

"No, I traveled south through Volochinsk, but I wrote to

Evgeniia Lvovna* and told her that I was coming here. By the way, on the way over I saw Stark. What's he doing? There is hardly any wood business around Rome. Does he visit you?"

"Occasionally. If you come tomorrow you'll see him."

"I want to chat with you as we did last summer, in S. Are you going to Petersburg soon?"

"I don't know. As soon as I finish the painting I'll go for a short time, but then return here," I said dejectedly.

"You're coming back!" he exclaimed happily.

"Yes, in the spring," I recovered myself, "but only to get the painting."

He looked at me searchingly, but I pretended not to notice and rang for lunch to be served.

Civilian attire doesn't become Sidorenko; he wears uniforms better. With his ruddy complexion and curly hair, he looks good in a tunic and high boots, and even handsome in a peasant blouse. But this suit fits him badly, and the tie is incredibly gaudy; I can see now why he offended Vasenka's aesthetic sensibilities.

While I was brewing the coffee and setting the plates with cold hors d'oeuvres, Sidorenko turned to Vasenka, "Are you a permanent resident of Rome?"

"Yes," he answered, tossing a contemptuous glance at Sidorenko; "I've already lived here fifteen years."

"Don't you miss Russia?"

"What have I forgotten there?"

"It's still the motherland. I couldn't survive a year away from it."

"What do you do for the motherland? You get your salary as a state bureaucrat. Have you spilled your blood for it?"

"We all do little for our homeland," Sidorenko smiled, "but we love it instinctively. Does a child who loves its mother give up something for her? It simply loves a familiar face. I love Russia, the width and breadth of its open spaces. . . ."

"Width and open spaces? Why not travel around the pampas or the Sahara?"

<hr>

*Zhenia's full name.

"Oh, a toast to the Russian song, Russian boldness, the expansive Russian soul, a Russian woman! I love the country roads, groves, and rivers. I'm from the Volga region, and for me there is no sweeter music than that of the barge haulers."

"Where do you publish?" Vasenka suddenly asked, very serious.

"What?" Sidorenko was surprised.

"Your poetry. I think I've read it somewhere: 'I didn't go into the sleepy forest with a bludgeon. . . .'"

"Vasenka," I whispered, horrified.

But nothing could stop him now.

"I remember the one about the boyar's daughter, who had been kissed by the gardener:

> He kissed her, he caressed her,
>
> and sang songs from the Volga.

"And just think, now I've met the author and I want to tell you how surprised I was that the boyar's daughter let him kiss and touch her—I'll bet you could have smelled him a verst away!"

"Get out of here, Vasenka," I said indignantly.

"I won't go," he said frostily. "When I asked to leave, you ordered me to sit, and now that it's raining outside you're driving me away."

Sidorenko saved the situation when he burst out laughing. Unwillingly, I also began to laugh and said, "Don't talk to him, Viktor Petrovich. He's in a foul mood today. Believe me, when he wants to be, he's one of the kindest people in the world."

Vasenka arose, came to me and ceremoniously kissed my hand.

"Forgive me, Mama. I won't say another word. And you, sir poet, don't be angry with me. These are my German ancestors misbehaving."

⋅→═◑ ◐═→⋅

Today I managed to win some free time for myself and worked from noon till five. Then I was in Stark's study, drinking after-dinner coffee and warming myself by the fire. It was already the second day that I had felt so miserable. Nothing really hurt, but my head would spin and I felt completely exhausted. Closing my eyes, I stretched out on the couch and tried to drive all thoughts away. . . .

"Do you want to sleep, dear?" Stark asked, sitting down softly beside me and taking my hand.

"No," I drew him closer to me.

"I want to ask you, Tata, if you will please accept a small gift from me," he said ingratiatingly.

"No, please, it's not necessary. You spend enough money on foolish things."

It's just one of his whims: when I come to him, I don't wear a single thread that he hasn't bought for me. The elegant toiletries, shoes, and fantastic clothes made of the softest silk, gossamer, and lace cost incredible sums. I know that flowers here are cheap, but he fills the rooms with them!

"It's just a little thing, Tatusia, and it only cost pennies," he pleaded, smiling and kissing my fingers.

"Still you shouldn't buy it."

"But I already have!" he laughed and took from his pocket a small flat parchment box. It held a slender gold chain with three pale rose-colored corals. He fastened it around my neck.

"What a simple but elegant trinket—but you still shouldn't have done it," I kissed him.

"I wanted you to have something from me that you could wear forever. Promise me, Tata, that you'll never take it off."

"All right, darling."

"No, seriously, I want your word of honor that you'll wear it even when you've fallen out of love with me."

"What nonsense!"

"It might be nonsense, but give me your word," he insisted stubbornly.

"Okay, I give you my word."

"You see, I thought about this for a long time, and I bought these corals with one thought in mind."

"What is it?"

He looked at me somberly, almost sternly. "Let me tell you about it later. It's my dream, and it's terribly important to me."

Resting his elbows on his knees, he raised his head, and looking into the fire, said, "Tata, I have no religion. No one ever told me about God. My father was an Englishman, and my mother a Russian Karaite.*

That's where he got those doleful Eastern eyes, I thought.

"I grew up and was educated in France, and I didn't hear anything about Him in school. Mother didn't want me to be a Christian, and father didn't want me to be a Jew, so they left me without any religion. I was sixteen when my mother died, and my father's sister insisted that he baptize me in the Anglican Church. And that was the only time I've ever been in a church for a ritual. Well, once I was the best man at a Russian wedding in Petersburg. I had forgotten the prayers that I had studied so hurriedly before my baptism. I don't know a single prayer in any language. But not long ago I prayed, Tata, I prayed, holding you in my arms and lavishing you with the most passionate caresses. I prayed to the terrible God of Israel, and to the meek Christian God. And unless all religions lie, my prayers must be answered."

He stood, straightened up, and raised his head proudly. I couldn't speak or take my eyes off him, he was so handsome.

"What did you pray for, dear?" I asked after a long silence.

"Don't ask me, Tata," he said, rubbing his forehead and sitting back down beside me. "For some reason I don't want to talk, as if I'm afraid to discuss even this."

"As you like, dear."

If I paint his portrait, it absolutely must be his profile, and with that stern-but-tender expression.

"Now we've caught you, signora!" Scarlatti's loud voice boomed. I turned around and saw him, small, round, always jolly, and with long gray hair and a pointed goatee.

*This is a small Jewish sect that emphasizes the Torah over the Talmud and the rabbinic tradition.

"We went to your studio, and Verber told us that the signora had gone to the Villa Borghese. Dio mio! Why? We figured that the signora wanted to look at something in the museum, so we went there. But no, the signora's sitting in the garden, dreaming."

"I was in the museum, maestro, but now I'm tired. I walked here," I said, smiling and answering his companion's bow.

The gentleman stood before me, his cap raised. What an interesting face! His head was almost bald, but he had a nice thick beard that reached his chest. The beard was dark, although what was left of his hair was quite gray. His face was long, with regular features: a straight nose and cold, steely eyes beneath dark straight brows. I liked his face, despite its pallor and his sunken cheeks. It was an intelligent face. He was tall and thin, slightly hunched over, and dressed in the kind of refined simplicity that I love in men's clothing.

"Meet your compatriot, signora, your ardent admirer. I have the honor to present Signor Latchinov. The signor was ecstatic when he saw the work in your studio, and now he sees that your beauty equals your talent."

"Oh, maestro, and I thought that you didn't consider me very talented," I laughed, and he shook his finger at me, crying, "Oh, she's clever, she's as smart as she is pretty and talented."

These compliments didn't bother me; it was simply the Italian manner of speaking courteously to women.

"Maestro," I said, as he took out a handkerchief and blew his nose, "I am extremely hungry because I didn't eat breakfast this morning."

"Of course, of course!" he jumped up. "Signor Alexandro has a carriage. Where do you want to eat? at Faggiano's?"

"No, treat me to whipped cream and a glass of marsala here, at the farm."

There were a number of people at the farm, but we found a table. I ate hungrily. I hadn't been able to touch my breakfast this morning—just drank some coffee. It had been difficult to get up, and I had been so pale that Stark hadn't wanted me to go to the studio. But that had passed, and now I was laughing, chatting, and watching my new acquaintance.

His hands were beautifully shaped and covered with expensive rings. I love precious stones.

"I wanted to ask you a favor, to sell me one of your paintings," Latchinov said to me.

"Unfortunately, I don't have anything here but sketches."

"And in Petersburg?"

"Some, not much."

"I have a respectable collection there, which includes one of your works."

"Not really!"

"A small, long canvas with a bunch of children running. I can't say that it's a masterpiece, but it shows a lot of originality and movement. The long, narrow shape resembles a fresco. Equal strips of blue sky and green grass. Flying bodies. It works very well. Even then I predicted your success. I don't like female painters, but there's nothing feminine in your style."

"Do you also paint?"

"No. If anything, my speciality is music; but I love art in general. Only art makes life beautiful and, if you will, love. Of course, for those who are still young."

"Sometimes one impedes the other," I smiled.

"Yes, when one is put ahead of the other. But when they flow together, the harmony is amazing. I think that the best works of art are dictated by love. I don't mean love in the narrow sense, but in the broadest—love for the homeland or for a woman, it doesn't matter."

"I don't completely agree with you. It's possible to love art for its own sake."

"You're entirely correct but, while creating something, you have to love something or it will be a lifeless thing. Think about it, all the brilliant works, about which we know the history, were painted either by lovers or religious or political fanatics."

"But, for example, there are dazzling portraits of men painted by other men."

My companion started laughing. "What does that mean?

Maybe the artist was in love with the sister or the mother of the man he was painting, or maybe the subject represented some religious or political doctrine that the artist believed in. A hero to his country. Don't forget, I'm not talking about the more or less talented, but the brilliant works, or at least those approaching genius."

I wanted to argue the point and speak with him some more, but the whipped cream and the marsala in the stomach were making their presence known. My temples began to ache—a migraine.

I stood up, shook Latchinov's hand, and said, "I have to run, but I so enjoyed talking to you that I want to exact a promise from you to visit me as soon as possible."

By the time I returned home the migraine, to my surprise, had passed. Thank God! I needed to get to work on my Dionysus. More to the point, I had to tell Eddy that everything was almost ready and that very soon he would have to start posing.

I didn't understand why he got so testy when I asked him to pose. I had to beg him, even lose my temper.

Sidorenko dropped by, but I said to tell him I wasn't home. I have to work, work!

Vasenka stretched the cloth backdrop across the scaffolding while I stood at my easel, growing very agitated. The agitation was a good sign that my work was coming along successfully. Stark was changing in the alcove, behind the drape, and grumbling the whole time about how he was uncomfortable, cold, how foolish he felt. . . .

Let him grouse, I thought, and then I'll give him a kiss.

"Do I have these stupid things on properly?" he asked, coming out from behind the drape.

I gasped in ecstasy. A panther skin fell across his shoulder, fastened across his hip by a gold buckle, and golden buskins reaching the middle of his calves made his slender legs even more beautiful. I was afraid to breathe.

"Come, come quickly," I implored, "strike the pose. Good, good, better, excellent!"

He reluctantly climbed onto the scaffolding, picked up the thyrsus* and, getting ready to lie down on the settee, said, "Please don't take long, Tata. I really don't like being a model."

"Just for an hour, darling."

"A whole hour!" he whined, nearly paralyzed in stupefaction. He was standing with his knee on the settee, his head tossed back slightly. Vasenka walked in right then. He dropped the hammer and nails and cried out in a voice that was not his, "Freeze!"

"Tatiana Alexandrovna," he ran toward me, "don't use the old stance. Paint him as he is right now. For heaven's sake don't change your pose—just raise your arms a little higher."

He flew to the scaffolding, then ran back, almost tangling his long legs in the backdrop. He paused, looked at it again for a moment and then returned to me. "Toss aside your earlier notions about the pose. This is what you want, as he is now."

"You've lost your mind, Vasenka. I've already painted the background."

"To hell with the background! It would be a crime not to use this pose!" he was almost crying. "Mama, dear, paint the scoundrel as he's standing. How handsome that damned rascal is! How did God create such beauty?"

"Watch your language, Verber," said Stark, curling his lips.

"If you have a conscience, you won't move a muscle! Mama, paint him quickly, damn!"

"You've gone too far!" Stark cried, aiming his thyrsus at Vasenka.

"There it is! Dionysus's wrath! Mama, start painting his head. You don't need Giovanni's mug. Get it all down now, the face, the face!"

---

*The staff Dionysus carried, with ivy wound around it and topped with a pinecone.

"And the nose, Vasenka?" I became infected by his enthusiasm. "Never mind, get the nose, too!"

"But it has to be classical, straight, in line with his forehead."

"Oh, hell," Vasenka clasped his head. "Why do you have such a nose?" he asked Stark, in desperation. "You're spoiling everything with that nose of yours. Where'd you get it?"

"I've had enough of this," said Stark, flinging aside the thyrsus and climbing down.

"Eddy, dearest," I blocked his path, "for heaven's sake, how can you cause me so much trouble over such trifles?" Almost in tears, I grabbed his hand.

"It's stupid, Tata, no more," he said angrily, trying to pull his hand away.

"Dionysus, my handsome one, don't be angry with me! Turn me into a beast and all will be well. I was swearing from a surplus of emotions, but you've captivated me with your beauty. Don't be angry—do you want me to throw myself at your feet?" and Vasenka fell to his knees in front of Stark.

At first Stark glowered, but then he couldn't contain his laughter and climbed back on the scaffolding.

I painted nonstop for five days, eating nothing but fruit, terrified that I would fall ill before completing the picture. The models couldn't leave my studio before sundown. Vasenka helped enormously, chasing people away so that they wouldn't interrupt me and keeping a fresh glass of lemonade on the table beside me.

I couldn't think about anything but my work; only when night fell and I could no longer paint would I come to my senses. My first thought would be about Eddy. He didn't bother me now, didn't lose his temper, and posed without speaking. When he wasn't posing, he would sit quietly on the divan with a book. He understood my situation and didn't want to interfere, but he was still troubled and jealous. Poor fellow!

"Am I interrupting you?" asked Latchinov, entering the studio.

"No, no, I'm extremely glad to see you. Just give me a minute to finish this."

"Go on, work."

Stark stood frozen in his pose, staring at Latchinov. Alexander Vikentevich had visited me several times, and we had long and serious conversations about subjects that interested us both, especially art. He looked at everything from such an interesting point of view. Sometimes I thought he was embellishing his stories, but what he had to say was always intelligent, original, and interesting. His interpretations and opinions differed so much from other peoples' that I was always interested to hear them.

"You have such an amazing model," said Latchinov.

"Yes indeed!"

"And the pose works so well. The delicate body is exquisite, and how strikingly his hip stands out against the slit in the soft pelt."

"And his legs," I said, "look at them closely. I've never seen such pretty knees on a man."

"Yes, everything is flawless. Odd that although he is no longer a youth, he has the body of one. Where'd you find this model?"

My heart froze—Stark was losing his temper.

"Forgive my absent-mindedness," I jumped up, dropping my brushes. "I haven't introduced you: Alexander Vikentevich Latchinov, meet Edgar Karlovich Stark."

They bowed.

"Edgar Karlovich was extremely kind to agree to pose for me. I'm torturing him a great deal."

"That's certainly true. I didn't realize that it would be so exhausting," Stark said casually, climbing down from the scaffolding. "At least it's warm today. Once I almost froze." He picked up a cigarette from the table and continued sardonically, "At least I can still smoke when she doesn't need my head or hands. I feel like a doll, taken apart in parts. Let me see your arm, now your shoulder, step. . . ." He was laughing and stretching as he spoke, as if showing off, but I could tell by his voice that he was angry. Hoping to drive away his bad mood, I interjected, "Verber's coming. Let's have lunch."

"Will you permit me to change clothes, Tatiana Alexandrovna," Stark asked deferentially, "or is my demonstration not yet over?"

"Please," I answered.

He went to the alcove, drew back the drape and said caustically, "I can only put up with the footwear. They're really very comfortable, and look quite nice with slacks."

Laughing, he tossed his head back, but both the laughter and the movement smacked of spite. I looked at Latchinov; he stood stock still, yet I could see some kind of alarm flicker in his cool, unflinching eyes. He saw me looking at him and said politely, "I congratulate you, Tatiana Alexandrovna. With a model like that, your painting will be outstanding. I love art, but when nature itself gets into the business, the result is something that completely eclipses human creativity."

Vasenka called us in to lunch.

"Are you coming, Dionysus?" he asked, looking at the curtain. "Do you need me to send an old woman in to buckle up your boots?"

"Go to hell," I heard the voice say quietly.

"We're waiting to have lunch with you."

"Thanks, but I'm going home now. I have business to attend to."

I shrugged my shoulders, wondering what he was so upset about—just because Latchinov had taken him for a model?

Stark came out with his hat and walking stick in hand.

"Stay to breakfast," I asked.

"I can't, Tatiana Alexandrovna, but with your permission I'll return this evening."

Oh, but he was embittered, and I was so tired of his everlasting capriciousness.

The three of us ate together, and I began feeling ill again. Tomorrow I'll go to the doctor—I'm worried that I'll get sick and won't be able to finish the picture.

When we went back into the studio, Latchinov stopped and stood for a long time in front of the painting. "Tatiana Alexandrovna, how much would you charge for this painting? Name the price and I'll buy it."

"Really, I hadn't even thought about that. The painting isn't finished yet—it could still fail."

"No, it's obvious that that's not possible with this one. If I can give you one bit of advice, I'd move the fat satyr in the foreground to the corner. He's too placid."

"He's stupefied from the wine, which affects everyone of them differently."

"But you made a mistake here. You've captured the moment, when insanity has possessed everyone. It's obvious from Dionysus's pose that his damnation has just frozen on his lips."

"That's what I said," cried Vasenka, "that old guy has been bothering me for a long time, but I couldn't put my finger on why. He ruins the impression! Mama, put him down on his hands and knees and let him howl—foolishly, joyfully. Let those two drunken bacchantes beat him with their thyrsuses, kick him— one laughing, and the other becoming livid with anger."

"You're right," I agreed.

Saying good-bye, Latchinov reminded me that if I wanted to sell it, he would buy it early and give me more than anyone else.

"What do you think of him?" I asked Vasenka after Latchinov had left.

"Oh, what do I care. Let him be. I've known him by sight for a long time—he's been hanging out with the local artists for years."

⊷⊜⊜⊶

"Stop pouting, Eddy."

Stark was seated, reading the newspaper, not speaking.

"What are you so upset about? Because someone mistook you for a model? Or are you jealous of Latchinov?"

"Listen, Tata," he said sharply, "I'm surprised that someone as sensitive as you are can't figure out why I got so insulted."

"Yes, why?"

"Imagine that I were the artist and you, out of love for me, agreed to my whim and posed for me. Suddenly a strange man walks in. . . ."

"But you're not a woman, Eddy!"

"Don't cavil with words, not in this context. Let's say a woman who is a friend of mine, but with whom you aren't acquainted, came by and the two of us started analyzing your body parts as though you were a thoroughbred. Would you enjoy that?"

"I'm sorry, Eddy, I was distracted, but I tried immediately to rectify my mistake and apologized."

"What was it to me that you were sorry? I don't care whether it was you or him talking, it was unpleasant and insulting for me."

"Our admiration insulted you?"

"Admiration? Why didn't you say proudly, 'He loves me, he's a good man, he's devoted to me, he's ready to give his life for me. . . .' No, you weren't admiring these qualities. You place greater store in my knees than you do in my soul!"

"It would have been much better for you to have said this than to spend the whole day sulking, Eddy. Let's drop it. Really, yesterday I felt so sick that I wanted to see a doctor."

"Yes, Tata," he hastened to agree, "go to the doctor."

"I'll go at some point. I feel better today. It's probably a fever—I'll take some quinine."

"No, Tatochka, please don't take anything. It'll be better to see a doctor. Can you go tomorrow?"

"Why are you so nervous?"

"Just go, for my sake."

"Okay, okay."

⊷══◉ ◯══⊷

Poor Sidorenko! In S., only Zhenia intervened to keep him from me, but here I'm never alone. He persists in seeking an explanation; has he really not noticed anything? Really, I've got to ask Eddy why, although he doesn't hide our relationship from anyone else, he always behaves in front of Sidorenko as though we simply have a proper friendship.

As, for example, right now:

"You arrived just in time. We're getting ready to go see the new church at the Casa Santa Cecilia. Would you like to come with us, Viktor Petrovich?"

"All I do since I've been here is visit the sights of Rome, Tatiana Alexandrovna. I'm still waiting for a clarification regarding my business here," said Sidorenko.

I sensed danger in those opening remarks, so I didn't let go of Vasenka's arm the whole time.

⊷═◑ ◐═⊷

Evening had already fallen when we returned. Walking past his apartment, Stark said happily, "I've got a bottle of champagne—let's go drink it."

I didn't want to stay with Stark today. I was tired and wanted to sleep. I wasn't in the mood to be romantic, and we'd have another scene . . . more reproaches. Is my desire really weakening? No, that's stupid, I'm just sick.

We went into his house. Stark and Vasenka went off to do something, leaving me alone with Sidorenko.

"Tatiana Alexandrovna," he began, "do you remember how in S. . . . ."

Oh, God, I was thinking, what can I do? Where are they?

"While we were still in S.," he continued, "I asked you to allow me to speak to you about something very important to me."

If only someone would come in! I looked around helplessly and said, "Of course, I'm at your service. But we have to name a time because I'm very busy now."

He stared at me intently and said, "I don't know if it's accidentally or on purpose, but it seems to me that you're trying to avoid this conversation."

Oh, he will say it now! I thought to myself desperately. "If that's what you think, then perhaps we shouldn't talk at all."

110

Wasn't that clear? But Sidorenko is so guileless that he continued looking at me and persisted, "Do you consider me a person whom you can trust?"

"We've known each other for such a short time," I was so happy to see Eddy standing in the doorway, "that I never considered that I had the right to ask anything of you."

"Oh, to hell with caution, Tatiana Alexandrovna," he shook his curls, "if only . . . I'll tell you. . . ."

"Tatochka, dear," Stark interrupted, "where do you want to drink the wine, here or in the dining room?"

"Here, here is more comfortable, Eddy."

How clever he is—he rescued me. I should have used words like that earlier.*

Stark and Vasenka brought in the wine and dessert; Vasenka filled our glasses. I dared to look at Sidorenko's face—he was completely taken aback. He drank his wine in one gulp and stood up.

"Where are you going?" Stark asked politely; "it's still early."

"No, it's time for me to leave," he answered, his voice quavering.

"Oh, have another glass of wine," Vasenka offered.

"No, no. . . . I promised. . . . I can't . . . excuse me," and not looking at any of us, he bid farewell and practically ran out onto the terrace.

Stark and I stood up to accompany him.

"Drop by tomorrow, Viktor Petrovich," I asked.

"Yes, I'll come. . . . I'm leaving tomorrow."

"Your leave is already over?"

"No, but the business I'd come here to pursue didn't work out, so I'm going to spend the rest of the time traveling around Europe." He left.

"What, the poet's stomach became upset so suddenly that he had to run away? They say that champagne acts on some like seltzer," said Vasenka.

---

*Sidorenko is able to deduce that Tania and Stark have an intimate relationship because they are using familiar terms with one another.

"I'm very grateful to you, Eddy, for saving me from his declaration of love."

"I saw he had you pinned to the wall and decided the time had come. I've wanted to drop a hint for a long time, but I felt so sorry for him. He believed so hard in his chances."

"Well, I'm exceedingly happy to be rid of him," I laughed. "Your words truly scalded him."

"What? You have no pity for him?" Stark cried out suddenly. "He's suffering at the moment."

"What are you yelling about? That's in the first place; and in the second, I'm not guilty of anything. I didn't do anything to lead him on—just the opposite. I did everything I could to keep him away from me."

"So you really can't feel sorry for him? His feelings deserve only ridicule? That's very cruel."

"Stop it, Eddy, I'm tired of this."

"Yes, I know how sick of it you are. I can see very plainly that you're moving away from me. And maybe in a few days you'll be saying how glad you are to be rid of me."

"Listen," I said, losing my temper, "it's these scenes of yours that are driving me away. I'm sick of them—daily scenes, hourly scenes, over every little thing. Vasenka, take me home. I can't take this any more."

I stormed toward the door.

"Don't go, Tata, please, for God's sake, don't go! I won't say another word. Just don't go today. . . ." His face was so pale, his eyes strange.

I stayed, because God knows what he might do without me. I felt sorry for him . . . but I'd had enough.

⤛══◉══⤜

Sidorenko dropped over to say good-bye. His behavior was bizarre, as though he had done something wrong. We had a very polite conversation in Vasenka's presence. In the hall, after he had already put one arm in his coat sleeve, he turned to me and said eagerly, "Tatiana Alexandrovna, if you ever need a true friend, call on me. All this," he waved his hand around, "seems like a fairy tale to me, one that I can't believe in. Tell me, is it true? You didn't ask Stark to play a trick to try to get me away from you?" He was trying not to cry.

"What are you saying, dear Viktor Petrovich? How can you think such things?"

"Of course; but like a drowning man, I'm reaching for straws. Why not? Stark is handsome . . . but I know him, and he's incapable of love. . . . I will not ask you to love me . . . you'll burn up in this passion . . . and then, at that time, let me know. You're a widow, I'm a bachelor. Good-bye!" He ran away without putting his other arm in the sleeve.

I took a cab home from the doctor. My legs had buckled, and a hammer was pounding in my head. In a daze, I kept asking myself, "Why didn't I think of that?"

Walking into Stark's study, I mechanically removed my boa, hat, and muff. He was happy that I had come so early and sat me in a chair close to the fireplace. Suddenly, looking closely at my face, he asked nervously, "What happened, Tata?"

"I went to the doctor."

"And he discovered a terrible illness? Tell me now!"

"No, I'm not sick. I'm pregnant."

What was he doing?

"Eddy, dear, what's the matter with you?"

He had fallen at my feet and was sobbing. I tried to get him up, but he pressed his head tightly in my lap, shaking from head to foot. I wanted to get up, but his hands were around my waist, holding me down tightly. Such a profound pity overwhelmed me that I was ready to cry myself.

"Please, Eddy," I said tearfully, "be careful of my nerves."

He raised his head. Tears glistened in his eyes, but his face beamed with extraordinary joy.

"And your nerves, too," I said smiling, wiping his eyes with my handkerchief. "What are you so upset about?"

He got up off his knees and without taking his eyes off me, said almost gravely, "Do you remember when I told you that I had prayed?"

I nodded.

"This is what I prayed for. I asked for a child, knowing that it would keep us together always. That you, who don't love me. . . ."

I started.

"Don't lie, Tata. You don't love me. You love my body, but not myself. I don't know exactly what sparked your desire for me, but only my looks could sustain it. You don't like the prose in life, and in my love you found poetry. You always said that my love was 'beautiful,' but cared nothing for its depth, honesty, or devotion."

I sat, hanging my head because I knew he was right.

"Lately," he continued, "this passion has been for Dionysus and not me at all. And me? Of course at first I too felt only desire, but from that grew such an attachment to you, such commitment, maybe the same sort of feelings that you have for 'that man' in Petersburg."

He put his hand on his forehead, his expression one of such torment that my heart contracted until it ached. This was the first time in our fairy tale affair that he had mentioned Ilya.

"I wanted this baby so badly. I hoped that you would be able to love me because of it, to love the father of your child. Your art has taken you away from me, but the baby would bring you back. We could share something equally dear to both of us. We could live and work together for it. And God heard me!" he raised his hand. "It isn't emptiness up there, He heard us! I believe, and I'm ecstatic to be a believer. My reckless love wasn't a sin, my passionate caresses weren't indecent, because I wanted to give life to this being that would consecrate our love. I don't have a homeland, or religion, but I'll give them to my child. Let him believe. You'll love the baby, Tata, I know you will."

"My children don't live, Eddy," I said softly.

"This one will. There's not just nothingness out there, but

God, and he won't let this one die. I believe!" He lay his head on my lap.

How strong his maternal heritage! How touching his faith! Why can't I believe like that? Why can't I feel happy? Earlier I had wanted to have children. Earlier, but not now, when I have dedicated my whole being to art. A baby will take me away from this. Poor Eddy could never compete with this rival, but a baby— small, helpless, and weak is still the strongest thing on earth. I've lost my freedom, and I'm tied forever to Stark. Forever!

"It'll be a boy," Stark told me the next morning at breakfast, over coffee.

"And what if it's a girl?" I objected.

"No, I want a boy, Tata, and he'll look like you."

"It'll be better if he resembles you," I took a deep breath.

"All right," he agreed, "since you like my face so much. But the girl will look like you."

"What girl?" I asked, dumbfounded.

"Our second child will be a girl," he answered placidly.

"And then another boy and another girl?" I laughed bitterly.

"What can be better than a family with a lot of kids?"

I looked at him and said sarcastically, "I'm painting a picture. One child is playing in the paint, two are misbehaving, I'm feeding the fourth, the fifth is sitting on the palette, the sixth has brought home bad grades from school, the seventh. . . ."

"Tata!" he interrupted me sharply, "why all this irony? You know how it hurts me when you get this way."

"I'm simply drawing you a picture of the life of the artist who has a big family. I don't want a passel of kids."

He stopped talking and picked up the newspaper. Let him pout, I thought to myself, irritated. I'm going to my studio. While I was getting dressed he didn't raise his eyes from the paper.

"Good-bye," I kissed his forehead.

He grasped my hand and said plaintively, "Tata, you will love the baby, won't you?"

"Enough, dear. I might be a poor excuse for a woman, but I'll love my own baby. Even a dog cares for its offspring, and I'm not completely morally depraved."

⋆⟞⊜⟝⋆

This is intolerable! It seems I can't move, bend over, or turn around without him yelling that I'm going to hurt the baby. We had a terrible scene yesterday. I stumbled on the stairs and he turned white as a sheet and cried out, almost rudely, "Look where you're going!" He won't let me work: "Tata, come here. You've been sitting down for so long." We go for a walk: "Don't walk so quickly, careful, don't trip, watch out for that step, that stone."

"Eddy," I said in desperation, "I'm losing patience with you. Your great concern for my physical health is wearing on my nerves and making me sick."

"Oh, Tata, dearest, calm down and I'll be quiet. I won't say anything more—just go slower on the stairs."

"In the name of all that's holy, leave me alone!"

⋆⟞⊜⟝⋆

I'm finishing Dionysus. Whatever else happens, I'm going to finish the painting. Then I'll think about the future. I've written to Petersburg to tell them that I'll be staying a little longer. The figure of the satyr is keeping me, the one Latchinov and Vasenka persuaded me to change. I owe them both a great deal; they've helped me considerably in my work. Vasenka helped me with the details: he would run to the museum and copy something for me, or burrow through the libraries copying things down for me. Latchinov provided direct inspiration. He would sit for hours, telling me about the cult of Dionysus and the various ways he has been depicted.

"It seems that there's never been another cult as widespread as

116

that of Dionysus. This god personified all the procreative forces of nature. Everything grew and blossomed in his presence. Did you know that in antiquity he was portrayed as a mature man, heavy and bearded. At that time his cult celebrated work in the fields, the vineyards, the production of olive oil.

"But the human perception became more refined, perverted if you will, and the cult of a favorite resplendent god began to grow. Alcamenes was the first to depict him as a marvelous youth, delicate and effeminate; and by the time of Praxiteles no one wanted to portray him otherwise.˚ Praxiteles endowed him with a secret, mystical duality, and after this the cult became a complex mystical religion, sensual, secret, and seductive for the person seeking sharp sensations. The entire civilized world at that time was enthralled by the cult. The Eleusinian mysteries!˚˚ The dark grove of Semele!† At night torches, frenzied dances, the whistle of lashes on lovely youthful shoulders, songs, eulogies to the young Dionysus. And no one was allowed to divulge the secrets of these nighttime rituals—death to the traitors! The Roman Senate was later forced to outlaw this fantastic worship under the threat of severe punishment."

I loved it when Latchinov visited—my work flowed so smoothly with him nearby. Eddy listened to him attentively, didn't shout at me, and posed calmly for long hours. Latchinov, of course, had guessed our relationship long ago—Stark could hide nothing—but he treated us both with simple tact. He always brought a present of some sort, candy, fruit, or a journal with an amusing caricature. Several times he hinted that he would pay whatever I asked for "Dionysus," but Stark insisted that the painting was "ours" and would hang in "our" drawing room.

˚Alcamenes was a Greek sculptor who made a statue for a sanctuary to Dionysus in the second half of the fifth century B.C.E.; Praxiteles was a Greek sculptor of the fourth century B.C.E.

˚˚This refers to Eleusis, a city in Attica famous for celebrations in honor of the mysteries of Persephone and her mother, Demeter, whose stories are told in the *Odyssey*.

†Semele was Dionysus's mother; his father was Zeus.

We'll see. I'm not conceited, but I feel that my Dionysus deserves a better fate. Maybe I'm overestimating it, but I want to see it in a big gallery and not a bourgeois drawing room.

⊷⇒◦⇐⊷

"Tata, have you thought about the official documents?" We were taking a break; Stark was reading the newspaper, and I, obliging him, was taking small steps around the room. Vasenka was warming himself by the fire.

"What documents?"

"For the wedding."

"What wedding?"

"Ours. What's the matter with you, Tata?"

"Why, are we going to get married?" I was surprised.

"What do you mean, why? What about our baby?"

"What about it?"

"Don't you want him to have his father's name?"

"If we're going to live in France, why not just register it under your name?"

"But if we don't get married and you remain a Russian citizen, the child will be illegitimate. You surprise me, Tata," he said, swinging his legs in their golden buskins from the divan.

"Well, okay."

"You have an odd tone, as though you don't care about your child's affairs. I want him to be legitimate, so that no hooligan can call him a bastard, so that he won't be ashamed of his parents."

"I said okay, we'll get married whenever you want."

"Of course, as soon as possible. As soon as you finish up here, we'll go to Paris. They want me back there, and I can't afford to neglect my finances—I'll even have to work harder to provide well for the child. I hope that we'll be married in a month."

"All right."

"Where, besides city hall, should we have the ceremony? In an Orthodox and an Anglican church?"

"A church would be superfluous."

"No, no Tata," he pleaded, "I want a church wedding. You're hurting me."

"Never mind, Mama," interrupted Vasenka, "it'll be stronger that way."

I kept quiet. I didn't care. Marry me in an Orthodox church, an Anglican, a synagogue, a pagoda . . . a pyramid if you want!

Stark had gone off somewhere, and I took advantage of the opportunity to read a letter from Petersburg; I can't read them when he's around. The news has disturbed me deeply: Maria Vasilevna has fallen ill and Katia has taken her to Petersburg. Ilya says she has some kind of internal ailment, and the doctor in Tiflis has recommended an operation. He fears it's cancer because so many in her family have already died of it. It's evident from his letter that he's extremely depressed. "I'm even glad that you're staying longer in Rome, while mother has her operation," he wrote.

He doesn't need me, he didn't ask me to share his grief with him, doesn't want us to spend this difficult time together. So be it, but this is excruciatingly hard on me. I'll go, pack up my things, destroy the nest I had become so accustomed to, where I was happy, in which we lived together. I lived freely there, and worked freely. . . . *Why am I thinking about this? It's all over. It's unbearable for me, but I can't cry. . . .*

Stark is in a wonderful mood today. I assured him that it's the last time he has to pose for me, so he's ecstatic. He's been laughing, joking, and chasing Vasenka around with a sword.

Latchinov dropped by, bringing me a bouquet of orchids. He turned to Stark and said, "Of course, when you lived in another century, they brought you as sacrifice pomegranates, roses, young goats, but now, in your second incarnation in this more prosaic century—I bring you cigars. I just happened across them and they're not bad." He handed Stark a box, chuckling, "Dionysus isn't wrathful today, as usual, but happy."

"It's better to have him sitting around, quiet as an owl," said Vasenka, coming out of the alcove where Stark had chased him.

"Verber, I want to teach you how to fence," said Stark, "pick up the sword. En garde! One!" His face was flushed from running around, and his chest was heaving.

"Two!" he cried, lunging forward unexpectedly; "oh, you're back in the corner."

"Give me a sword," said Latchinov, "I used to fence pretty well."

They found masks, but I didn't have gloves or chest protectors. Stark was visibly vexed.

"Let's go to my place. I've got all the equipment, and we'll see whether or not I can handle myself if I'm ever challenged to a duel," Latchinov smiled. "Have you ever endured such an unpleasant experience?"

"Oh, no, I'm such a gentle being," answered Stark, feigning naiveté.

"Don't believe him, Alexander Vikentovich, he's a most skilled duellist," I interrupted. "Look at his hands, and the bullet wound on his shoulder, and the scar from sparring—two centimeters lower and it would have hit his heart. It's a good thing that I've been able to paint him now, because in a few years, if he hasn't been killed, this model will be quite defective."

"No, Tata," he seized my hand; "do you think that I'll risk my life now over trifles like I used to? As you well understand, my life is now very dear to me."

"I was almost challenged once over cards," said Latchinov.

"You're a gambler?"

"The only time I've ever gambled, I argued with my partner, and the only reason we didn't have our duel was because my opponent died of a heart attack on the eve of it. I was extremely sorry that I hadn't killed him."

"Oh, Alexander Vikentovich," I said, "do you really think it would feel good to kill a person?"

"I remember! That happened a year ago, here in Rome,"

Vasenka interjected suddenly; "everyone was talking about it. You were supposed to fight with Baron Z."

"Baron Z.?" Stark and I asked simultaneously.

"How do you know of him, Tata?"

"Sidorenko talked about him," I laughed.

"What a blabbermouth," Stark was also laughing, "and he loves to gossip. So Z. is dead. I have a funny story to tell you about him sometime."

Suddenly Stark began to laugh hysterically and fell onto the divan.

"What struck you so funny?" Vasenka was surprised. "Quiet down, or else after 'Wrath of Dionysus' Tatiana Alexandrovna will have to paint 'The Laughter of Dionysus.' That'll make you swear!"

It was true that every time he moved, he posed, and he looked especially graceful on the divan at the moment. But why didn't I feel the same passion I used to? Had my love really burned out? The butterfly loses its multicolored wings, the roses their petals, and fireworks burn out.

Stark calmed down for a minute, but then looked at Vasenka and started that laughter again.

"You're getting carried away, Dionysus," said Vasenka. "Remember, you're running around without your pants on and there's a lady present."

Stark, startled, jumped up and wrapped the panther skin around himself. His face was so flustered that I started to laugh, but my laughter froze when I turned and saw Latchinov. His face, normally so composed, now showed pain and fear. Why?

"Eddy," I said, "if you don't start posing properly now, I'll have to do this again tomorrow."

"No, no! Slaves! Where's my thyrsus?" he cried, springing onto the podium with one leap.

The letter from Zhenia, covered in stamps, was an entire manuscript.

"Dearest sister, I've spent three days writing this interminable letter, but I know you'll find the heart to read the whole thing."

It read like a poem of true love: "He" was still young, had just finished the university four years ago, but had already published some historical research that had attracted critical attention . . . then the newspapers had taken notice of his work. A girlfriend introduced them at a concert, but it turned out that they had known each other in the Caucasus when they were children.

"We heard a Beethoven symphony together!" She had wanted to write to me all about this for a long time but wasn't yet sure of her feelings. Convinced of them now, she had decided that I should be the first to know.

"And just imagine, Tatusia, he has a beard! Although I'm certain he'd shave it immediately if I asked him to."

They had postponed the wedding because of Maria Vasilevna's operation, which would be in a week, in the hospital where they had already put her. Reading the letter, I wanted to cry, but the tears caught in my throat and began to choke me. They don't need me; they haven't asked me to come.

Really, though, I had left of my own free will and was set now to deliver them a heavy blow. Maybe it won't be a blow at all. Maybe it'll be better this way. Before, when I was feeling like this, I could run to Stark and find forgetfulness in his embraces. But not any more.

"I'm so impetuous, Tatochka, that I can hurt you by squeezing you too hard."

At night he jumps out of bed and pleads, "Don't kiss me, dear, you know that I can no longer think rationally when you kiss me. Your words make my head spin and I forget all else, but now we must remember 'him.'"

He reproaches me constantly for not loving the baby enough. It isn't true! I love it enough to sacrifice my freedom, my homeland, my habits, maybe even my art, and I'm not damning the baby because of this. I love it already. Poor little thing! Why do I call it "poor"? It'll have all the comforts of life, good care, an adoring father and a loving mother . . . nevertheless, I still feel extremely sorry for it.

⊰⊱

"Dionysus" is finished. All my friends and even people I don't know came by the studio. I heard so much praise from the experts that I can't help but feel pleased. But when I made the final stroke and stepped back from the painting, I found myself completely overwhelmed by the sensation that now I must return to the real world, to people, and to my own problems and affairs.

And maybe I also sensed the strange feeling that I would never paint anything better, and my heart ached.

⊰⊱

In the evening, after everyone had left, Stark showed up, beaming happily with a small box tied with a blue ribbon. Inside was some magnificent antique Venetian lace.

"You've lost your mind," I exclaimed; "how much money did you throw away on this lace?"

"It's not just lace, Tata," he said tenderly, "it's your wedding veil."

You mean you didn't rent an orchestra? I wanted to ask, but that would have been cruel, so I thanked him sweetly.

"Do you really want such pomp at the wedding?" I asked him after a few minutes.

"We won't have an ostentatious display, nor do I want to hide. I'm so proud of you! You are my wife, and the mother of my child. . . ."

"That's the problem: by the time we get married, it's going to be rather conspicuous, and an elaborate ceremony will be comical."

"Nothing will be noticeable. In three days we'll go to Paris. I just received a telegram and can't put off my business there any longer. If I'm late, I'll lose a great deal, if not everything."

"You've forgotten that I have to go to Petersburg," I said, annoyed.

"What? You're still planning to go there?"

"Yes, it's imperative."

"Don't go," he turned pale.

"You know that I must."

"You could write."

"I should have written two and a half months ago. To leave it at that now would be, well, extremely rude. . . . Besides, I still have pictures there."

"You can send Verber after them."

"I can't go," said Vasenka. "In the first place, my passport expired fifteen years ago, and second, they won't let me in with my political background."

"You got into political trouble?"

"I sent some stuff from anarchists here to my former comrades. They dragged me down to the embassy and interrogated me about who I knew and what I'd sent."

"I never realized that you were politically oriented, Vasenka, and had anarchist friends," I laughed.

"What kind of friendship? We ate some pasta together once. They weren't bad fellows."

"I don't want you to go, Tata," Stark interrupted Vasenka.

"I must and I will go! You yourself pointed out that we need documents to get married in France, and the only thing I have here is my passport."

"When are you leaving?" he asked anxiously.

"Day after tomorrow."

"I'll go with you. Let the business fall apart, I can't let you go alone."

I was barely able to persuade Stark to let me go alone. I reminded him that he truly must go to Paris and that I didn't want him to lose all his money because of me. What was he afraid of? Did it really enter his head that I would remain there? As I explained to him, "Do you really think that you could forgive me if I showed up with someone else's baby?"

"A baby, no! Never! But . . . you alone . . . I don't know. You go, and I also have to go, but don't stay long there. Remember, Tata, how inexpressibly agonizing it is for me to be separated from you for even a minute. Tata, you are my wife, my happiness, my life."

⊹⇾⫘⊂⫘⇽⊹

I returned home. No, it's not my home any longer. I don't recollect how Ilya and Zhenia greeted me. As soon as I saw Ilya, I fell apart. I threw myself on him, lay my head on his chest and burst into tears. When they saw my face they both thought I was ill. In the carriage, Zhenia prattled on about nothing, but Ilya held me quietly in his arms.

Pressing against him, I thought, this is for the last time. In an hour or two you will have pushed me aside and we'll be like strangers. We have been so close up to this point. And the sweet, youthful being sitting across from me will turn away in contempt.

"It all came down on us at once," Ilya was saying, "mother falling ill and Katia getting arrested."

"What's this about Katia?"

"You know that she wasn't political at all, but one of her friends in the Caucasus got involved in something very serious. Don't worry. We've been petitioning the court and Katia will end up just being exiled abroad. I'm sure that she'll be allowed to return in a few years. And Zhenia, on the other hand . . . ," he smiled.

"I already know! Congratulations, dear, from the bottom of my heart," I said, extending my hand. She threw herself on me and began smothering me with kisses. Will she still kiss me tomorrow?

⊹⇾⫘⊂⫘⇽⊹

I couldn't eat anything at dinner. How can I tell him? So much fell on him at one blow, and here I sit with another stone poised to throw at his head. And something even more terrible has happened: one look at Ilya and I knew that I could never stop loving him. I could never leave him, and if it weren't for this baby, I would be even more unscrupulous and simply hide what happened in Rome from him. I'd steal my happiness and stay here, next to him.

With him, my heart could be resurrected for my art. He wasn't an expert on it and he didn't help out, but he never interfered and was never jealous. He understood that art was my vocation and he reconciled himself to that. "He" will never be reconciled.

Zhenia left to make arrangements about the housekeeping, and Ilya said hurriedly, "I didn't want to say anything in front of Zhenia, but mother is worse. It is cancer, and she'll die soon regardless of whether or not she has the operation. With it, she can live maybe a year or two longer."

I covered my face with my hands.

"I didn't want to call you, Tata, because I didn't want to tear you away from your painting . . . the picture must be successful, people are already talking about it here . . . but many times I wanted to send a telegram. It was so hard. Mama is speeding along Zhenia's wedding. I think she realizes her condition. . . . Zhenia is marrying Kunavin and they're leaving. . . . Katia's gone. . . . Mother. . . ." He stood up and began pacing.

"We'll be together, Tania, just the two of us. You're all I have left."

"No, I can't!" I jumped up. "Ilya, I have to talk to you."

"What's the matter, Tania, your face looks so strange," Ilya grabbed me. I was staggering.

"Darling, we shouldn't be talking about this now. You're ill," he led me into the bedroom. My movements were mechanical.

"Lie down, or better still, try to get some sleep."

"No, Ilya, I must speak with you this very minute. Shut the door."

Closing the door, he said, "You're frightening me. I'm anticipating something dreadful."

I took his hands and pressed my face against them. *Let me warm myself one more minute by your love! It will disappear now, be gone forever. This is how a prisoner must feel before the execution.*

"Take heart," he said tonelessly.

"I can't . . . don't love me, Ilya, I'm not worth it. I'm a rotten woman," I whispered.

"I can guess, Tania, you've lost your head over someone else."

I said nothing, pressing more tightly against his hands.

"What can we do?" he said after a pause. "We can't control our feelings, dear. It's fate." He stood up and took a few steps. I sat with my head down.

"I noticed it some time ago, Tania, still in S. When I came down, your nervous condition told me something was wrong. It had already begun?"

I nodded.

"I sensed something was wrong, and even wanted to ask you about it."

"Why didn't you ask me then," I said desperately; "I would have told you, and you could have helped, could have sobered me up!"

"Don't despair, dear. I see my mistake. I'm an even tempered man, sedate. I myself don't understand why I seem to fear extroversion. I'm afraid to appear ridiculous. Sometimes I even get annoyed with you for being so open, so impetuous. Sometimes out of an involuntary mulishness I try to put a stop to your caprices. Yes, the mistake was mine. I wasn't candid with you, and I feared your frankness.

"Sometimes you would come to me in a burst of joy or depression, and I would be cold to you on purpose, just because it seemed strange for an adult to be so emotional. Often you would try to get a conversation going about feelings, sensations, personal matters, but I would always lead it back to generalizations or would try to end it by joking. You would go away insulted, hurt. I felt sorry for you, but I thought it best to try to teach you have to live more circumspectly.

"I admit, Tania, that in trying to teach you to live more simply, I was taking the poetry out of your life. And I made the biggest mistake. 'He' spoke to you in 'the language of the gods'—you see, I'm so used to making jokes that I can't refrain from them even at the most serious moments. But it was your native language, and you responded to it with your whole heart."

He was quiet for a minute.

"Maybe this attraction only seems serious to you, Tania. Maybe it will fade away gradually, you'll forget about it, you'll manage to cope with it, and it won't have to destroy our life together. You're attracted to someone, but it won't last."

"You don't understand, Ilya, you and I must part. I lived with him in Rome and am carrying his child!"

Ilya recoiled. His face convulsed and he clutched his heart. Still at the table, I lay my head on my hands and said no more. The logs crackled in the stove. Zhenia was playing her exercises on the piano in the drawing room.

The silence was oppressive. I raised my head and saw Ilya, sitting in the chair, staring into the distance.

"Say something, Ilya. As you can see, nothing can be done. I'll leave as soon as possible, tomorrow if you want."

"Stop, Tania. This has stunned me so that I can't think," he said, not looking at me. "I have to think some more, to try to understand. I haven't become accustomed to that idea yet. . . . I was so far from thinking such things, but still. . . ." He started to go, then stopped. "As you can see, I'm in no condition to discuss this now. But I have one question: is he an honorable man?"

"Oh, you're being practical. He dreams of having wedding ceremonies in city hall and two churches."

"City hall? He's a foreigner?"

"Yes."

"And I thought . . . ," said Ilya, wiping his forehead.

"What were you thinking?"

"Nothing. Tania, we'll discuss this tomorrow. Try to get some sleep, you're quite ill."

He left. Left! It's over now, it's all over. I could hear him telling Zhenia not to disturb me because I was sick.

⋯⟫⊜⟪⋯

Zhenia dropped in on her way to the hospital to see Maria Vasilevna. My white face frightened her. "Lie down, Tatochka, get some rest."

"No, Zhenia, I'm better on my feet. Mama is waiting for you—give her a kiss from me."

She left and I, sitting in the armchair in my cozy bedroom, looked around despondently. Every object here told something about my life, my hopes and dreams. There, behind that door, was my large, airy studio, where I had experienced so much happiness that would never be repeated. I was supposed to be packing, to be putting the things I needed in my trunk, but I just couldn't. It was like trying to cut myself in two with a knife.

Someone's hand touched my head; I recognized whose it was straightaway. I grabbed it and kissed it, washing it with tears.

"Don't torment yourself, Taniusha," said Ilya, sitting down across from me. "Don't even think about me. See, I'm much calmer now. We just have a few small matters to discuss."

I stared at his face; it was pinched, as though it had aged somewhat, but it really was completely serene.

It's easier for him than for me, I thought dejectedly.

"Okay, let's talk," I sighed.

"Mama is very weak after the operation, and we have to protect her. Nor do I want to bring Zhenia into all this.

"Yes," I said prayerfully, "do me a favor, if you can, and hide this from her for as long as possible. I don't want to spoil her first days of married life."

"I've thought about that, too. Here's the plan: you'll stay here for another week, and then we'll say that the doctor has ordered you to undergo treatment until spring. Then, we'll work it out somehow."

I nodded. Ilya was stroking Fomka, the cat, which had jumped onto his lap.

"Ilya," I said, my voice quivering, "I have a request. It's stupid and silly under the circumstances, but—don't give Fomka away."

He smiled sadly. "Don't worry, Tania, I'll keep him always. He's the only one left of the family." His voice trembled.

I began sobbing vehemently.

"My darling, stop, don't cry. It was terribly stupid of me to say such 'pitiful' things. I know that you're tormenting yourself with pity for me. Now it's hard on you, very unpleasant, but not for long. Soon you'll be back with the man you love. . . ."

"But I don't love him, Ilya," I whimpered.

"What?"

"No, I don't love him," I cried, jumping up, "it was insanity, a momentary passion at first sight. I struggled with myself because I knew that it wasn't love. I thought I'd mastered my feelings and went to Rome confident, but then. . . . I don't know . . . it was desire, hypnosis, call it what you want, but it wasn't love! I'm going back, but not for happiness. I'm burying my talent! You're the only one I love, and that's why I'm crying, that's why my heart is breaking!"

Ilya unexpectedly seized my head and clasped it to his chest. "Tania, my darling, is this true?"

Ilya was crying. Can it be that he still loves me? I was afraid of those tears, I was shaking all over, losing consciousness, and with a moan I threw myself around his neck. When I came to, he was holding me in his arms like a child, stroking my head, his voice shaking: "If this is true, everything can be fixed, Tania. It does happen that a man and his wife get divorced, live separately, and then get back together."

"You're forgetting. . . ."

"No I'm not. Tell me this: if I had been attracted to someone else for a while, and then came back to you with a baby, and I told you that it was all over with the other woman, that I loved and love only you, would you not take the baby into our house?"

"Of course I would," I whispered.

"So why do you think you're better than I am?"

"But you won't love the baby."

"Tania, dearest, don't demand paternal emotions from me. But I will take care of it, and with the passage of time, when the pain is no longer so sharp, I will become like a real father. If the children from your first marriage had lived, do you think that would have stopped me from loving you?"

"Ilya, what can I say? Can I ask you to make such a sacrifice?"

"It's no sacrifice, Tania. Just remember one thing: that it would kill me to lose you. Yesterday I wasn't so much upset by what you were saying but by the idea that you were leaving."

"Are you sure that you mean this?" I asked, feeling my soul coming back to life, my sorrow waning. The future looked bright.

"No, Tania, you know me well enough to know that I don't go by first impressions. Are you certain that you're not making a mistake because you pity me?" he asked apprehensively.

"No, Ilya. Now my whole life is in you and for you."

I sent him a letter. Of course I knew very well that I was inflicting pain, but I had been ready to do that to the one I love most. It will be easier for Stark to bear this. He's so handsome, he's bound to find many women to comfort him. What could I do, sacrifice Ilya and art? I wrote him not to be concerned about the baby: Ilya and I are getting married, so the child will be legitimate. I admitted my guilt about hurting him, but he had done the same to someone else. I wept over the letter, and asked him to forget me and to forgive me, if he could.

Four days later I received a telegram: "My curse upon you!" It seemed very affected, theatrical. Somehow it soothed my conscience: no letter, no mention of the baby. Maybe in the past I would have found it attractive, but I've forgotten why.

The days are flying by. I've already been here a month. My heart is calm, but sometimes I get so depressed that it almost makes me sick . . . but there's a soft light that saves me, Ilya and his love.

He forgets all about himself and as soon as he sees that despair on my face, he drives it away with jokes or caresses. This is an extremely difficult pregnancy, but I'm still managing to get a lot of work done. I'm thinking of paintings I'll do when I'm better, and now I'm working on a portrait of a writer I'd started before I got sick.

Talk of my painting has made me famous, and I'm receiving many solicitations for portraits. I'm not agreeing to any of them though—what if I should die suddenly, in childbirth? or if this baby should be born dead like the others? I would be sad for it, but for Ilya that would probably be better.

Zhenia returned from the hospital today very depressed. She had spent the whole morning with her mother, and Katia is being sent away tomorrow. I wanted to cheer her up, so I started talking to her about her fiancé. I like him very much, but he tends to take himself too seriously. Last night, although apologetic for my candor, I decided to offer him frank advice: "Don't ever be afraid to be candid with your wife, don't repress your feelings, even if you fear that they might appear foolish. Otherwise, she might think that you don't love her enough. If she throws herself on you in a burst of either joy or despair, hold her and kiss her. Most of all, don't be afraid of words. When they aren't sincere, words are a lie, but if you love someone, they are music to her ears."

He kissed my hand and seemed to understand what I was trying to say. Now he seems to have dropped his academic pretensions in front of Zhenia and myself. God grant her happiness!

The servant brought me a calling card: Latchinov! Although I don't like encountering those who witnessed my fairy tale life in Rome, Latchinov has always been discreet. I enjoy conversing with him so much that I was genuinely glad to see him.

"Zhenia, let me introduce you to a very interesting gentleman."

"For me now all 'gentlemen' are tedious," she said contemptuously.

Latchinov, as always, was elegant and kind and, also as always, brought me flowers. We were having a very lively conversation and, despite Zhenia's "indifference" toward gentlemen, within ten minutes she had joined us, chatting about music, and was trying to drag him into the drawing room to play the piano. Then we heard the familiar doorbell and she excused herself and, flushed and happy, she whirled out of the studio like a hurricane.

"Tatiana Alexandrovna, I'm here on business," said Latchinov. "I've been ordered to give you a letter, and I must ask you to read it quickly and to give me an answer immediately, even if it's only oral."

He handed me a letter. My hands were shaking as I opened it.

"I am writing to you not because I want to remind you of

myself. I won't reproach you. Be happy—I don't want to destroy your happiness. I have no further business with you, but I am demanding that which belongs to me, that which I would never relinquish. I am demanding my child. How could you even think for a minute that I would agree to give up the only thing I have to live for? Did you think I would allow my child to think he was someone else's son, and to call him 'father'? How could you think I would permit this?

"I don't want to frighten or to threaten you, because I think that you'll agree to my conditions. If you don't, there's nothing I won't do: I'll create a scandal, I'll kill the other man if I have to and won't consider my actions criminal.

"I don't demand my wife; I don't have any power over her emotions, and I don't have the right to interfere in her life; but I do insist upon my child, and you cannot take him away from me!

"I'm still very ill and cannot write coherently. Please conclude the business aspects of these negotiations with Latchinov. I still can't forgive you, and I still hate and even curse you, but give me a healthy child of your own free will, and I will forgive everything from the bottom of my heart."

I sat, hanging my head, my thoughts flying everywhere. And I had thought that my misfortune had ended.

"Tatiana Alexandrovna," Latchinov called me back to reality, "may I say something?"

"Speak," I answered mechanically, putting the letter back in the envelope and twisting it about in my hands.

"I was having breakfast with Stark when he received your letter. While he was reading it I could tell by his face that something terrible had happened. When he finished it, he threw himself on his desk and wrote a telegram—just one line, he couldn't write any more. 'Send it anyway,' he said, putting the sheet of paper in my hand. Before I could take it he had fallen flat on the floor.

"He lay unconscious for several days. The doctor feared brain fever, but he came to and began to remember . . . then we feared even worse, that he had lost his mind. But he's got a healthy constitution so he recuperated. As soon as he was able, he wrote this letter. He directed me to tell you his conditions, if you want to hear them. I got Verber to come to Paris. He is a good man and will make certain that Stark is looked after properly.

"I hope that you can give me an answer today. I'm leaving tomorrow because I don't want to leave the sick man alone with his thoughts for too long."

I was sitting with my head down. *What could I do? Could I surrender my child? And if I didn't? Didn't I, too, have a moral right to the child? Legally he would be registered as Ilya's legitimate son. I was also prepared to create a scandal for this baby. But the threat! Because I knew Stark so well, I realized that these were not empty words.*

We still have five months to go before the baby is born. Maybe he'll change his mind, soften up . . . no, I'm just trying to console myself. He won't change his mind. This is my punishment. Is he going to demand that I never get to see my baby?

"Tell me his conditions," I said uneasily.

"First," Latchinov began evenly, "when it's time to give birth, you must be in France so that he can come and take the baby immediately. He will go to city hall and register the baby under his name, and at the same time you will give him a notarized letter in which you renounce all rights to the baby."

I covered my face with my hands.

"He'll give you the right to see the child whenever you want, but only at his home, which will always be open to you."

"And if Stark marries?" I asked. "Maybe I don't want my baby to call another woman 'Mother' either."

"That's already settled. If Stark were to marry, or even to bring a mistress into his house, you would get the child back. I reminded him of this, but he is convinced that he will never marry. His condition at the moment doesn't allow him to look into the future with a clear head."

I looked hopefully at Latchinov and noticed he was smiling bitterly. What was he smiling about?

"Stark has also promised to raise the child with the knowledge that you are his mother, and that circumstances, such as business or sick relatives, are keeping you away from him. Stark also gives his word that he will encourage the child to love you and that he will keep you informed about the child's health on a weekly basis. Moreover, he'll give you a say in how the child is raised and his future. That's all I have to tell you."

"Thank him for me and tell him that I accept his conditions," I said unhappily.

"There's one more point. I asked him not to make me tell you, but he insisted. Of course you'll forgive a sick man—he was so ill and so upset. You must forgive him, and also me, for telling you this."

"Tell me everything now!"

"He's afraid that you want to rid yourself of the child before it's born."

"How could he insult me like that!" I cried.

"Tatiana Alexandrovna, you have to remember that he isn't normal at the moment. He's been having terrible thoughts. He even wanted to be present at the birth because he was afraid that you would switch babies on him. You must excuse this.

"I took care of him during his illness. He begged me not to tell you about his suffering, but I must say it was delirium, hallucinations. We even had to put him in a straitjacket a few times. He's so strong and agile that we were afraid of dislocating his arms and legs when we tried to keep him down.

"You must agree that it's been too short a time after such a serious illness that he can't yet think straight. You mustn't be insulted. Shall I continue?"

"Yes."

"Of course he was threatening all sorts of atrocities if you attempted to rid yourself of the child, and I won't repeat them because I know that it was the rantings of a sick imagination. He also demands that you take good care of your health. That's all," Latchinov finished with the sigh of someone whose load has just been lightened.

I remained quiet for a long time.

"And what if the child is stillborn?" I was directing the question more to myself than to Latchinov.

"He doesn't fear that scenario at all. When I raised that possibility, he said, 'I have found God, and God will not permit that.'"

"But if?" I asked.

"Then . . . he himself will die," Latchinov said quietly; "as it is now, that child is the only thing keeping him from suicide."

We sat without speaking. The early winter twilight had begun to fall, and the flowers Latchinov had brought me were still lying on the table, fading. I don't know what was in Latchinov's heart, but mine was filled with apprehension, depression, and desperation.

"Why are you sitting in the dark, Tania?" asked Ilya, walking into the studio. Latchinov was long gone, and I was paralyzed in the armchair, Fomka purring on my knees. He turned on the lights and asked anxiously, "What happened to you?"

I shielded my eyes from the sudden light and said indifferently, "Something happened that I hadn't at all anticipated. I had forgotten that I'm not the only one who has rights over this child."

"I don't understand what you're talking about."

In the same tone, I told him everything, except, of course, about Stark's threat to kill him. He said nothing for a few minutes.

"What can we do, Tania," he finally said; "the man's completely correct. I think that you'll be doing the right thing if you agree to this." Ilya's voice sounded troubled, and he was twirling a letter opener in his hands.

"He won't forbid you to see the child whenever you want, and he's even allowing you to participate in the upbringing. As far as material resources are concerned. . . ."

"We don't have to think about them. The father has the means to support the child. If he didn't, he wouldn't be taking it," I said, staring intently at Ilya's face, which looked confused, maybe even guilty. *I understand how you feel, Iliusha. You've demonstrated superhuman strength. Because of your love for me you were willing to take this child into your home, but now you're glad, even relieved, that the opportunity has arisen for you to decline this bitter cup. Although you yourself would never have sug-*

gested this to me, now you're afraid that I'll refuse it. You're prepared to work night and day to provide the money so that you won't have to see my past in front of your eyes.

"I've already agreed, Ilya, because I realize that it's better this way."

"Wonderful, Tania! Don't worry about a thing. We'll go abroad in the spring. And when it's over, I'll come for you . . . and we'll never be parted again. Let's get married, Tania."

I smiled bitterly. "Tie me down, Iliusha, so that I don't run away again."

I had just returned from visiting Maria Vasilevna at the hospital. Things were going comparatively smoothly. She would be coming home soon, but Ilya and I knew that her days were numbered. Was she aware of this? I think so. She would caress us and say sweet things more often. Her reserve had disappeared and she begged us to take her home as soon as possible and to hurry up Zhenia's wedding. She wanted to spend the summer with us and kept telling us how nice it was to have everyone around her.

"Mama," Ilya told her, "Tania has to go abroad for part of the summer."

"Why?" she asked plaintively. "Can't you put off your work for my sake, dear?"

"It's not to work, Mama, but the doctor has ordered me to take the waters for my health."

"Yes, Tania, you look terribly peaked. What's the matter with you?"

"Nothing in particular—the fever left me anemic."

She stared at me as I fixed her something to drink.

"Tata, come here!" she said, her voice excited. I walked over to her, and she threw her shriveled hands around my neck and whispered through tears of joy, "I can see, Tata, I noticed it yesterday, and I'm so happy. I want to be able to live just a little longer so that I can take care of my granddaughter. I know it will be a girl."

"Mama, you'd do better to wait for grandchildren from Zhenia. My children don't live," I barely kept my tears from gushing.

"Of course I'll love Zhenia's children, but this will be Ilya's daughter. . . . I love all my children equally, but Ilya has always been closer to me than the others." She closed her eyes, smiling happily.

Feeling like a criminal, I couldn't look at her. What heartache! And the anguish that waited for me every day at Maria Vasilevna's bed. The sick woman could talk about nothing but the child, her son's baby. Why didn't Ilya say anything, couldn't he see how much I was suffering? Was it revenge? No, he isn't like that. I could see that he, too, was in agony.

⋆⇒◎⇐⋆

We were saying our good-byes, getting ready to leave. Maria Vasilevna grasped Ilya's hand and said reproachfully, "It's amazing how apathetic men are to their children. I'm surprised at you, Ilya. You seem more displeased than happy."

"Mama," he said decisively, "we didn't want to upset you, but the doctor has said that Tania will lose this baby. She's going abroad in a few days, and she has to hurry. Your hopes are breaking our hearts—have pity on us."

Maria Vasilevna said no more, tears streaming from her eyes.

We went out into the corridor. Ilya embraced me and whispered softly, "Poor thing, be brave! I love you so, even more than before, if that's possible."

"I believe you, Ilya, because you've just done something you've never done for anyone: you lied to your mother."

⋆⇒◎⇐⋆

(Five years have passed—Trans.)
The express train flew along, but it still seemed to me that I was moving very slowly. I felt as nervous as a schoolgirl sent

home for the holidays. This was my holiday—I was on my way to spend two months with my child. I'd been able to steal a week last winter and visit him, but what's a week? I'd love to be able to stay with him always, but I can't leave my husband. These next two months without me will be very difficult for him, but I'm comforted by the fact that he'll spend the time with Zhenia in the country.

In the past five years Zhenia has had three children, and a fourth is on the way. She abandoned her music and lives only for her husband and children. Sometimes she grumbles about how she has no time to read or to play the piano, but it's obvious that this doesn't really bother her much. Her husband loves her very much, but why does he use such a patronizing tone with her, and treat her with such condescension?

Once I reminded him of our earlier conversation. "You're splitting hairs, sister-in-law. You're someone with a calling, a vocation, but Zhenia's simply a woman."

"What do you mean, Sergei Ivanovich? That a woman should be nothing more than a housekeeper and a nanny?"

"Good God, not that old question again! The answer is yes, if she has no talent or special vocation."

"What about Zhenia's music?"

"How can that be her vocation? She's given it up completely."

"Why didn't you encourage her? Why did you bring her to live in the country?"

"You're saying curious things, Tatiana Alexandrovna. What do you want—for me to take care of the kids while she gives concerts?"

"Zhenia's not an actress, or an opera singer, or a dancer whose whole employment takes place outside the home and who has trouble making time for her children—although some of them manage to. Female musicians, writers, and painters can be mothers if there is sufficient financial support and they don't have to wash the diapers or prepare dinner themselves. And if the husband doesn't bother them. . . . I've noticed, Sergei Ivanovich, that you take up more of Zhenia's time than the children do. In fact, you even take her away from the children."

"Oh, indeed?" he responded sarcastically.

"Of course. When you're working in your study, she has to walk around on tiptoes, afraid to breathe. Her job is to keep the children from crying, or the servant from slamming the door. When does she have time for music? She has to keep the children hidden away and, like a dragon, has to guard the door to your precious study. And if you hear a child crying, you start hollering about how anyone involved in intellectual work needs a corner away from the family. Your words upset Zhenia, and she starts crying. Now you soothe her and kiss her, but you've only been married for five years! Will you still be consoling her after ten years, or will you have already wounded her heart so badly that it cannot heal?"

"If I demand peace and quiet while I'm working, this doesn't mean that I'm taking up all my wife's time. You love to exaggerate, sister-in-law."

"From where I stand, I can see that Zhenia spends more time worrying about you than about the children."

"That's ridiculous."

"When you're not working, you demand that she be with you. You never give the servant orders; all reprimands are directed at Zhenia. She has to pour the glass and bring it herself. If a maid brings it you ask, 'What are you doing?' You see dust and tell her to get a cloth and wipe it off. Yesterday she spent the whole evening darning your socks because you enjoy watching her do that."

"So now I'm supposed to walk around in torn socks? Female logic," he said contemptuously.

"The servant could have darned the socks, but you would have gotten angry if she'd given them to someone else while she played Chopin."

"This is all very astute, Tatiana Alexandrovna, but where are you going with it?"

"Do you want me to be frank?"

"Please."

"Another woman would have an affair after a few years. But not Zhenia. She'll continue to love you, to look after you and the kids, and to take care of the cooking and your socks."

"In other words, everything will be fine."

"Not exactly, Sergei Ivanovich. When her cheeks start to lose their color, and you notice the gray in her hair and a wrinkle or two, you'll say to yourself, 'My wife is just a cook and a nanny. She's incapable of understanding me, and she's bringing me down. . . .'"

"Do finish this, Tatiana Alexandrovna!"

"And you'll take on a mistress."

"You're painting a wonderful panorama for us," he said maliciously; "have you told my wife this also?"

"No, only you."

"I'll thank you not to say anything in front of her. It's a pity that she loves you so much. That philosophy of yours could have a bad influence on her," he said, walking out of the room.

Oh, if you knew everything, you wouldn't let her see me at all. You cherish her virtue because it satisfies your needs at the moment. But when your wife's youthfulness begins to fade, you will reproach her for that same virtue. You will decide that you need more unconventional women, primitive passions, frenzied love, and you'll go anywhere, spend anything for it. And you're going to delude yourself into thinking that they love you for your mind, your looks. . . .

This train is moving so slowly!

Zhenia is withdrawing from all of us: from me, Andrei, Ilya— she can't even mention Katia's name in front of her husband. Mother was spared this retreat by dying. She lived long enough to see Zhenia's first son, Iliusha, but died when he was seven months old. We were all around her at the time, so she died happy. All of us but Katia, although she didn't have to worry about her.

Katia has a good position in Paris. I wrote to Latchinov about her, and he arranged for her to give Russian lessons and also made her something like his secretary. She earns a significant amount of money, and Latchinov fixed it so that she could return to Russia if she wanted to; but since her mother died, she has preferred not to. In fact, she even asked Andrei to come to live with her. But he finished the gymnasium and has enrolled in the Technological Institute and is living with us.

Why is this train moving so slowly!

⋅⇥═◉═⇤⋅

Latchinov! How could I have known then that our chance introduction at the Villa Borghese would turn into such a friendship. No, this isn't exactly a friendship, but we have friendly relations: he's always very reserved and proper with me, but he's always there for me at the most difficult times. He always does everything he can, and I never have to ask for favors. Because he's independently wealthy he doesn't have to work, so he's always at the service of whoever needs him.

For the past three years he's played the role of our good fairy. For example, just before I left, he wrote to say that in my absence he'll go to Zhenia's house in the country and "entertain" Ilya for a couple of weeks. These weren't empty words; Ilya enjoys his company very much because he respects his talent and knowledge. Zhenia refers to him as "Brockhaus and Efron."*

"When did you have time to learn all this?" asked Ilya, who often turns to him for information and advice.

"Fate, Ilya Lvovich, emancipated me from the need to worry about my daily bread. So what else did I have to do? I've got a good memory, I'm sufficiently intelligent, and science has always been easy for me. We have to spend our time somehow while we're on this earth."

Sergei Ivanovich is always fawning all over him, and I find it extremely amusing when he drops his authoritative manner in front of Latchinov.

---

*"Brockhaus and Efron" was a multivolume Russian encyclopedia published around the turn of the century.

There are other things that Latchinov never talks about, and we discovered them only by accident: his generous contributions to charity, and the confidential aid he gives to the poor and to students.

We all love him very much and talk about our most intimate affairs with him, but he's never once said a single word about his life or his emotions. We know only that he is a widower, whose wife died long ago. I've even seen her portrait in his Petersburg apartment. Could it be that this woman, with her thin lips and the haughty expression on her seemingly English face, wounded him so severely with her death that he still can't find happiness ten years later? And something is gnawing at him, tormenting him—I've noticed it many times. Why does his face show such intense pain at times? I owe him a great deal. He kept me from breaking my head against the wall when they took away my baby.

This insufferable train is crawling along at a turtle's pace!

If I did Stark wrong, he's certainly made me pay. And bitterly! For the past four years his continuous harassment has seemed to be unconscious, but what he put me through in the first few days after my Lulu was born—I can never forgive him for that. I pleaded with him to take the baby away immediately, before I could become too attached to him, but Stark insisted that I nurse the little one myself. I was permitted to see the baby only while he was feeding, and as soon as he fell asleep, Stark took him away immediately.

All the time I was feeding, Stark would sit beside me, not saying a word. Thin, with dark circles under his large, feverish eyes, he looked terrible, alien even. He was still handsome, but now he had a different kind of beauty.

I was terrified to feed my baby—would my milk kill him? I begged, pleaded, but Latchinov, who was trying to keep both of us calm, was unable to do anything with Stark.

"She must feed her baby. He must know that his mother fed him," the latter insisted.

Finally, with help from a doctor, Latchinov persuaded Stark that the baby could become ill and rescued me from that torture. Four days later Stark found a wet nurse and took the baby away.

Latchinov! I still don't see how he was able to keep his head, caught as he was between the two of us. He spent the worst night with me, and it was the first time I ever saw tenderness and compassion on his face. How pitiful I was that night.

And how slowly this train is moving!

But that's all in the past, and tomorrow I will be with my little boy, my treasure, with him whom I love more than anyone else on earth!

"A child born of such love as ours must be beautiful," Stark had once said. No, my child is more beautiful than that love. It's striking how much Lulu looks like his father; but he is even more handsome. The only thing he got from me was the color of his eyes which, although large, like his father's, are blue-green. And they are so pretty, shaded by his long dark lashes. The child is absolutely amazing—so smart, so good-natured, so sweet.

Time flies; this little person is already four years old. I worry about the future, though, when he grows up and starts wondering about his beloved mother. . . . I'm so grateful to Stark for encouraging him to love me . . . will it ever be possible to live with him permanently? At some point he's going to stop believing in the existence of the sick grandparents who are keeping his mother so far away from him.

Stark presents me to his friends as Lulu's godmother, or sometimes as the sister of the boy's dead mother. The story goes that the boy calls me "Mama" because we are concealing his mother's death from him. It's so stupid, but I do it for Ilya. I'm stunned at how frightened he is that someone might suspect the truth. Certainly no one in Petersburg has any inkling, but here it's an

open secret. . . . Stark is incapable of hiding anything. It's difficult for him to restrain himself and not taunt me. . . .

*This is supposed to be an express train, so why is it making
so many stops?*

⋅⊱══◉═⊰⋅

When Katia first arrived, it was impossible for me to avoid
seeing her. Latchinov apologized profusely for not arranging it so
that we would not run into each other at Stark's.

"Imagine," I'd never seen him so upset, "that I completely
forgot that Katerina Lvovna was your husband's sister." Katia
had deduced everything.

One day the boy fell down and hurt himself, not badly. We
pacified him and forgot all about it. Then Stark returned from
work to the dacha at seven as usual. When he saw the small
bruise on Lulu's chin he blew up. Venomously, he accused us
women of being too wrapped up in conversations about clothes,
and visibly upset, he began to question the boy.

I wanted to make fun of the situation: "Only an abnormal
father such as you could have become so distressed over such a
petty incident."

"You're the abnormal parent," he screamed maliciously. "You
wouldn't have cared if your son had died!"

I looked at Lulu—he was terrified, his eyes filled with tears.
He couldn't bear such nasty quarrels, such foul language, and
wanted us to kiss and make up.

I put him in my lap. "Don't cry, sweetie, Papa's just teasing.
He's mad at the rock that struck you."

Lulu calmed down, and looked at me with his large, trusting
eyes. I turned to Stark and said in Russian, because the boy can
barely understand it, "You'd better stop picking on me in front
of the baby. Do you want him to stop loving me?"

"He's young now, but when he grows up he'll realize that for
his mother he is only a pleasurable toy."

"If you please," I said indignantly, "the next time you want to perform a drama for my edification, please hire a child actor, if you need a child to hurt me."

He wanted to respond but Katia, surprised and upset, stood up. We had both been so angry that we had forgotten she was there.

"Katia," I said, "I'm sorry that Edgar Karlovich made you a witness to a family quarrel," and I took the child into the next room. I was so angry that my hands were shaking as I tried to arrange the toys on the floor. I tried to laugh it off, joke about it, but the boy wasn't fooled. He looked anxiously at me and asked, "Are you mad at the rock too, Mama?" If it was difficult to deceive him now, what about later?

That hadn't been the first scene with Stark. When Lulu was still a baby and I came for my visits, I would spend the days with him while Stark was at work, then leave right before Stark returned. But the baby became attached to me and would cry when I left. I started staying longer. Stark would try to work in his study, but Lulu wanted the two of us together. The more the child understood, the more upset I became.

The boy is extremely sensitive and high-strung. How could he not be nervous, given the state of my mind when I was carrying him. And when I'm around, Stark seems willfully anxiety-ridden and malicious. Sometimes I think he's jealous of the boy, and at other times I think it's vengeance. Stark and I rarely speak together alone, and when we do it's always about business and the conversations always end in fights. In front of other people he's always very polite to me, but he can't refrain from making innuendoes.

It's the same when he writes, and it hurts me. He only writes about the baby, but he'll drop little asides: "Yesterday a couple and their child were sitting across from me on the train. The mother was kissing him, and I felt jealous and depressed. The baby was playing with my walking stick—'Don't you like children?' the wife asked, because I had drawn back into the corner. I felt terrible for having insulted her. 'No ma'am, it's just that I'm envious, watching you cuddle your baby. Mine doesn't have a mother.'"

Why would he put this in a letter? I understand why he wants to punish me, but why hurt the baby? Latchinov once said to me very decisively, "Tatiana Alexandrovna, you must tell Stark to stop complaining in front of the child about how his life is ruined, and about how if he dies, the child will be forsaken and alone. And put a stop to the evening prayers! The boy is a Protestant and the father without any religion, yet he insists upon praying before an Orthodox icon to an unknown goddess."

There's something perverted about the love he's trying to inspire in the boy for me. I'm a fairy, flitting in and out.

Lulu gets exceedingly nervous when I first arrive. He won't leave my side and at night, when he's going to bed, he asks, "You won't leave tomorrow, will you?"

This train is moving so slowly!

I sat there thinking about the time that Stark had made the scene in front of Katia. All I had wanted to do then was to soothe Lulu, which I did. He started laughing—he has the same charming laugh as his father, and he tosses his head back and crinkles his eyes.

Our games were in full swing when Katia came in. I was surprised to notice that she had been crying.

"Why didn't you try to make up with him?"

"I didn't want to argue, so I don't feel any need to reconcile. It will only provoke another scene, and I'll again have to run up against his gall."

"Gall!" she exclaimed, laughing nervously. "Tata, like all people who have been overindulged, you take every remark to be impudent. Why are you looking at me so surprised? You think you're the center of the universe and that everyone should bow down before you."

"Lulu," I turned to the child, "run to the nanny and tell her it's stopped raining. We can go for a walk."

When he left I turned to Katia. "You're wrong. I certainly don't require worship. . . ."

"No, you do demand it," she interrupted me; "women like

you comprehend only their own passions and fancies. They wreck the lives of those around them and then are surprised when those whom they've hurt cry out. Women like you care only about themselves."

"Listen, Katia, I'm not going to discuss with you what I've been through and what I'm going through. I realize that you can never be objective about me, after what I did to your brother. But he's forgiven me, so why can't you?"

"My brother is his own person, just as I am," she answered. "He forgave you because he loves you and can't live without you. I can't forgive you, but not because of my brother. You went back to him and you take good care of him. I must be fair to you on this point, you're an ideal wife. But I can't forgive you for what you did to the other one—you ruined his life just because he has pretty eyes!"

"So you think it would have been better for me to leave your brother?"

"Of course. Your place is here, with your child. Edgar Karlovich told me the whole story. He said he lays no claim on you as a woman, but he's very distressed by the thought that his child has no mother. Women are condemned when they abandon their children for their lovers, and I denounce you, even though your lover is my brother!" She slammed the door as she walked out.

That scene remains sharp in my memory. . . . Night has fallen, and everyone except me is asleep. I can't sleep—I'm on my way to my son. How slowly this train creeps along!

Katia became more subdued after our scene. She had been able to justify her antipathy toward me and at the same time express the maternal instincts that she felt toward my son, in the way that spinsters sometimes become attached to other people's children. And who couldn't love that charming creature!

Stark loves him more like the most intense mother than like a father. I'm losing the hope that he will ever marry. Sometimes his love for the child exceeds all boundaries. I'll never forget when Lulu got the measles. Stark went crazy and sent me a wild telegram. And what was I thinking as I was hurrying to Paris then? The doctor was there when I arrived, and he calmed me down, assuring me that it was a light case and the child was in no danger whatsoever. I wanted to console Stark, but he had said such nasty things to me about my supposed indifference toward the boy.

The train is still moving so slowly!

I jumped off the train, forgetting about my luggage and everything else in the world. Since morning I hadn't been able to eat or drink anything, or to sit still. Then I saw a group of people on the platform. A small figure dressed in white stood apart from the others. Another second—I was crushing my child to my breast, trying to hold back my tears and covering him with kisses. He wrapped his arms around me and pressed his dark head against my neck. Someone was saying something to me, but I was blocking everything out. I came to my senses when I heard Latchinov's quiet voice saying, "Tatiana Alexandrovna, you're suffocating Lulu. We are also here and want to kiss your hand."

Refusing to relinquish Lulu, I laughed and said, "Here's my cheek, Alexander Vikentovich, you can kiss it. And I'm also very glad to see you."

Laughing, he kissed me.

"You kiss me too, Edgar," I said to Stark, "and let's agree not to bicker during my visit."

His lips barely touched my cheek and he asked, "Where are your things, Tatiana Alexandrovna?"

"Oh, I'd forgotten! They're still in the train car," I waved a hand, and then hugged my treasure again.

At breakfast I still couldn't tear myself away from Lulu.

"Neither one of you is eating, you're still just kissing," Stark smiled; "I'd better separate you."

"Oh, no, Papa, I'm eating everything," and a small hand clutched me tightly.

"I'm eating, I'm eating!" I repeated. "And after breakfast, we'll open the trunk and see what's there. What do you want more than anything?" knowing that he wanted a boat big enough to float in the pool. "Tell me."

"For you to come."

"And after that?"

"A sleigh?"

"But it's summer now."

"Oh, a live horse!"

Stark and Latchinov saw that I was so depressed that I couldn't pull a horse out of my trunk that they started laughing.

"You've bungled it, Mama," said Vasenka, "I can't believe you didn't pack a horse." After Stark's illness Vasenka remained in Paris, although he was constantly swearing about *piccoli francesi.*

I stared closely at Vasenka and then exclaimed, "You're getting better looking. In fact, you look quite elegant."

During these years in Paris he had been terribly impoverished. Stark and Latchinov had done everything they could, but it was difficult to get him to take help. He would only agree to eat at Stark's. Vasenska looked at me and said proudly, "Now I'm wealthier."

"How?"

"I'm earning a lot and don't know what to do with my money. Just today I earned one hundred francs. You don't believe me? Well, what's this?" He pulled a hundred-franc bill from his pocket.

"Don't tell me that the Parisians also like the Colosseum in the moonlight?"

---

*"Little Frenchies," or "Frogs" in English slang.

"For heaven's sake! No, now I'm drawing pornographic pictures."

"You?"

"Why not? A woman in a chemise writing a letter . . . a woman in knickers smelling a rose . . . a woman not wearing anything going to bathe . . . to hell with them. I got a hundred francs for drawing that group."

"What makes it pornographic?"

"Do you think I'm painting those women for aesthetic purposes? Just a solace for old men. Michelangelo's *Leda* isn't pornography, but a work of art. My women, however, are wanton subjects."

"Did they sell well?"

"Couldn't have been better—you saw: a hundred francs for a set of four."

"Were they pretty?"

"Depends on your customer's taste. One customer criticized me because he said that the hat my model was wearing was no longer fashionable. She was wearing nothing else. Another squabbled that women are no longer wearing such knickers. So I began leafing through fashion magazines to get the correct accessories, and at the same time I started drawing faces from the magazines."

"What happened?"

"They liked them so much that they raised the prices and now I'm working for five stores!"

⊷══◐ ◖══⊷

I put Lulu to bed. We were laughing and kissing. Dressed in his long night shirt, he jumped on the bed. He wasn't sleepy at all.

"Come on, go to sleep, my little one."

"Look at me, Mama, I'm lying down. Where's Papa? He always puts me to bed."

"Well today I am. Doesn't that make you happy?"

"Oh, happy, yes," he threw his arms around my neck, "but Papa must come too."

I opened the door to Stark's study. He was sitting at his desk, his head propped up in his hands.

"Come, Edgar, the dauphin is going to sleep and he demands your presence," I laughed.

Stark jumped up and hurried to Lulu's bedside. The boy stuck his hand out toward his father and scolded him, "Why didn't you come? I want both of you together!" He put one arm around me, the other around his father, and kissed us in turn. I moved to free myself, but Stark said sternly, "Don't spoil the child's happiness. Your punctiliousness is out of place."

I surrendered. Our heads touched, and the boy's warm lips alternated between our faces.

"Enough, Lulu, go to sleep," said Stark.

"I am, I am . . . but, Papa, now kiss Mama."

Stark's lips pecked my hair. Lulu smiled happily and said, "Tomorrow we'll go to the zoo."

During this visit Stark and I didn't argue as much as usual. He had changed his attitude toward me and was very polite, solicitous, and attentive. His outward appearance had also changed for the better; he was once again fussing about his clothes. I also noticed how occasionally some of his old flirtatiousness, his smile and gestures, would creep back into his mannerisms.

Why? Maybe he had at last reconciled himself with the situation. Perhaps he was having an affair? That wouldn't be so bad. If only he would get married—then Lulu would be mine forever!

"How wonderful that would be," I said out loud, inadvertently.

"What are you talking about?" asked the surprised Latchinov. We were sitting out on the terrace as we usually did after breakfast, he with his newspaper and me with my work. I put my drawing aside and began telling him about my speculations, pointing out to him the various slight changes in Stark's behavior in the past few days. Latchinov sat with his eyes down, but with the pained expression on his face that always frightened me.

"What's the matter, do you feel sick, Alexander Vikentevich?"

It was obvious that he was struggling with himself, but then he said, "Don't worry about me, my friend; I've been ill for a long time. It's better to talk about you. You've noticed a change in Stark and are hopeful that he'll get married and give you Lulu?" He was having great difficulty speaking. "I'll tell you straight: no, that will never happen. He'll never bring a stepmother to his son. He told me once that as far as he's concerned, if a woman loves a man, she can never truly love any child he has by another woman. Of course she can fulfill her maternal obligations commendably, even be sweet to it, but she can never love it.

"I objected to this, giving him examples of loving stepmothers, but he responded that such women had either noticed that their husbands were indifferent to the child or these women were meek, frigid, or submissive. He told me that he could never love such a woman, and the opposite sort of woman could never reconcile herself to his passionate love for his son."

"All right. I guess I'd better not count on complete happiness," I said. "But has he started an affair? And would that be so bad? He would be better able to adjust to the past, and not prey on my nerves and, more important, the boy's."

Latchinov said nothing for a few minutes, but then looked at me and declared, "Tatiana Alexandrovna, I don't like to meddle in other people's business, and I certainly don't like to betray confidences, but our friendship and the circumstances have forced me to warn you—may I ask you a question first?"

"Please."

"Tell me, would you really be indifferent if I told you that yes, Stark has fallen in love with another woman? Don't answer right away, think about it."

I frowned and said, "I'll be completely honest with you: yes, it would hurt my ego a little . . . maybe not my ego, but my feminine pride. See, I'm being open. But that would be a petty emotion indeed in contrast to how I would feel if I were ashamed of a painting. It's nothing in comparison to the happiness I would feel if Lulu did not have to have such a depressed, dissatisfied, and nervous father always by his side. I'm confident that as time goes by I will be able to win the right to have the child with me and to spend most of my time with him. Maybe Stark would surrender Lulu and he would be mine, mine!"

In my excitement I squeezed Latchinov's slender hand, which was lying on the arm of the chair.

"Tatiana Alexandrovna," I suddenly heard his voice, toneless and unfamiliar, "don't start celebrating too early."

"Why not?"

He was quiet, as if suffering an internal debate, but then he raised his head resolutely. Despite his poise, a sad smile played on his lips. "Here's the situation. I'm going to spill Stark's secret. I don't like doing this, but it's unavoidable.

"For the past four years I have almost always been at his side. He's not one of those people who can hide his emotions, and he never concealed anything from me. All this time he's been living only for the child. Of course he had a few 'one-night stands,' but they never counted.

"You've complained to me often about his practical jokes, which were sometimes cruel. You accused him of taking out his revenge on you, but couldn't you see that he did this out of passion, not revenge? He spent all these years living in the memory of those three months in Rome. He talked about that incessantly. Sometimes he would forget that I was there and rave on about what you said, your caresses, your kisses. He still keeps some of your clothes and a few trinkets that belonged to you in a cupboard in his office. Last year he finally agreed with my opinion that he would go out of his mind if he continued to kiss your clothes every night, and he gave me the key.

"Often he told me that it took all his strength not to dwell on the fact that you belonged to someone else, and that only his love for the boy prevented him from murder. Several times he wanted to go to kill your husband. Lulu has kept him from both murder and suicide, and if the boy were to die tomorrow, Stark would put a bullet in his head.

"You've been celebrating the changes, Tatiana Alexandrovna, but I'll tell you why they occurred. On the eve of your arrival, he came into my room at night. As happy as he was about the upcoming meeting with you, he was equally distressed about the usual problems: to have you alongside him but still inaccessible for him. . . . I advised him to go away. 'I can't,' he said, 'I have but one joy, and that's seeing the child in her arms. I try not to think about her, I spend the rest of the year taking care of my business, but for these two or three months I can live under the illusion that she's my wife, the mistress of my house.'

"I was so unbearably sorry for him that I quite possibly made an enormous mistake by giving him hope. . . ." Latchinov stopped.

"For what?"

"That he might earn your love back by not trying to hurt you all the time. I suggested that he tease you, pretend to be in love with someone else, but he knew better. 'I can't do that,' he said, 'that would only make her happy,' he said sardonically.

"And that's why he's trying to restrain himself, play up to you, look after you, and even flirt, the poor thing. He's hoping. . . . "

"You know very well that that's impossible, Alexander Vikentovich."

"I don't know, Tatiana Alexandrovna. Here's my opinion: if I were a woman, I would give all I had for a love such as Stark's, but women are capricious creatures, and I refuse to try to understand them."

"But you know Ilya, and my relationship with him! How could you raise Stark's hopes?"

"I admit that I made a terrible mistake, but I felt so sorry for him. I just wanted to comfort him and ease the strain on you during your vacation. Please don't be angry with me, my friend." And he kissed my hand respectfully.

Katia had arrived. She would come down from the city twice a week to consult with Latchinov about his extraordinary correspondence and to collect the material she would take back to type up. She always left after dinner. But this time she had come for two weeks because she had to work through material with Latchinov that he had been collecting for many years. I know that he's working on a magnum opus on the history of music, and he often jokes that after he dies Stark will have to publish it and I will do the illustrations. With Vasenka's help I've already begun.

Latchinov was sitting on the terrace dictating something to Katia. Lulu, Vasenka, and I were in the gazebo playing at sculpting wild animals out of clay. Lulu became extremely excited about every animal and finally, when he molded something that resembled a pig, I became as excited as he was. Vasenka observed in a most serious tone, "yes, you've got talent—a future Rodin. Your pig is an exact copy of his statue of Balzac." We were having a marvelous time, all smeared with clay.

We heard the gate slam; Stark had returned for dinner. Lulu jumped up and bounded into his embrace, streaking his elegant suit with clay. But Stark didn't pay any attention. He took the boy in his arms, kissed him affectionately, and carrying him out onto the terrace, asked Katia proudly, "Don't you think he's growing even more handsome? Don't you agree, Mademoiselle Katia, that he's a dream?"

"That's not very polite, Edgar," laughed Latchinov, "you're fishing for compliments. He's your spitting image."

"Oh no," said Stark excitedly, "he'll be a hundred times better looking than I. He's got blue eyes, and his mother's small hands and feet. . . ." Looking at me, he became embarrassed and, turning back to the child, said, "He'll be taller, kinder, and better than I am . . . and smarter, much smarter!" he added bitingly.

A dig at me!

--✦⊜ ⊜✦--

Today Stark fell apart and we had an especially ugly scene. I had taken Lulu for a walk, forgetting my watch. We found a lovely spot in the park, lost track of time, and were late for dinner. Katia and Latchinov were waiting for me at the gate. It turned out that Stark had sent out the servants and taken a bicycle to look for us himself.

"What absurdity," I chuckled, "am I a small child?"

Stark returned half an hour later. He clasped Lulu so hard to his chest and kissed him as though the boy had just been rescued from a terrible danger. Lulu, sensing his father's tension, became so frightened he started to cry and asked, "What's the matter, Papa?"

Stark said nothing, pressing the boy closer, and he also began to weep bitterly.

"Stop this display of nerves," I commanded acidly.

"And to whom do I owe this pleasure?" he cried out. "You took the boy for the whole day so that you could enjoy the pleasure of being with him all by yourself. You didn't care that I was worried to death. How could I know what was going on with you? Maybe you'd fallen into the water or been hit by a car! Or else you could have stolen my baby! You were thinking only about yourself, unconcerned that he might be tired, worn out. You don't really love him. You spend time with him only because he's handsome. If he were deformed, you would never hold him in your arms, never kiss him!"

"Pull yourself together and stop screaming at me!"

"You're lucky that I'm only screaming. I'd hit you, except that I can't raise my hand to a woman."

"Shut up!" I could hold back no longer, "I'm leaving right this minute. I ask you to bring the child to my hotel in the morning. I never want to see you again."

Stark grew white, fell down in the chair, his head thrown against the back of it, and began to sob hysterically. Katia ran to get some water. I wanted to take Lulu away, but he was crying, wrestling away from my arms, clinging to his father. I gave up, returned to my room, and collapsed on my bed.

Did I really have to leave? How else could I spare my son from scenes like that one?

Stark was standing in front of me begging for my forgiveness. He claimed that he himself didn't know what he was saying, didn't know what had happened to him, and was swearing that it would never happen again. I didn't believe him. True, nothing this outrageous had happened before, but how could I guarantee that poor Lulu wouldn't have to undergo this pleasure again?

The child was sleeping in his little bed. He had forced us to kiss and make up and had fallen asleep holding both our hands. And now? I looked in on him a few minutes ago; he was tossing and turning in his sleep.

"Let's end this farce now," I said to Stark, "next I'm going to have to endure beatings for Lulu's sake." I turned to Katia, who was pacing the room. "So, Katia, are you going to blame me this time?"

"No, Edgar Karlovich is the guilty party. No one should ever scream like that. The truth can be told more calmly," and she continued to pace.

⋆⇥◉⇤⋆

My clever ploy succeeded; everything was going off without a hitch. Peace and quiet. I had a feeling that it wouldn't stay this way, but all was going smoothly at the moment. I wasn't feeding Stark's hopes, but . . . sometimes I'd allow myself to joke around with him, give him a compliment, or ask him to read to me while I was drawing. And while he was at home, I didn't take the boy anywhere.

⋆⇥◉⇤⋆

The heat was unbearable. It was Sunday and Stark was at home. We were all lounging in light clothing, all except Latchinov, who remained proper in his dark suit. It was so hot no one even wanted to talk. Katia suffered from heat the most, and she cursed it incessantly.

"Go take a shower," I advised, "I've already bathed three times."

"That's a good idea," she responded, "maybe after a bath I'll be able to do something." She went into the house.

"Papa, I want a bath," asked Lulu, "please let me go."

"It's too cold for a shower, but I'll draw you a bath."

"But the nanny's gone—today's Sunday."

"If your mama helps me, I'll give you the bath."

All day long Stark had been very pleasant to me, and now he was carrying water to the tub and clowning around. I was getting a Turkish robe ready for Lulu, who was wildly excited. Like

158

all children, he especially enjoys seeing the regular routines over-turned, and a bath in the middle of the day was an event.

Lulu was racing about the room, trying to catch the sunbeams as they reflected off the water. His bedroom was bathed in sunlight. Actually, it wasn't a bedroom so much as it was the nursery; we called it the bedroom because next to the boy's little trundle bed, his father kept a narrow white cot. All the furniture was white. The room had no drapes or carpets. Everything was clean, simple, and hygienic.

I have to give Stark credit—he took excellent care of the boy's physical needs. He appreciated to the smallest detail what Lulu would require at any given moment. But what sort of care was he taking of the boy's young soul, his loving and tender heart?

This young soul slid out of his father's grasp and started running barefoot around the room. He looked so sweet, wearing nothing but a long shirt. I chased after him, kissing him, while he squealed merrily.

"If you don't behave yourself, you won't get to have your bath," Stark declared. Lulu calmed down and let us put him in the tub; he flinched slightly from the cold water.

Stark took off his jacket, picked up the pitcher and began to pour the water on Lulu.

"Let me roll up your sleeves, Edgar," I offered.

"No thanks, I can do it myself," and with his wet hands he pulled back his shirtsleeves.

Lulu could not restrain himself any longer and he suddenly began splashing water in my face. I answered in kind. He leapt up and, throwing his wet arms around my neck, began yelling, "Mama, you get in the tub, too!"

"How sweet he is! maybe it's because I'm his mother, but I've never seen a more beautiful child," I said. "I should sketch him in the bath like this."

"No, please, don't start drawing him," said Stark derisively.

"Why not?"

"You'll stop loving him then," he said, not looking at me.

He just couldn't resist getting a barb in. But I was in a good mood so I didn't answer him.

"No, Mama will never stop loving me. This will protect me,"

and Lulu showed me the coral he wore around his neck. It was one of the three that Stark had given me in Rome. The day that I had given birth he had torn the chain from my neck and had given it back only just before I had left. Only one pink orb remained. Lulu always wore a second one. The third. . . .

"Where's the third?" I asked. Stark said nothing.

"I protect my coral," Lulu continued insistently, "because Papa told me that you'll stop loving me if I lose it."

"What a silly thing to say, child! Papa was joking; Mama will never stop loving you."

"Papa has told me all about it . . . on winter evenings, he tells me stories. . . ."

"Son, jump out of the tub," said Stark.

"In a minute, Papa. He told me about how when God gave you to him, he gave you these three corals . . . there were roses all around. It was night, wasn't it, Papa? And what did you say about the stars and the moon?"

"Enough chatter, hop out of the tub," Stark said impatiently, blushing slightly.

"What kind of strange fantasies are you filling the boy's head with?" I asked testily, drying Lulu with the robe.

Stark walked to the closet and got out some clothes for the boy. I couldn't see his face, but I could hear the embarrassment in his voice.

"In the winter I spend almost every evening alone with him. Maybe I fantasize out loud—the past won't always stay peacefully in the past."

I said nothing for a few minutes and then turned to Lulu. "Now you're clean and dry. Papa, give us his stockings."

Stark handed me his socks and we began to put on his shoes. I was seated on the divan next to Lulu, and Stark was kneeling in front of us.

"Papa wears the third bead himself. Mine's the biggest, yours is smaller," Lulu pulled out my chain, "and Papa's is like yours. Show her, Papa."

"I don't have mine any more. Get dressed, put on your socks."

"Where is it?"

"Stop this, Lulu. I lost it," said Stark impatiently.

"Papa, Papa, how did you lose it!" Lulu threw up his hands, ready to start crying.

"Papa was joking, Lulu, he didn't lose it. Stand up and let me button your shirt."

"No, no, he lost it! He always used to wear it!" Lulu broke out in tears.

"For heaven's sake show him the coral if you still have it," I said irritatedly, "you're the one who sows all this sentimentality, and now you have to reap it!"

Stark wouldn't talk; his eyes were lowered, his lips pursed. Lulu was sobbing.

"Why this idiotic stubbornness?" I exclaimed and, seeing the delicate chain around his neck, I thrust my hands under his collar. What happened? Memories of forgotten sensations? The power of this beautiful body? My hand involuntarily pressed against his chest. A minute later I had recovered and pulled out his chain, and said with a forced laugh, "There you go, Lulu. Papa was only joking. Here's his coral, intact."

Lulu's mood changed instantaneously from tears to bliss. Even before his tears could dry he was bounding on the couch in his unbuttoned shirt. The expression had flashed across my face for only a second, but that was long enough for Stark to catch it. Good Lord, what am I going to do now? More than hope, I had given him confidence. While I was trying to catch Lulu to button his shirt, Stark was watching me with a familiar gaze, through half-closed eyes. I grabbed Lulu and quickly whisked him out of the room, babbling about something.

All day long I stayed in a weird mood. Had I really begun experiencing those feelings again? Was I truly no more than an animal? I could rationalize my attraction to Stark and my cheating on Ilya by thinking of it as a kind of poetic love, spoken in "the languages of the gods." But how could I explain yesterday's feelings? And it wasn't just yesterday! I caught myself today. Throwing caution to the wind, today I found myself looking at

Stark's lips and wanting them. It wasn't, however, the same sharp sensation I'd felt in the past, but an aching, a hunger. . . . Thank God he hasn't noticed it today; yesterday I certainly gave myself away. When he said good-bye, he kissed my palm so long and ardently that I had to draw it away.

What can I do? I'm not so much worried about myself as I am afraid of new scenes. Should I go away? And leave Lulu? I simply cannot.

"Tatiana Alexandrovna, what happened between you and Stark, if it's not a secret?" Latchinov asked during our after dinner siesta.

"Nothing special, Alexander Vikentovich."

"Forgive me, dear friend, for asking an indelicate question, but you've spoiled me with your candor."

"Maybe I still want to be forthright with you, but I'm embarrassed."

Latchinov did not answer.

"I'm mortified," I cried acrimoniously; "I was angry with you for raising Stark's hopes, and yesterday I myself . . . did an incredibly stupid thing. I realized that I'm nothing more than an animal, and I'm ashamed of myself, but I also hold you in part responsible."

"Pardon me, but I don't understand a thing."

"Yesterday I, completely unexpectedly, for one fleeting moment, felt my desire for Stark rekindle, and he realized it."

"So what did I have to do with that?" Latchinov asked with a sickly smile.

"Remember our recent conversation? I thought that Stark had grown cold to me, but you persuaded me otherwise. I'll use Zhenia's words: 'When I'm not saying anything, I don't usually notice anything either. But as soon as my friends start talking, I start imagining things.'"

"What's that supposed to mean?" Latchinov raised his head sharply.

"The scenes are now becoming even more intense than before."

"I've noticed," he said quietly, dropping his head again.

"When?"

"This morning I inadvertently caught your glance when you were watching Stark."

I blushed, covering my face. "If only you knew how disgusted I was with myself, Alexander Vikentovich. It won't happen again."

"Why not? Do you really think you can fight it?"

"How can you be saying this, you who are so controlled and balanced!"

"Tatiana Alexandrovna, sometimes self-control and equanimity are only manifestations of having made peace out of a sense of hopelessness, as when a person is standing in front of a brick wall. But you're standing before screen doors, so it is worthwhile to push against them. . . ."

"But I don't want to push them. However exasperating and unpleasant those feelings are for me, I only have to endure them for brief moments."

"The more I hear, the more I believe in my theory."

"What theory?"

"Permit me to explain it to you at some other time. Now I suggest, if I may be so bold as to advise you, that you try to make Stark happy. That will end the matter." He closed his eyes and leaned his head back.

"You're joking, Alexander Vikentevich."

"Not in the least. Don't you know *how* Stark loves? I doubt that you remember him with disgust. In fact, I'm even convinced that you've sometimes wanted to relive some of the moments."

"You seem to have forgotten that I'm Ilya's wife, and I love him."

"I don't doubt that for a minute, but that didn't stop you before. . . ."

"Stop. At that time I thought I loved Stark, but now I realize that what I felt was plain and simply sensuality."

"Then give him back at least that; it'll make him happy."

"What about Ilya? You are very well aware that after all this happened, and after his mother died to boot, he contracted a heart disease. You know that he's alone now, living only for me. He loves me and trusts me enough to send me here."

"He doesn't trust you."

"What?"

"He's simply resigned himself to this so that he won't lose you completely."

"That's impossible. I'm always faithful to him."

"I don't doubt that, but he does."

Stunned, I stared at Latchinov; his face was calm, as before, and his eyes closed. "Do you remember the time, just before your departure, when he came to you with the proposition to take the baby? He realized his mistake then. He was referring to the fact that you were going to be away for a long time, and he could see how anxious and lonesome you get when you're separated from your son. You answered that you had neither the legal nor the moral authority to take the baby. You kissed his hand, deeply touched by the depth of his sacrifice. You didn't understand how much easier it would have been for him to have had your son around constantly than the torments he suffers in your absence, imagining you in the arms of the child's father."

"What can I do if it isn't true?" I despaired. "I'll prove to him that it isn't so."

"What kind of evidence do you think you can provide? The more you dwell on it, the more you'll feed his worst suspicions."

"What can I do? I don't want to hurt Ilya. Alexander Vikentevich, dear, tell me what to do," I pleaded, clutching his hand. "Tell me what I can do."

"Lie to him."

"To whom?"

"To your husband. Tell him that Stark has a mistress, whom he adores, but he won't marry her because he doesn't want a stepmother for his child. Mention this casually, in the course of a conversation, and then later build it up with a few details."

"I can't lie to Ilya, he'll figure it out," I said, shaking my head.

"Do you want me to tell the lie for you?" Latchinov asked suddenly. "I'm getting ready to go to Russia on business. I'll go to the country for a visit and will reassure Ilya completely on this subject."

"Do you see no other way out?"

"Only if you're prepared to sacrifice the child."

"Never."

"That makes the lie mandatory. In any case, you shouldn't kill a man slowly."

"You're right. Do what you think best, you've always known how to resolve these situations. We don't call you our good fairy for nothing."

"I'll do what I think appropriate. I don't want the people around me to suffer, so I do what I can to prevent this. That's my one satisfaction in life; my personal life ended long ago."

"If only I could end mine, too," I said unhappily.

"There are various kinds of endings. Some move away from passion, others from love, or from excitement or devotion—you simply have to consider the welfare of those around you and throw yourself into the whirlpool. That's how to end your personal life."

"That's not a bad idea, and in fact it works well for a 'paradoxical woman,' as the late Sidorenko used to call me," I said bitterly.

"Is he really dead?" Latchinov asked absent-mindedly.

"Why am I burying him? He's alive and got married not long ago. I buried him in my imagination because our past happened so long ago that it's as if it had already died," I observed introspectively.

"All right, Tatiana Alexandrovna, I'll take care of Ilya Lvovich, cheer him up, so what are you going to do about Stark?"

"What can I do?" I shrugged. "I guess I'll go back to avoiding him."

"That means he's going to be the only loser in this."

"Listen, you have already surprised me once today, so I'm asking again: are you joking?"

"Not at all."

"This is just great. You're telling me that Ilya suspects me of being unfaithful but has reconciled himself to this. Stark, however, if he becomes intimate with me, won't accept this situation?"

"He'll come around. He's so tormented," Latchinov said softly.

"And if he doesn't?"

"Lie."

"To him too?"

"Him too. You can't lie to Stark? Or do you want me to?"

"It's fine, but what am I supposed to tell him?"

"Tell him that you're staying with your husband out of pity for his illness and his loneliness. Say you can't leave him because you love him as you would your father or brother, almost as you do your child, but that you don't have conjugal relations."

"And I become the wife of two men???"

"Tatiana Alexandrovna, people are composed of two parts, body and soul. The two aren't always in harmony, but we find a way to live anyway, we don't just fall apart."

"Now I know you're joking, Alexander Vikentevich," I stood up.

"Think whatever you want to, my dear friend, but don't get mad at me. Believe that I love you, am devoted to you with my whole soul, and that if I ever at any time open my soul to anyone, it will be to you alone."

That frightened me. I never expected to hear anything like that from Latchinov. The expression on his face, in his eyes, was so sad that I lay my head on his shoulder and began to weep. My nerves were still stretched to the breaking point from yesterday.

He stroked my head and said in his familiar impassive voice, "It's good for you to cry, it will soothe your nerves. You're a very lucky woman, even if you don't realize it."

"Thanks for the luck," I said, wiping my eyes.

"You have two main purposes in life: your child and your art."

"Let's be honest, dear friend, and speak candidly: my art has died. I'll never paint anything exceptional again, I can feel it."

"No, you have one painting left to accomplish."

"What?"

"A portrait of Dionysus's son."

⊷⇒◓⇐⊶

Vasenka had stretched the canvas across the frame for me very artistically. I was preparing to paint my son's portrait—a large but modest picture. Lulu would be wearing a simple white blouse, sitting on the big, dark divan in his father's study with his beloved Amour, a mischievous bulldog, next to him.

Stark had paid a neighbor one thousand francs for the dog simply because the animal, mean and sullen around others, even snarling at his masters, had developed an uncommon attachment to Lulu. The boy could do whatever he liked to the dog, who only panted along blissfully. Vasenka named him Amour because the dog had the same inexplicable hatred for him that he had for Sidorenko.

"Je suis toujours malheureux en amour,"* he would say, walking cautiously past the dog. "Get your charming toy out of here, Lulu, I'm wearing new pants."

I didn't make my baby suffer through long sittings, and I tried to keep him entertained by telling him stories while I was drawing him. The stories were always cheerful and amusing. Lulu laughed happily and said, "When you tell stories, Mama, I understand them and I don't get scared."

I know, I know, child, I thought to myself, the stories your father tells you on those long winter nights are frightening and bewildering, all about love and passion and suffering. You won't hear any of those from me; I'll give my body and soul to guarantee you a happy childhood. . . .

⌁⌁⌁

We all persuaded Katia to come live with us because Latchinov is in a terrible hurry to finish his book and his health doesn't permit him to write for long periods of time. She kept making excuses, but finally agreed. She loved Lulu very much but seemed to be ashamed of these feelings. When she thought no one was watching, her normally stern countenance would light up with surprising tenderness. Had she really lived her whole life like this, never allowing anyone to become attached to her smooth exterior,

---

*"I am always unhappy in love."

other than her mother and Ilya? In my opinion, she didn't really love Andrei and Zhenia. I was always fascinated by her thoughts and emotions, but she would never open herself up to me.

She can't, however, hide her love for my son. Recently Stark asked her to come by mornings this winter to give him practice speaking Russian, and she agreed immediately, unable to disguise her pleasure. Even if she lacks sensitivity, Lulu has awakened her maternal instincts. I'm very happy that she'll be with my son. At first I feared that she might try to turn him against me, but then I chased that thought away. Katia is scrupulously honorable and would not do that. She will be an excellent teacher, and her more sober attitude toward the child will provide a splendid corrective to his father's fantasies.

Someone picked up my hand from the arm of the chair and kissed it. I shuddered. It was Stark. He put his briefcase on the table and said jokingly, "You were completely lost in thought, not seeing or hearing anything. Congratulate me, I got away from work early today. Here are your books, Mademoiselle Katia, but I'm not sure that they're the ones you want. What do you say, shall we have dinner in Versailles? Tatiana Alexandrovna, what's on your mind?" He adjusted the comb that was about to fall out of my hair.

"I'm thinking about Lulu, only about Lulu. Always and everywhere," I answered, pulling my head away.

He withdrew his hand quickly and asked derisively, "About Lulu himself or his portrait? I'm sure that the latter is much more interesting to you."

"Why so spiteful, Edgar? You've developed the habit of stinging me. May God forgive you. I'm going to change clothes. Lulu will be delighted."

⋅→⇒ ◯⇐←⋅

Indeed, the boy was ecstatic: a train ride, fountains, a boat ride, dinner in a restaurant. He gathered flowers and demanded that Katia weave them into a garland.

"I can't, Lulu, you picked them with their stems too short. If we had some thread. . . ."

"Hold it! I've got thread—strong stuff I bought," said Vasenka, rolling up his pant leg and beginning to unravel his socks.

"Vasenka, where did you find those socks?" I asked, astonished. The socks were made of thick, coarse material, unevenly bound.

"My roommate knit them as a present for me."

"A roommate? Who?"

"Sir Cavalier de Monte-Sarano-Croce del Bambo!"

"And he knits stockings?"

"What else should he be doing?"

"And why is he living with you? Doesn't he have a family?"

"He had a daughter, a widow and a seamstress, but she died recently and left a whole brood of grandchildren. He and I got three of them placed; the kids will be fine. But the two oldest—we have to ask Alexander Vikentevich to do something about them."

"But who is he, your cavalier?"

"I already told you—he's a genuine aristocrat. And you should hear him swearing about the republic—malicious stuff!"

"And he knits stockings?"

"He knits. He's got to do something to keep from being bored. I take him out for a walk once a day. I feed him, while he sits in his chair."

"He does nothing besides knitting stockings?"

"What else can he do, he's blind."

"Vasenka, where did you find this blind old man and his grandchildren?"

"Not far. . . . What's bothering you? He's just a guy, not hurting anyone. . . . What's the matter with that?"

"Lulu," I said, "come give Vasenka a kiss."

Lulu jumped in Vasenka's arms, happy to kiss him. Vasenka patted him on the back, saying, "Come by and see my cavalier. Only don't bring Amour, or the cavalier will bite him. He's even meaner than your dog."

Evening had already fallen by the time we returned, and it was completely dark outside. The train car was filled with lively conversations, jokes, and laughter from the people returning from their excursion. Despite the noise, though, Lulu fell asleep as soon as we sat down. Although he's thin, he's a very solid boy, and it's uncomfortable for me to hold him.

"Give him to me," said Stark, seated across from me.

I wanted to hand him over, but Lulu clung to me, mumbling something in his sleep.

"Move over, a little, Edgar, so that I can have room to put my legs up on your seat," I said.

Stark moved aside. Now I felt comfortable; I was holding my child close to me, had wound my shawl around him, and closed my eyes. When Lulu is sleeping in my arms I'm happy and don't think about anything else. Vasenka and Katia were arguing about something. Laughter and noise all around.

My skirt kept sliding off my legs as the train jerked along, and Stark would readjust it. Drowsiness began overtaking me. Then suddenly I felt Stark's hand, cold and shaking, on my leg. A familiar sharp sensation seized me, but now I was afraid of these feelings. I quickly pulled my legs from the seat and, handing him the boy, said, "Take him, I'm tired."

He accepted Lulu obediently, not even glancing at me. I huddled in a corner, trying to fix it so that not even my dress would touch Stark's knees, and again closed my eyes. After a long time I decided to look at him. He was staring at me with his eyes wide open, not with love or desire, but with the eyes of a person who had gone mad from hunger.

⋯⇒◦ ◦⇐⋯

That night I thought I heard someone trying to open the door to my bedroom. I sat up in bed and froze with fear. But what was I afraid of? It's impossible to inflict violence on a woman, one-on-one. Stark wouldn't try to knock me out with a blow or to suffocate me. He wouldn't use such means. But what if he wants to ask me, to plead with me for a kiss? I realize now that his beautiful body still exercises power over me, and that he's also aware of this. And if he succeeds, I know I'll surrender with the same blind passion.

This can't happen, though, because it would mean the death of Ilya and I could never forgive myself. I don't have for either one of them whatever it is that people call "love." I've finally reached that conclusion: I don't truly love either one.

Latchinov is right. I love Ilya like a friend, a brother, a father. I feel sorry for him, and love him as much as I do my son. Stark? I don't love him at all. That which I feel for him can never be called love, despite the intensity of the feeling. Either I don't understand love, or it simply doesn't exist. But in any case, I have to resolve the present dilemma.

Should I abandon the child or Ilya? If I leave Ilya, it'll kill him. If I forsake Lulu, I'll have no reason to live. The easiest way out of this would be for me to die, but my death would also kill Ilya. Who knows what would happen? Maybe after my death Stark would calm down, and then perhaps another passion, as strong as ours, would flare up. What would then become of Lulu?

Was there truly only one exit, that which Latchinov suggested?

I spent all day thinking and thinking; my head was splitting. Stark will return at six and follow me around constantly, trying to touch my hands, my hair. Yesterday I used the excuse that I wanted to get into the city with Katia after dinner to see Vasenka's protégés. Today I'll get out an hour before he returns, and I won't offer any explanation. Maybe he'll catch on. But I can't do this every day. The only thing left is to leave, to shorten my happiness by a whole month and again to languish there, next to the other being I love so much, who will himself become depressed when he watches me pining away.

In truth, I'm not living, I'm languishing. I come alive only when those dear, sweet eyes are looking at me and that little voice is babbling, "Mama, my dearest Mama, I love you very much."

"If you please, Marie, clear this away and bring me my house coat," I said to the maid. I had just returned from the city, exhausted. All my friends have gone their various ways. I'd had to eat in an unfamiliar restaurant. I'd dropped by to see Vasenka but he wasn't home. His cavalier, a wreck of a man who had served at the court of Napoleon III, practically threw me out. Then I went to see a production of a Molière play at the Comédie Française, but as soon as I calculated that everyone at our house had gone to bed, I returned home.

The only light in the dark house was burning in Latchinov's room. I wanted to kiss Lulu very badly. The poor little thing was probably very upset that I hadn't put him to bed as usual. Maybe he even cried?

A knock at my door. "Tatiana Alexandrovna, I must speak with you."

"Please, Edgar, I've already undressed and I'm completely exhausted."

"It's very important," he entered my room.

"You can't put it off until tomorrow?"

"No. Dismiss the servant."

I faltered.

"Marie, the lady doesn't need you any more. You can go."

After she'd left he stood for a while without saying a word. We weren't even looking at each other.

"I came to tell you," Stark began, "that we can't continue like this any longer. My health and my nerves can't stand it."

"I said that a long time ago, and more than once I've suggested that I go to a hotel. Katia can bring the child by every day from morning until six. I've even said that you can have him on Sundays."

"I can't allow the child to be dragged around like that, every day in all kinds of weather," he said through his teeth.

"I agree. I can come here every day from ten until five. We'll start with this routine. Please, enough already. I'll move tomorrow, but today I'm tired and want to sleep."

"My God, what agony!" he cried out suddenly, his voice sobbing, wringing his hands.

"Edgar, I'm asking you to please leave me alone."

"Tata, Tata, you understand me, what I. . . ."

He took a step toward me. I put a chair between us for protection and said, "I asked you, and now I order you to leave, now!"

He kicked the chair away and grasped my hands.

"Tata," he pleaded desperately, "be mine! If only for a day, for an hour, out of kindness or compassion. Think about the baby. I can't take this much longer; I'm either going to go crazy or die. I know that you don't love me . . . but you don't love the other one, either. Latchinov told me today that you are no longer a wife to him, but he's ill. . . . I agree to everything, Tata. Be near to him. I know that he's the only one to whom you are truly devoted. You'll continue to come here as you always have, but I'll know that for these few months you'll belong to me, that you'll be mine, as you were before.

"I know you haven't completely fallen out of love with me, Tata, I can sense that. I can tell that you aren't indifferent to my kisses, my caresses. They'll be even hotter, wilder, because I've suffered all the horrors of life without you. My dear!"

Give me one last ounce of strength or everything will be lost. I pointed to the door and insisted, "This won't happen. Get out!"

He recoiled from me. We stood for a few minutes, neither one of us speaking. Then he lowered his eyes and said, "I'll go, but I have a few more things I must say. Like a beggar, I just pleaded for your love. I thought that you would take pity on me, but now I see that I hoped in vain. You feel neither love nor pity for me. The truth of the matter is, you don't feel them for anyone. You have only illusions. You decided to remain faithful to a man who cannot be a husband to you, and because of self-imposed penance you torture yourself, me, and our child. Fine, hurt yourself, feel noble for your self-sacrifice, your deed, but I can't put up with this any longer. . . . I'm going to take the baby some place where you can never find us. Good-bye."

I jumped up. "Are you trying to blackmail me?" I asked.

"Call it what you like and think what you want. It's my last word," he started for the door.

"In that case," I screamed, beside myself with rage, "take what you want, now, this minute!" I tore open my peignoir.

"What kind of kisses are you commanding me to give you, what caresses are you demanding of me? Don't be shy, give your orders! When you threaten to take away my baby, there's nothing I won't do." I choked on my rage. I ripped off my nightgown and burst out sobbing, reaching out my arms to him.

"Quickly, quickly, I'm ready!"

He flung himself toward me, grabbed me, his teeth searching for my lips, but then he unclenched his hands, turned and staggered toward the door. He had already grasped the knob when he collapsed, with a moan, on the carpet.

⤑═◉═⤐

Oh God! Is it possible that he may die? My scream aroused the entire household. Latchinov called the doctor, who told us that he had simply fainted and would soon come around. But perhaps he was consoling me? Why was Latchinov so worried, and Katia looking at me with such unbridled hatred? And his face! So pale, his eyes rolled back, showing their whites beneath his dark lashes. . . .

What if he dies? Am I to be blamed for his death? I couldn't have acted otherwise. I never wanted his death. If he dies, I lose all hope of getting my son back. According to the will Stark drew up at Lulu's birth, in the event of Stark's death the boy will be sent to a private school and watched over by two guardians: Latchinov and MacPherson, one of Stark's relatives. I'm not mentioned anywhere. I had hoped that with the passage of time Stark would concede to giving me some sort of rights with respect to the child. Nor did the will offer me any hope of coaxing the guardians to allow me to spend the holidays with him; according to Stark's instructions, the boy is to spend holidays either at school or with MacPherson's family.

Good heavens, my poor little boy! I've done your father a great deal of harm, and who knows what he wrote in the letter that he gave Latchinov when he handed over a copy of his will. You're supposed to read that letter when you're eighteen. Maybe he's telling you the story of our affair. When you read it, you'll have so much contempt for me. But do I deserve this disdain? I just got all tangled up in my feelings and in the circumstances; caught in the mess, I couldn't make sense of it either. Life is so complicated!

"He's regaining consciousness, come here!"

I looked up and saw Katia next to me. Was that her face? White with agony, she was shaking all over.

"Is he dying?" I clung to her hand.

"No, you still haven't killed him with your conjuring tricks. But the doctor warned us that he passed out from a severe shock and that when he comes to we're going to have to calm his fears about whatever it was that upset him so much. We watched him all evening and noticed that something was bothering him very much. He wouldn't eat or drink, and lay face down on the couch the whole time. We were all still awake when you got back because we knew something would happen to explain his behavior.

"Latchinov was pacing quietly in his room, but I . . . I was standing in the corridor, behind the door, waiting for something terrible. . . . Enough. Go to him now and tell him that you were just clowning around, maybe flirting too much, or trying to do the decent thing, or acting from a sense of duty. Or maybe just because you like to put on airs. But tell him you realize now how stupid this was and that you love him."

"Katia!"

"Go now! You've tortured him enough. What do you want, for him to suffer more after he comes to? Or do you want him to go mad? Latchinov is worried that he will and ordered me to tell you this."

"Katia, you think that after this I should live with Stark?"

"Of course you must. Now go," she jerked me up by the hand.

"What about Ilya?"

"What about him? What's his tepid love in comparison to this desperation, this love to the point of insanity? Ilya can reconcile himself to the situation. He isn't a child, like that one in there. Ilya can even be kind to you under the present circumstances."

"Katia, where's your love for your brother?"

"When we must make sacrifices, we sacrifice those who are less dear to us."

"You love Stark!"

"Yes, I love him, but not the way you imagine, you depraved woman. I love him in the same way that I do his son; for me, they're both children—clever, sweet children, one bigger than the other. In the past few years they've both become remarkably dear to me. No one except my mother has ever occupied that place in my heart. I am a sexless creature, a true old maid. I never sought the kinds of attachments that you have with men. I gave my heart to those who were close to me and everyone, save Mama, pushed me away. Ilya left me for you. Andrei and Zhenia—I still don't understand why— maybe it was because I was the oldest and was strict with them. Papa never loved any of us except Zhenia, and only then because she was pretty. No one ever showed me overt affection, not even Mama, and my ego would not let me ask for it.

"But then this child treated me like a close relative, always demonstrating affection. And in Stark I found brotherly love and concern. They didn't pay any attention to my external moroseness and antisocial behavior. They simply cared about me, and for this I gave them my whole heart. Now go in there!"

"Katia, you don't know the whole story. You don't know Ilya. He has the same disposition as you. It was because I showed him affection that he fell in love with me. And now? Now you don't understand the present situation either. Ilya's sick, he's got a heart disease. It'll kill him this time if this comes out."

"Damn you!" She clutched her head, as I stood before her, as a prisoner before a hanging judge.

"What to do, my God, what to do?" she hissed through clenched teeth.

"Latchinov advised me to lie, to lie to both of them," I whispered, almost delirious.

"Yes," she cried out, "tell them both lies! That's the only way that you can make them both happy. Yes, of course!"

"Katia, that's a disgraceful thing to do."

"Oh, you want to remain honorable? You don't want to soil yourself? You want to maintain your self-respect, even if it costs the life of someone who loves you. I know how honest and upright you are. But this time play the dirty trick and then spend the rest of your life punishing yourself with the realization what you did.

"Tell the lies! However base you consider this action, it's still the only way that you can act unselfishly." She exhaled sharply. My legs were shaking so I sat down.

"Have you no mercy? Are you an animal or a human? If I didn't know that I would hurt people I love by doing so, I'd happily strangle you on the spot, I hate you so much. I despise your ruthless honesty, your stupid sense of obligation. Where thousands of people are dying 'for the idea,' pity cannot be shown to the single individual. Under those circumstances I would sacrifice those whom I love just as I would my own life. But to sacrifice the lives of others for my own personal morals. . . .

"Maybe if you felt disgust toward Stark I could understand you. I can sympathize with the girl who hesitates to sell her body, even though she could save her family by doing so. I understand Judith, and Sonia Marmeladova. . . .* But you? You don't have that excuse. You're struggling within yourself because you're hungry for his touch. Look at him lying there, so soft and handsome, your Dionysus. And you're burning with the desire to go in there. What's holding you back? Surely not feminine modesty.

"Do the right thing, Tania, for once in your life. Tell the lies. I despise you, but if you . . . if. . . ." Suddenly she dropped to her knees before me. "Tania, I implore you. I hate you, but I'll be your slave for life if both of them are happy. I . . . it seems that I . . . can grow to love you. . . ." Tears poured from her eyes as she dropped to my feet.

---

*Judith is from the Old Testament and Sonia Marmeladova from F. M. Dostoevsky's novel *Crime and Punishment*. Their fictional lives placed them in a dilemma, much like Tania's, of whether or not the body should be prostituted for a higher goal.

"Let's go," I arose. "You're right. I'll go in there, and I'll lie to both of them, and spend the rest of my life hating myself."

I deserved this.

⋆⇒◎ ⊜⇐⋆

I couldn't fight the circumstances any longer. Things are fine; I simply don't allow myself to think about it. I feel dreadful, and suffer . . . but all around me are happy. And that's the way it should be.

Those eyes, submissive and passionate, shine with happiness. And that small sweet face is always cheerful now. Lately they've both become healthier and better looking. The child, with his intuitive sensitivity, seems instinctively aware that something terrible has been erased. In happy amazement, he sees that both his mama and his papa are with him and that he can make them kiss each other without the former tension. Moreover, the sharp words and gestures between them that used to frighten him have disappeared. He can talk about whatever he wants without the abrupt order to be quiet. He no longer has to be divided in the evenings between his parents; now they both smile at him, his baby talk, his hugs.

Katia? She can never love me, that's impossible. But she appears somehow embarrassed and touched. It's as though she's thawed out; she responds shyly to Stark's and Lulu's kind words and no longer tries to avoid our company. Vasenka pretends that he notices nothing, but his face is radiant. Katia and Vasenka won't have much to do with me, but the people they love are happy, so they are too.

Yesterday Vasenka saw me sitting with my head in my hands. I don't know what he read on my face, but he nudged my side and said, "Pull yourself together, Mama. What if Dionysus should see you?" Vasenka, who was always so alert to my joys and sorrows, now cares only whether or not the expression on my face will upset Stark. My feelings no longer matter to him; I must put on a good face, and that's all.

178

Tomorrow Latchinov is leaving for Russia. I want to cry because I'll miss him so, but I know that he will be visiting Ilya and will be able to comfort and console him. In other words, now everyone will be satisfied, happy.

In the past few days Latchinov's health has grown worse; he now walks with a cane and his jaundiced face is as yellow as a lemon. He has a serious liver ailment but hates to treat it. Despite his health, he's calm and chipper, as before.

We tried to persuade him to postpone his trip.

"This is sheer idiocy, Alexander; you could get even more ill on the road," Stark told him.

"I have to leave quickly—I have business in Russia."

"Really, your business can't wait for two weeks? At least then you could travel with Tatochka instead of alone."

"Believe me, it can't."

"You're leaving, and then Tata—it's going to be so lonely. Mademoiselle Katia, I won't permit you to take off for London with your students. If you absolutely must see London, just wait a little: I'll finish up with my most urgent business and we'll take Lulu there together. We can introduce Lulu to his grandmother. Please Katia, be sweet and don't leave me all alone. I know Alexander just thought this trip up so he wouldn't have to console me after Tatochka leaves." Stark begged, pleaded, and threatened, but Latchinov would not change his mind.

In the evening, when Latchinov and I were alone, he smiled and told me, "I'm afraid of becoming very ill or dying before I can execute my mission. We'll see each other in Petersburg." His tone was joking, but there was also such decisiveness in his voice that I no longer tried to insist.

My heart sank. In two weeks I would have to part with my little boy. But there was nothing I could do, because I didn't want to force Ilya to wait a minute longer than necessary.

Stark had already decided that I would come to him for the Christmas holidays, for about ten days, and then in February he would come to Petersburg and stay with Latchinov. This latter plan scared me, and I tried to talk him out of it. "Don't worry, Tata," he assured me. "Do you really think that I would disturb 'the other man's' peace? There, in Petersburg, we will simply be friends. But you yourself understand that now I can't be apart from you for long periods of time. I'd like to stop you from going there altogether, but I know how much that would hurt you, and now that I understand that only your sense of duty and pity for a sick man keep you far from me, I can freely agree to this situation. I know that the kind of love that I've dreamed about, that which a person experiences but once in a lifetime, you have for him. I take what you can give me, your tenderness and your passion. You love me just a little, don't you, Tata, as a man?"

"Now I love you as the father of my child, Eddy," I said. I was telling the truth, and it was nice not to have to lie for a change.

"This is our last siesta," I said to Latchinov. "Tomorrow I'll be taking mine alone. Frankly, Alexander Vikentevich, this is terribly difficult for me. You're the only person to whom I don't have to lie. I've grown so accustomed to you, I value our friendship so. . . ."

Tears began streaming from my eyes.

"I don't know what we did to deserve your friendship. We put you through so much aggravation, straining your nerves. Anyone else would have brushed us aside. More than that, I think that Stark owes his life and his sanity to you. He loves you so, admires you, is devoted to you."

"Tatiana Alexandrovna, stop talking about Stark. Let's talk about you in this last hour that we'll have together alone."

"What's there to say about me, Alexander Vikentevich? As far as I'm concerned, my life is over—I no longer think about myself. I will live for the child, and these two people who, to my misfortune, love me. I believe no woman has ever found herself in a situation like mine. My life has turned out very strange and unnatural."

Latchinov suddenly interrupted me. "Tatiana Alexandrovna, do you want me to tell you now what I've long wanted to, my theory?"

"All right, Alexander Vikentevich."

"You just said that no other woman has found herself in this situation, in which life turned out so peculiar, unnatural. But the point is, that you're a *woman*. Put yourself in a man's place and the problem sorts itself out, everything becomes normal.

"Really, tens—what am I saying?—hundreds, thousands of men live like that. They undergo precisely what you have. Let's suppose for a minute that you're a man, and we'll retell your story: you're married, living quietly and happily with an unusually intelligent and kind wife. Your love is good, solid, 'conscious.' You devote yourself completely to your art, and your wife doesn't bother you. She's a bit bourgeois and can't always understand the demands of your artistic nature, but you know that she loves you faithfully—she lives for you, protects your tranquility, respects your occupation, your tastes and habits.

"Then suddenly you meet another woman—stunning, captivating, smart, passionate! This woman is in love with you, and she doesn't hide her feelings. She says things to you that your dear, meek little wife never would. She promises a world of delights. Her beauty is so extraordinary, her lust—infectious. What man could resist her? And you don't!

"You struggle with yourself, you suffer. You haven't stopped loving your wife, but 'the other woman' is everything—desire, beauty, poetry. But at the same time, she's a lovely despot who wants to possess you completely. Your body is not enough for her—she demands your soul. It doesn't matter that you've sacrificed your wife and family, she wants your art. You can't accept this. The tears begin, the scenes, all those things that men can't stand. You start growing cool to her. The tears and scenes double, triple. You're ready to break it all off, to run away, when suddenly a baby appears. You love it. Here the situation becomes different. Now you have to recognize that your love is stronger and more passionate than a man's would be in this situation. You yourself gave birth. For purely physiological reasons Stark could not have given birth for you. But if he could. . . .

"Yes, you love the baby. You pity it. This pity for the child and its mother supersedes all other feelings, and you decide to sacrifice both your art and your wife. But when you see your wife, the earlier emotions grip you with renewed intensity. What's more, you also see the possibility of devoting yourself to art again as before.

"Add to this that, because of extraneous circumstances, your wife has remained alone. You don't have the heart to break up with her, so you give up the other woman . . . and you do so cheerfully. This consoles you, except that you don't get custody of the baby. The attachment to the child keeps growing, and you realize that the peace and happiness of this child can only be bought at one price: getting back together with the mother, who is again alluring you with her beauty. To return to her means to kill your dear, devoted wife. Yet alienating her means sacrificing the child. You agonize, vacillate, and search for a compromise. . . . This story is banal, very common for tens of thousands of men."

"But I am a woman, Alexander Vikentevich," I said.

"No, Tatiana Alexandrovna, you are a *man*. You only have the body of a woman. You're feminine, soft, and gracious—but you're still a man. If one looks at you as a woman, your character appears quite original and complex. But as a man, you're plain and simple. A good man, poetic, with an amorous, sensitive disposition, but decent and kind—even though a little coarse, like all men. Have you ever paid attention to how you swear? My dear, you curse like a sailor. I'll never forget the time in Petersburg, during the white nights, we were walking along the embankment. You were in a melancholy, poetic mood. You were so sweet and tender. You recited to me, 'Look over there, at the end of the path; the shrubs are spread out in nighttime beauty; They've taken the shape of night fairies. . . .' At that moment a cabbie ran into us. 'Where do you think you're going, you oaf!' you hollered at him, and then continued softly, 'Beloved, you don't understand my melancholy.' How I wanted to burst out laughing! But you were so absorbed in the verse, the poetry around us, that I didn't want to destroy your mood.

"Remember how often in our long conversations we've discussed your masculine characteristics, how in childhood, when we all had terrible crushes, you only fell in love with women. You understand and appreciate feminine beauty and paint women as though spellbound. During our conversations in your studio, I listened closely; you evaluate women strictly from a man's perspective. Remember the French girl that your sculptor friend brought over? You watched her walk out and said, 'She's too made-up and no longer young, but I understand why he fell head-over-heels for her. There's something strangely attractive about her.' You should have been a lesbian."

"Alexander Vikentevich!"

"Calm down, my dear. The word frightens you, not the idea. You didn't become one simply because of your upbringing, circumstances, and gentility. Before you met Stark, your inclinations were still latent and didn't set you down this path. Besides, this never entered your head. You didn't know you had a 'secret.'

"Kismet led you to Stark. Here I find a truly remarkable coincidence, a kind of diabolical joke, because Stark is exactly among men what you are among women. Strong, courageous, he has more of a female nature than you do. There's nothing masculine in your appearance, whereas Stark's body, his manners are more refined and delicate than most men's. Most people consider femininity in a man unbecoming, but look at how everyone is attracted to Stark. Even people with completely opposite personalities like him. And his love for the child? Is this really a father's love? No, he's the mother, and a most passionate mother. Before he met you, overwhelmed by his ardent temperament, he chased one woman after another but then walked away angry, morally unsatiated. It might be strange that fate brought you together, but there's nothing surprising in how you threw yourselves at each other, despite all obstacles. It would have been more unusual if that had not happened. You would never have felt such passion for another man, nor he for another woman. You're a lucky woman, my dear."

I sat there just listening to Latchinov, recognizing the element of truth in what he said.

"But I could never be a lesbian, never!" I exclaimed.

"You're lucky that you never became aware of your secret,

as it would have caused tremendous anguish. It would have pulled at you like wine does a drunkard. If you'd had to struggle with it, with your sense of morality, you would have fallen into despair. Your luck is that you never figured it out—and you met Stark. I repeat, you're a lucky woman."

"If your theory is correct, Alexander Vikentevich, then Stark didn't realize that he could have been happy with Baron Z."

"No, Tatiana Alexandrovna. There's a subtle difference. Women can love another woman, but men . . . it's not easy to explain this, but Baron Z. could have only aroused disgust and ridicule in Stark."

I said nothing.

"Such is my theory. Many people in this world have changed their sex. Some know this, others don't even suspect it. I don't know whether my theory is true or false, but if you accept it, you won't have to agonize trying to figure yourself out."

He stopped talking for a minute, then began again, smiling, "Maybe I have surprised you for now, but I feel terribly ill. I realize that this is the beginning of the end. I recently went to the doctor and demanded the truth about my health. Aesculapius said that if he performs the operation immediately, I'll live a long time. If not, I'll have only six months at most."

"Alexander Vikentevich! You agreed to the operation?!"

"No, my friend. The doctor has promised me an end without suffering, and I wouldn't give up the opportunity to terminate as quickly as possible this mess that we call life."

I wanted to talk, to beg him, but my voice betrayed me. I simply took his slender hands, with their beautiful rings, and squeezed them sadly. He looked at me with the same expression that I had seen only once before, that unforgettable night that Stark took the baby away. That night he held me on the bed, and said, "My poor dear. Pity them. I think they need you more than you realize. If not for them, I wouldn't have kept you here. I don't have poison or a revolver; I would have taken you to the rocks above the sea. But I know that your life is necessary for others."

At last I was able to speak. "Stay alive, if only for us. You've always lived for other people."

"My dear, I'm so tired that I just want peace. Don't call me back to life. I wanted to die back there, in Rome."

I lifted my head and, surprised and depressed, looked at his face, which still looked so sweet, yet melancholy. He gently stroked my head.

"Do you remember the day when Stark posed for you for the last time? How happy he was?"

I nodded.

"Well, that very day, when I got home, I wanted to kill myself."

"Why, why?" I asked him dejectedly.

He pensively stroked my head.

"My dearest friend! It's true, that among all my acquaintances, I've never loved any as I do you. I myself don't know why. You alone make me want to say things that I never thought I would tell anyone, ever. I attribute the fact that I want to talk to my illness, my weakness. My days are numbered, and I don't want to take anything earthly with me 'there.' For some reason, I believe that there's something 'there.' Of course, not heaven or hell, but I cannot believe that my thoughts, memory, and imagination will disappear with my body. That seems terribly stupid to me—that's the word I want, stupid.

"You see, Tata—let me call you that—I've become chatty, like all who are senile or dying. But I can't, I don't want to take with me the things that made me either happy or sad. I loved Stark madly, Tata, a thousand times more than you did. I see how surprised you are, but I want to tell you everything. You didn't know your 'secret,' but I've been aware of mine since childhood. I wanted to be 'pure,' and this was my torture. As a child, in my naive infatuations, like you I went for those of my own sex. But you switched your attraction to the opposite sex, while I always remained with men. When they sent me to one of the privileged boarding schools, and I saw the perversion among boys of my age, I shrank away in terror. I had good, intelligent parents; they gave me a moral upbringing, and therefore I recoiled from these boys. But much later, when I became an adult, I became horrified when I realized that female beauty had no effect on my emotions. Only the beautiful bodies of youths attracted me. I began trying to court women with a vengeance, involved myself in liaisons, lived with them, purchased them for a day. I was afraid of myself, ashamed of myself. It was the most horrible time of my life.

"I took these women like a disgusting medicine, which I hoped would cure me of my sickness, my shame. I experienced everything that a normal person would do if forced to engage in perversion. I tried to work, to go into government service. But work and service are productive only when they satisfy a thirst for money or ambition. I already had too much of the former and none of the latter.

"I threw myself into science, into art. But science was too easy for me and art . . . it spoke about love, and at times, sorrow. I tried physical labor. I lived in a Tolstoyan colony for two years.* I gave a third of my estate to the peasants. I tried to concentrate on my soul, but my body spoke louder and louder.

"At this point, my parents began to insist on marriage. They even found me a fiancée. One of my father's friends, Prince Ukolov, died ruined, heavily in debt. His daughter, Princess Varvara, was literally out on the street when my mother took her in. I refused this union point blank. Could I ruin the life of an innocent eighteen-year-old simply to please my parents? But this girl herself came to my study, where I'd retired following a row with mother, and said, 'I heard your conversation; I was eavesdropping. You don't love me, nor I you. You're afraid of destroying my life, but as far as I'm concerned, you could make me happy. I'm not especially pretty, and I'm poor. Who would marry me? A derelict? I want wealth and freedom. Your parents want to continue the line. Fine. We'll try to give them an heir. I think two would be sufficient, in case one dies. If they're girls, then we'll stipulate that when they marry, they'll keep your family name—at the least, they'll take a double surname. And then we won't bother each other.'

*Several of Lev Tolstoi's more fanatical disciples established semi-utopian colonies, where members lived according to the master's ideals of Christian anarchism. Not surprisingly, these anti-statist colonies often ran afoul of the tsarist government.

"Stunned, I looked at this slender girl, who appeared so chaste and innocent. 'You aren't mistaken,' she said quietly. 'I am completely virginal. But I'm not stupid. I know that I have to think about my future, and I've always wanted to be rich.'

"Then I told her that I don't like women in general. 'Are you really a . . . ?' She spoke the Greek word—although it didn't apply to me directly—with singular composure. 'Never mind. I know you can still have children.'

"She gave me a thought: what if I have children and find through them a meaning to life? So I agreed. But this hope was never realized. My wife threw herself into social life with such reckless abandon, that after she gave birth prematurely to a stillborn baby, the doctor told her she could never again conceive. When I visited her after the birth, she told me, 'I've wronged you, Alexander. I didn't do my part properly, and it looks like I seduced you into a bad bargain. Can this be corrected? Can you impregnate another woman, and I'll simulate pregnancy and birth?'

'That would be a crime,' I answered her. 'Your conscientiousness is carrying you away. Let us accept the situation.'

"We lived together under the same roof for many years, meeting for dinner and to receive guests. We went to the theater and visited friends together. We enjoyed chatting in the evenings. She was dry, far from stupid, and I liked her malicious mind. You could call us a compatible pair.

"Did she have affairs? I don't know. No one ever said anything about her. But in society, I often met men to whom I felt a sudden attraction. What could I do? If I opened myself up to a woman, confessing my passion for her, and she did not want to return these feelings, she could still think about my rash declaration with a contemptuous smile, or perhaps even an involuntary sigh. But a young man? a proper youth? He would run from me with disgust and fear—at the very least with laughter, that same laughter Stark howled when remembering the baron.

"Tata, Tata, you're so lucky that you did not understand yourself when happenstance led you to Stark. Fate corrected this 'mistake' of nature; it didn't want to deprive you of the happy experience of shared passions."

Latchinov reflected for a moment, then continued.

"After my wife's unsuccessful pregnancy, I gave up and began to travel. And for the first time I met those creatures called 'queens.'* They repelled me more than women did. I wanted to love Ganymede,** Antinous,† but I saw before me caricatures of the women from whom I'd run away. This imitation, the women's dresses and wigs, revolted me; I wanted divine youth! What's more, I didn't want what they were proposing to me. I wanted to prostrate myself before a beautiful body, before the proud face of a demigod. I wanted to forget myself, caress my idol into oblivion, expecting only kisses and caresses from him. I wanted friendship, more sweet than love, and poetry in my devotion. . . .

"But these warped creatures, these painted dolls tried to sell me something else. They didn't understand the ancient cults, they knew only the vulgar customs of the Orient, inspired by the shortage of women. I fled from them with more disgust than I did from their female counterparts.

"Then I met an American, Johnny. He was also one of those miserable impersonators, but more clever than the others. He understood what I wanted and tricked me—or I fooled myself. He was an avaricious, capricious, intolerable creature, but I loved him for two years. He grew bored with me. He couldn't pretend forever that he enjoyed the cloistered life, with books, music. . . . In my naiveté I wanted to make him my companion, my friend. But he wanted to play cards, drink, and often told me that our love was 'too platonic,' that he liked a completely different sort. He stayed with me only because of the money, and I denied him nothing. Finally, Baron Z. seduced him and took him away from me.

"Stupidly—and I know how stupid it was, but I couldn't forget—years later, when I met Z., I used a card game as the pretext to challenge him to a duel.

---

*The French word he uses is *chattes,* female cats.

**Ganymede was a beautiful boy kidnapped by other gods to serve as Zeus's cupbearer and lover.

†In another reference to the *Odyssey,* Antinous was one of Penelope's suitors when Odysseus was away fighting the Trojan War.

"After Johnny left, I turned to doctors, then to a hypnotist. I don't know whether he did it or I hypnotized myself, but for a long time I lived peacefully with my books, paintings, and music. I traveled almost all the time. Suddenly, in your studio, I saw Stark and the torment began, worse this time than before . . . the wall . . . the futility. . . .

"Oh, Tata, it was horrible. Despair and joy at the same time. My pathetic happiness consisted of the fact that I could have him near me, be his one true friend. You left him, and he was lonely, depressed. You know how childlike his affections are. I stole touches, kind words, a smile. Sometimes I went into his bedroom, after he had already retired. I sat by his bed, and we had long, friendly conversations. On purpose, I would get him to speak about you, to see the fire in those fabulous eyes. Sometimes I was cruel enough to drive him to despair, so that then I would be able to caress his hands, kiss his forehead, hold him tight to me as he sobbed on my shoulder. Oh, I would feel so guilty the next morning, looking at his troubled face.

"During his illness, despite the fact that he was in grave danger, I was happy. Only then was I truly happy. Oblivious, he would lie in my arms for hours. I could kiss him as much as I wanted. I reveled in gazing at him for hours; there was only the night around us . . . and peace.

"Tata! My only and dearest friend! Forgive me. I got carried away and said too much. But you know that soon it will all be over—my endless love for him, and also my life."

Latchinov closed his eyes and sat there quietly. Troubled and feeling very sorry for him, I stroked his thin, pale hands.

I'm standing on the terrace of our dacha in Neuilly and waiting impatiently for that tall, slender figure in the uniform from the Polytechnical Institute to appear at the end of the lane. I'm burning with excitement; I'm waiting for my son.

Today marks the thirteenth anniversary of Latchinov's death, and I've been disconcerted all day, thinking about him. It seems like only yesterday! How much water has flowed under the bridge in these past thirteen years! Now, I no longer need to tell the lies.

Ilya's dead. He died in my arms, peaceful and happy, confident of my love and devotion. As for me, I took comfort in learning that he did not die of heart disease but rather of the cancer that runs in his family.

Soon it will be seven years since I became Stark's wife. As he had dreamed, we were married in city hall and then held ceremonies in two churches. His love for me hasn't changed, which I find alternately touching and amusing. Stark's a year older than I am, but I look younger than my age and I take care of myself, because my son takes great pleasure in my looks.

Sometimes Stark still pitches jealous fits, but I get neither angry nor embarrassed. I've come to terms with Latchinov's theory, which has explained a number of small particulars about my husband's life, mine, and our son's. . . .

Here he comes, my treasure! Laughing, he picks me up and kisses me, kisses me incessantly. We gaze into each other's joyful eyes—it's been a whole week since we've seen each other!

He's a full head taller than his father but not nearly as handsome as I thought he would be. His forehead, brows, and eyes are good-looking, but his chin juts out too far, and he has a snub nose and a big mouth. He's significantly less attractive than his father. What made Eddy's features so appealing was their delicacy and gentleness; but I am very happy that Lulu's face is more coarse and masculine, though it comes at the expense of his looks.

Even our son's relationship to both of us supports Latchinov's theory. For example, after telling me about a confrontation he's had with one of his teachers, he added, "As you see, Mama, the affair didn't amount to anything serious, but please don't tell Papa. He'll get unnecessarily upset and nervous and then go and demand an explanation. We'll tell him about it later."

Lulu adores his father, but he doesn't want "Daddy Dearest" to get upset over trivialities. He realizes that it's better to seek Mama's advice and to discuss with her whatever difficulties he might have at school.

Stark's hair has turned completely gray, and Lulu and I always treat him with kindness and consideration. It's as if two men were taking care of a fragile woman they both love.

Katia, my son, and I always try to keep him away from things that could upset him. It seems that Katia is more devoted to him now than to Lulu; the boy grew up, but Stark remains a child.

Vasenka is completely cold to me now—he does not care for me any longer. The reason for his attitude seems to be that I no longer show the talent I once did.

Yes, I'm through with art. I sensed this happening long ago, when I finished my Dionysus. My painting, "And You Will Be Like Me," which I finally displayed after two years, made my reputation and enjoyed thunderous applause. But I realized that this success was only superficial; the success of the painter of "Wrath of Dionysus" lay in the contrast between the beautiful female bodies and the grotesque old woman in the foreground. I did not exhibit any more paintings after that.

The public has never seen my final major work, the portrait of Lulu hanging in his father's study. Life is coming to an end. Maybe I lived mine too tempestuously, unconventionally. I don't know who's accountable for that: maybe me, maybe nature, according to Latchinov's theory. But his melancholy shadow often stands before me, and I seem to hear his soft, quiet voice: "Nevertheless, you're a lucky woman, my friend."

Louise McReynolds is Associate Professor of History
at the University of Hawaii and author of *The News under
Russia's Old Regime: The Development of a Mass-Circulation
Press.* She is currently writing a book on leisure-time
activities in late Imperial Russia.